Detroit Cracked - Book 1
By: Marsell Morris (Mojo)
Mojo7books.com

No part of this book, except the cover, may be reproduced in any form without written permission from the author.
For more information, write to: Marsellmorris@aol.com

Distributed by:
CreateSpace.com
ISBN-13: 978-1480077300
ISBN-10: 1480077305
&
Smashwords.com

The characters and dialogues contained here-in are products of the author's imagination, and are not to be construed as real. Any resemblance to an actual person, living or dead, or an establishment, existing, or defunct, is entirely coincidental. The situations here-in, although fictional, mirror real life situations.

Copyright © 2008 All rights reserved.
Printed in the United States of America

Other works by Marsell

Detroit Cracked — Book 2 — Big-D's Return
Detroit Cracked — Book 3 — Boss-man's Rise
Detroit Cracked — Book 4 — Boss-lady's Rise
Detroit Nympho
Detroit's Sin Hotel
Snakes Don't Walk
Midnight Sex in Detroit
Rage in Detroit
Alien Plot — Man's Extinction
Alien Plot — Man's Extinction — Episode Two
Alien Plot — Man's Extinction — Episode Three
Alien Plot — Man's Extinction — Episode Four
Beyond the Beginning - Brock's Adventures - Earth Two

This novel is written for entertainment purposes only, and should not be considered, or used as a reference material. Be forewarned, to keep it real, some of the language contained here in is in the street vernacular, but with few, if any, vulgarities.

Some might find the sex references candid, and the violence graphic, but necessary to the telling of the whole story. It's because of the sex and violence, this material should not be considered proper reading for minors.

Acknowledgments

The author is extremely grateful to all of you, who shall go unnamed, for your assistance in unraveling the intricacies of the drug life, and sex trades. Without your aid, I would not have been able to write this work. You know who you are.

And for those of you, who don't want me to publish, thinking I have exposed too much, thank you for your concern, which reinforces my desire to tell it like it is. Besides, all the characters are fictional. Only those who might have been in similar situations as those depicted in this work may know of what I'm writing.

Thank you.

Dedication

    This novel is dedicated to all who've fallen victim to, or may fall victim to the every expanding crack epidemic. It is hoped those who read this work may change their minds about experimenting with crack, or better yet, any drug for that mater.

    I speak of the misery and utter futility of addiction, not for closed eyes who will not see, or covered ears that will not hear, but for those who seek the truth.

    The author.

Detroit Cracked - Book 1
By: Marsell Morris (Mojo)
Mojo7books.com

Table of Contents

Introduction

Prologue

Chapter 1	Nancy and Rob, pay the price.
Chapter 2	Tiny and a crack-whore.
Chapter 3	James loses to a lesbian.
Chapter 4	JC meets his match.
Chapter 5	T and Jam get jammed.
Chapter 6	Jeff, Quick, and Amos, looking for trouble.
Chapter 7	Big-D on the scene.
Chapter 8	Edward and his dope house.
Chapter 9	Officers Drake and Johnson on the job.
Chapter 10	Slow gets laid.
Chapter 11	Big-D is being watched.
Chapter 12	Big brother flexes his muscles.
Chapter 13	The sting.
Chapter 14	Candy and Shirley only want the rock.
Chapter 15	Big gets a dose of reality.

Introduction

Most people have heard of crack cocaine, but how many know how crack is rocked and smoked? How it affects the people who distribute and use the drug.

The reader will see through a series of individual experiences, how the drug affects the people in the life — will peep into the lives of the mid-level supplier, the drug house operator, and all the way down to the bottom layer of the pyramid, the street user, whom some might call the victim.

The reader will witness through these cautionary tales how sex is traded for drugs. Will see how the lives of most people in the drug world usually end in tragedy.

Prologue

...Unknown to JC, as he was negotiating with the woman, he was being watched by two men in an old car parked in the lot across from him.

"Hey Benny, I think that's the mutha who sold me those peanuts about a week ago," Willie told his buddy, while sitting his half-cup of gin on the dash. "Hold on a minute. I'm going to get my money back from that punk."

"Taking the gun?" asked, Benny, while reaching under his seat to retrieve the deadly pistol the men had been riding around all day with while, unconsciously, looking for a reason to use it.

"No, I'll be back for it, if he gives me any crap," Willie said, while climbing out of the ancient vehicle...

Chapter 1

Nancy and Rob, pay the price.

Rick jumped behind a loud knock on the front door of the abandoned house he and his woman, Nancy, were squatting in. He'd just finished smoking a 51, a concoction of weed and crack rolled into a joint, and was jittery. Smoking either crack or weed, individually, has a tendency to make most people paranoid. Smoking them together was really doing a job on Rick. All kinds of thoughts, some rational, others not so rational, raced through his mind.

"Damn, who is that?" Rick thought, aloud. His first thought was it might be the police, which was quickly replaced by a thought of someone attempting to come in and rob him. He being minor crack dealer who sold rocks to support his and his woman's habit, and just barely at that, had no shotgun protection in his dope house. He'd never be more than a step above an addict. He had a problem — he smoked as much as he sold, leaving very little profit to re-up.

He, at twenty-two, and his thin body showing the results of his constant drug use, knew he'd told his customers to never knock on his front door. He told them to always go around to the back. So, who the hell was this, he wondered?

"Nancy!... Nancy!" Rick yelled, as loud as he dared, while jumping up from a folding TV table, and starting for the bedroom, and looking back at the front door.

One of his feet entangled one of the table's, wobbly, legs, almost tipping the it over, and nearly spilling the plate of crack and weed he had there, causing his already racing hart to practically leaped out of his chest, but he managed to catch the table at just before that critical moment.

Now beginning to get angry, he called again, "Nancy! Woman! Get your ass up, and see who's at the door!" he yelled over his shoulder as he headed for the bedroom.

Asleep on the broken down, thread bare, couch, Nancy stirred a little, and rolled over onto her back, and stretched with a loud yawn and quickly fell back into a half-sleep. To look at her face, one could tell she was mixed. A very beautiful and intelligent, red-boned, young lady, of nineteen, she at about five-foot, one-hundred and three pounds, had long, naturally straight, black, hair, inherited from her white mother. Her large, bright, green, eyes, were framed by naturally long lashes. She could have become an excellent model with a couple more inches of height, but instead, thanks to Rick, she was a strung out crack addict.

Nancy was introduced into the drug world by Rick. He was using crack at the time they met, but only recreationally, as he struggled to become a major roller in his neighborhood already filled with dope houses. He wouldn't become a heavy user until later.

The first time Rick laid eyes on Nancy, his first thought, *he had to have him some of that.* He was out taking a casual drive in his pimped out, vintage, Jaguar, with massive, double-nickel, spinner wheels, and she was walking to the store one summer day. He had his oversize speakers in the trunk booming to a recent rap tune, and he was in full player mode. He pulled over to the curb, and his confidence showing on his angular face, asked her if she'd like a ride.

Because Rick wasn't a bad looking young man, at just under six-foot, with a medium build at that time, and a dreadlocked framed face, which was the platform for a face splitting smile, and because she liked the car, and had a distance to walk, she accepted his offer.

Little did Nancy know the ride she was accepting would change her life forever. Before she met Rick, she was planning to go to college and major in criminal justice. She hadn't decided what aspect of law she was going to pursue, but she'd make up her mind once she was in school. Those lofty dreams, now, long forgotten, her only ambition now was for the next hit of rock cocaine.

———

After yelling at her once more from the bedroom, Nancy moaned, rubbed her face with one hand, and finally got up from the couch. She was naked from the waste down, and burning eyed tired, and had a crook in her neck from her odd sleeping position. The night before, Rick had demanded she bend over the couch while he made her from behind, as he took a particularly strong hit of a stone from his stem, causing him to immediately finished. The drug sometimes had that affect on men, particularly, if the drug was of high quality. But the insidious side of the drug is it affects the pleasure center of the brain while tricking the user into thinking he wanted sex, to sometimes, rob him of his ability to perform until the affects of the drug wore off. Rick rewarded her with a couple dime rocks, which took her all night to smoke by the time she'd pushed her stem several times, rinsed, and pushed several more times, while trying to extract another cloud from the weak residue. She'd just managed to shake the ever-present desire for another hit, and hand shaking weary, fell asleep on the couch without bothering to cover her nakedness.

Nancy picked up her shorts from floor near the couch, quickly slipping them on, and not bothering with her underpants. She stumbled to the window beside the two-by-four barricaded door. With her eyes half closed, she pulled back the ripped bed sheet they used as a window covering, while peeping in the direction of the knocker.

"Who is it!? " she yelled, irritated she had to answer the door. *That damn Rick is getting worse with his paranoid ass,* she thought.

"Rob," came the reply.

"Damn, fool, you know better than to come to the front door. Go around to the back," Nancy responded, releasing the sheet and heading for the side door, now more irritated Rick wouldn't answer the knock himself. She eyed the pile of crack on the TV table as she passed, wondering if Rick would set her out a piece after Rob was gone — her anger now dissipated by the sight of the crumbs on the table.

"Who is it?" Rick, quietly, asked, as she passed the bedroom on the way to the side door.

"That thieving crack-head, Rob," Nancy, replied in a tired voice.

"That dumb asshole," Rick said, as he frantically slipped on his pants. *I told him a hundred times to always go to the back door, and he still comes to the front. He'd better have cash or something good for me this time, or I ain't letting him in anymore. I'm sick of this crap. I ain't letting him go short either,* he added, almost as an afterthought, as he searched for his shoes.

After climbing over the pile of stolen property nearly blocking the hallway and spilled into the kitchen, Nancy made it to the rear door. She wet a thumb with her tongue, and ran it over a scratch she'd received when she failed to completely step over a microwave. Seeing there would be no blood, she turned to the door, and stood looking at it, not wanting to get a splinter from the bracing two-by-fours placed across the door to prevent unwanted entrance.

After realizing most of his customers rarely had much money, Rick began receiving stolen property in place of cash for his drugs. He could later take the holdings to the pawnshop, and get more money for the property than what he gave out in drugs. The problem was he was beginning to do more and more of the stash he had for sale, and made fewer trips to the pawnshop, resulting in the growing pile of stolen goods in the hall, and kitchen, and less dope to sell. Without he noticing, the drug was already robbing him of the ability to conduct business, and would only get worse with continued use.

After carefully removing the three two-by-fours, Nancy opened the door. She then, without saying a word, wheeled around and started back towards the living room, stepping this way, and that, to avoid being scratched again.

Rob, who knew the routine, closed the door and replaced the lumber. He then made his way to the living room behind Nancy, as he watched her shapely behind and well-formed legs hanging below her skimpy shorts. *Damn, she's fine,* he thought, his mind going where it shouldn't. *I'd ride that all day and every day if she was my winch.*

Rob entered the livingroom, wearing only a stained T-shirt, a filthy, torn, threadbare, waist length, cotton jacket, on which the broken zipper was hanging loose. A pair of dirty sneakers with no shoestrings covered his bare feet. His oversized jeans had a large hole at the right knee exposing a unwashed, rusty, leg, underneath. It was early winter, and cold outside. Anyone who saw him knew he was either homeless, or a drug addict, possibly both. He had a laptop computer tucked under one arm.

Rick was back at his table rolling another 51. Now, slightly less stressed out, he looked up at the approaching Rob. His eyes locked on the computer under Rob's arm. His previous thoughts of getting into Rob's case about coming to the front door, now gone. He'd been wanting a laptop for some time, and until now, no one had brought one to him, and he wasn't about to let this one get away, no matter the cost.

Rick's mind went into calculation mode, wondering how much dope Rob was going to ask for, and what's the least amount Rob would accept for the computer? He knew the computer was stolen, but he also knew Rob could take it to any other drug dealer in the neighborhood and get a deal. He couldn't let that happen. *Time to barter,* he thought. "My man Rob, what's up?" Rick said, enthusiastically.

"I'm cool," Rob responded.

Although, Rick knew what it was Rob had brought him, he tried to not act excited.

"I know you got cash this time?" Rick said, as he looked down to the 51 he was rolling. He, also, knew Rob would be focusing on the plate of dope he had on the table. *Be cool,* he thought, *let him stew a while longer.*

"Come on man. No, I ain't got no money," Rob replied, "but I got something you might want."

Rick had finished rolling his 51. He slowly lit the joint, inhaled deeply, turned towards Rob, and blew the smoke into Rob's face. He was hoping the odor of the weed and crack would send Rob's cravings in to overdrive.

"I told you before, I got all the junk I need," Rick said, a little louder than necessary, and in a choked voice. *Be cool*, he reminded himself.

"I know, I know, but you gotta take a look at this, Rick. It's a computer, and I know it works, and it's heavy too. Come on man, take a look," Rob said, almost in one word. The smoke in his face having the desired affect.

"All right, let me see what you got," Rick said, in an uninterested tone. On the inside, he felt like it was Christmas, and he was receiving a valuable present. *Be, cool, be, cool,* was all he could think. "It better work," Rick continued, as he looked for the latch to open the laptop. "I don't see the power cord, or the battery charger adapter," Rick mumbled, as he turned the weighty computer over in his hands. He was really trying to act as if he didn't want the it. He knew those accessories could be purchased later. He found the latch, and raised the shiny cover and hit what he thought was the power button. It, not being protected by a password, lit up like a Christmas tree, the Windows program chiming as it came into view. The battery seemed to be on full charge. His heart began beating faster. A bead of car window glass fell to the floor. *Rob must have just stolen it from the back seat of some poor fool, who thought his car would be safe in this neighborhood with the doors locked, and alarm set,* Rick thought.

———

Anyone, who lives in their neighborhood, knows you don't leave anything, unguarded, on your car seats — never. There were thieving crack-heads, who rode bikes up and down the streets while looking into the parked cars as they passed, hoping to find something they could steal and trade for a rock. They didn't care if the car had an alarm. They knew they could smash the window, grab anything on the seat, and be gone before the owner came to investigate.

Rick quickly closed the computer, and handed it back to Rob.

"What you want for it?" Rick asked, trying to act indifferent, and taking another long drag of the crack filled joint while, again, blowing the smoke into Rob's face.

Rob's eyes got as large as saucers. He started to fidget nervously. His mind started to race. He tried to figure out how much the computer was worth, and had no idea? This was the first time he'd even laid eyes on one. *How much dope would Rick give me, without shortchanging myself,* he wondered? He decided to ask for much more than he'd settle for.

"Ca... ca... can I get an 8th?" (One eight of an ounce, about $140.00 of crack) Rob managed to ask after stuttering a couple times.

Rick chuckled to himself. He was up on what Rob was trying to do. After all, he'd been rolling drugs since a littler after he met Nancy this past summer...

When Rick met Nancy, he used, but not heavily. The main reason he got into heavy dealing was to impress her with extra money. Once he started to role, and had access to more dope, he started to use more. Then the unexpected happened. It happened so gradually he didn't see it coming — he got hooked.

Because he had less money with which to impress Nancy, the result of his increased habit, he was afraid he might loose her. Rather than loose her, he decided to make her dependent on him in another way. He introduced her to the drug. At first, she was reluctant, but behind Rick's constant pressure for her to try it just one time, she relented, and once was all it took for her to become hopelessly hooked. Her extra use took all of the extra money he was making. He was now dealing to support both their habits. He could no longer afford to lavish her with gifts, and she didn't miss them. The drug was now the most important thing in her life and all she wanted.

Because crack is extremely addictive, and she had the addictive gene, it didn't take long for Nancy to become increasingly more strung out and was willing to do whatever was necessary to get more. Because Rick was supplying her, she was able to keep her youthful appearance. She didn't have to do the things rock-stars or crack-whores had to do, such as turn tricks in the streets to support there habits. Giving Rick a little sex every now and then was no problem. Besides, when he was smoking, he couldn't do much of anything most of the time, anyway.

Rick expected Rob to ask for more drugs than he normally does, but he didn't expect him to be savvy enough to ask for that much. Rob's request caught Rick off guard. He had to rethink his bargaining strategies. He was hoping Rob would ask for, maybe a 16th (around $45 to $55 worth) and settle for three dimes ($30.00 worth)

"You want what? Hell no, I ain't giving you no 8th for a computer I don't know I can use, and don't have a power cord too."

Rick was betting on the fact Rob didn't know the computer was worth anywhere from eight-hundred to fifteen-hundred-dollars.

"Tell you what," Rick said, after a long pause. He could see Rob was getting more agitated. "I'll give you what I have on this plate." The way the drug was spread out over the plate, it appeared to be much more than what was there.

Rob, who was a long time user, could spot quantity no matter how it was presented, but as Rick had planed, his craving was making his stomach churn. He looked down at the plate of dope, only about 50 cents worth ($50.00), seemed to hesitate for a moment, and then decided to take the deal.

"Damn, Rick. You're doing me wrong. I know I can get more for this bad assed computer. But it's cold outside — I don't feel like running around to get a better deal. I'll take what you got there on the plate, even though I know it ain't much."

"Cool," Rick said, a little more enthusiastically than he intended. He quickly picked up a playing card, and began to scrape the dope into a pile, and then said, "hold on while I find something to bag it," he said, while standing to go to the bedroom, but hesitated. "Aw hell naw. You go stand over by the door, while I'm gone. I don't trust your thieving ass."

"Come on man, you ain't got to put me down like that, Rick," is all Rob said, but not denying the accuracy of Rick's statement. He moved over to a spot near the hall door. As he waited, he looked longingly at the sleeping Nancy. *Damn, she's fine. I wish I had a woman like that. I'd be on her every day for sure,* he imagined, again, as he watched her firm, tank-toped, covered, breast, rise and fall as she slept on her back, with one shapely leg hanging over the side of the couch and the juncture just below her stomach looking overwhelmingly inviting.

Rick, came back from the bedroom with a sandwich bag, and proceeded to scoop the dope into it. Rob, who by now was licking his lips, and shuffling from one foot to the other, asked Rick if he could take a hit, now?

"Man, you know I don't allow that in my place. That's the last thing I need, a bunch of crack-heads sitting around begging, and stinking up the place."

"I know. I thought I might ask, anyway," Rob replied, while pocketing his booty and heading for the back door with Rick following.

After replacing the two by's, behind Rob, Rick returned to the living room. He took a quick glance at Nancy on the couch, on her back, one leg hanging down. He walked over to where she was sleeping, leaned over, and ran his hand between her parted legs. He could feel himself start to get excited. *Damn, she's fine,* he thought, his manhood rising.

He thought about pulling down her shorts and trying to do something while she was asleep, but not wanting to wake her because she might want more dope, he decided to leave her alone. While gently massaging his stiffness, he picked up the computer, and went to the bedroom to check out his new toy.

Damn, I got to go out later and see if I can find a charger for this damn thing, he thought, while falling across the sheet-less, bed, on top of the single blanket, and opening it up.

After Rob left Rick's, he had to decide where to go to smoke in peace. He considered going by Dave's, but decided against it. Dave would let him smoke if he gave him a rock. The problem came after Dave had smoked his rock. He'd begin to beg, and wouldn't stop until he was given more — this, Rob wasn't ready to deal with. He felt he'd met with a small stroke of luck while finding the computer just setting there, unprotected, and for the first time in a while, he'd gotten a quantity of drugs, and didn't want to share any more than necessary.

Rob knew he could go to Edward's, a dope house operator whose place was a few blocks over, and where he'd have taken the computer in the first place if Edward took contraband in place of money for his dope, but that wouldn't work either. *Edward would let him smoke in his place, but didn't like anyone bringing in their own supply. He might try Tiny's.* He discharged that thought, also. He'd seen Tiny with that freak, Elisabeth, earlier. He knew Tiny wouldn't let him in if he was doing what Tiny liked to do, party with her and eat snatch. He was running out or ideas, and about to find an alley with an empty garage, and smoke there. It would be cold, but his cravings were about to get the best of him — he needed a hit now, but where?

I know, Rob thought, a grin coming over his face, *I'll go by Phyllis and Roy's. Yeah, Phyllis, and Roy would be happy to let me smoke at their place for a rock apiece. They'd beg, but not too bad,* he thought.

A destination in mind, he began walking fast, heading for Roy's. His feet and hands felt like they were freezing, but the thought of hitting the first stone bolstered him against the weather. As he walked, he kept pulling the small bag out of his pocket to make sure he hadn't dropped it. He was getting paranoid, and he hadn't begun smoking yet.

Phyllis and Roy lived in an abandoned garage, behind a house that'd been seriously fire damaged. They heated the garage with a small electric heater Roy had found in the trash, and repaired. Whoever had abandoned the house had left the electric and water on. They cooked on a nearly burned out, single burner, hot plate. The couple, also, used the toilet in the house. It was remarkable the pipes hadn't frozen, considering the heat was not on in the house. Maybe it was the dripping faucets that saved the pipes from busting.

To halfway support themselves, they, as a team, panhandled in front of liquor stores and super markets to get money for food/Ramens, cigarettes, liquor, and of course, drugs. For the moment, the pair were reasonably comfortable in their garage home — better than being on the streets, but, if the electric or Water Company showed, they'd have to move somewhere else, probably another abandoned house. Lord knows there were enough of them around — some still having the utilities on.

Both, Phyllis, and Roy, had been disowned by their families because of their constant stealing of the family's property to by drugs, something they had in common before they met. They were both somewhat easygoing and a little slow-witted. They decided to live together because they felt better together than being alone. They'd want some of Rob's dope if he wanted to smoke with them, but they were slow smokers, and most likely wouldn't beg later, well not as hard as Dave, anyway. They'd be glad to have anything to smoke at all.

Rob arrived at the garage, and knocked on the side door — no response.

He yelled, in a whisper, "Roy... Phyllis!" Still no answer. He didn't panic. He knew where he could find them. The same place they were any time they weren't in the garage — out panhandling somewhere not too far away.

Rob headed towards the liquor store a couple blocks away, on Chalmers Street. Rounding the corner, sure enough, there they stood. One, working customers coming from one direction, and the other soliciting customers coming from the opposite direction. Roy, a short, dark-skinned man in his forties, who had several of his front teeth missing, and Phyllis, a heavy-breasted woman in her late thirties with unruly hair and protruding stomach, were a team all right. Not a single customer was missed, as they were approached with request for any loose change. As soon as the pair collected enough for a nickel or two, and maybe a half-pint of liquor, and on a good night, a pack of cheap cigarettes, they would cop their dope and head back to the garage to get high. After the dope and liquor was gone, they would return to the front of the store to begin the process again until the store closed. Day in and day out they did the same thing. The store's manager had tried to get them to move, and they would for a few minutes, but would return as soon as he'd gone back into the store. Eventually, he gave up trying to get them to stay away as long as he didn't receive too many complaints from his customers.

Rob approached Roy, "Hey playa, make enough to buy some cigarettes, or get a half pint?"

"My man Rob" Roy, responded, turning around to see Rob approaching. "Yeah, we got enough to get a pack of Smokers Choice, and a pint of Indian," (Mowhawk Vodka) Roy continued, "I know you must have something to smoke?"

"You know it, playa. Come on, let's go to your place, and get high," Rob encouraged.

"Word? Hold on a second," Roy said, as he looked over Rob's shoulder, and saw another customer approaching. Roy took off towards the man. He went into his begging mode, "please, Sir," Roy said, in his pleading voice, "can you help me? I'm only one dollar short of a pack of Kite." (Rolling tobacco). Roy hoped the customer was a smoker. Most smokers were more sympathetic, because they understood how not having a cigarette felt. Roy continued to beg, almost in a jog, as the customer walked fast, and waiving him off at the same time.

"Thank you anyway, maybe I can get a quarter when you come out?" Roy finished, as the customer disappeared inside the store. "Cheap ass punk," he said, under his breath, as he turned to Rob.

"Come on man. I'm ready to get high," Rob said, impatiently, his hands in his pockets, and doing a little jig to keep warm.

Roy turned around and called Phyllis over. "Give me what you got. Rob has something for us to smoke. I'm going in to get a pack of cigarettes, and a half-pint."

Phyllis gave what change she had to Roy, who went into the store to buy the liquor, and the cheap cigarettes. Roy coming out of the store, the trio headed for the garage.

"Where you been keeping yourself?" Roy, asked, Rob, as they walked.

"Man, all over the place since I got kicked out of the shelter. Mostly wherever I can get my high on — you know what I mean?" Rob replied.

"Yeah I know what you mean. Man we was lucky to find this garage we're staying in. No rent, no light bill, all we got to do is get money to buy us some Ramens and some dope. We got it made," Roy, bragged.

"A-men that," added Phyllis, "I just wish we had a better bed. Them rats, sometimes, run right across us when we're making love, or trying to get some sleep. Scares me so bad I can't sleep for the rest of the night."

"They smells that fishy booty of yours," Rob teased, jokingly, with a laugh.

"Boy you alta quit, you know you wish you could get some of this tight twat," Phyllis retorted, while pulling her thin coat tighter around her.

"Sho, you right, Rob said. "Hey Roy, you going to let me tap some of your old ladies good stank. I ain't had none in about a year, and I'm tired of whacking off," he said, truthfully, but in a joking manor.

"Don't bring me into y'alls mess," Roy said. "It's up to her, as long as she gets paid, I don't care what she does. She knows I'll still love her."

Rob laughed, "I don't know, I might take you up on that one day when I hit it big," he said, as he gave Phyllis a light tap on her rump as they walked.

"That's gonna cost you a nickel," Phyllis teased.

"Damn, girl, you is expensive," laughed Rob.

They continued to walk, now in silence, and not thinking about the weather, each thinking about that first blast of white smoke from their stems.

"Aw, damn," Rob said, after a while, "I got a lighter but it's damn near dead. It ain't got enough fluid for all three of us. Y'all got one?"

"Naw, I ain't got one," said Roy.

"What we gonna to do? We gotta have something to flame the rocks. I know this lighter ain't gonna last for all of us." Rob said, stopping in his tracks and holding up his nearly empty lighter, and then sticking his hands deep in the pockets of his flimsy jacket. "Hold on for a moment. Let me see how much change I got left," he said, pulling out the few cents he had left after buying the liquor and cigarettes. "Good, I'm only about fifteen cents short of fifty cents. I tell y'all what — y'all wait here for me. I'm going back to the store and beg up enough to get a lighter. It shouldn't take no more than five minutes. I can get that much easy. Someone will probably give me a quarter real quick. I'll be right back," he said, turning around to walk back to the store with a slight limp. Earlier tonight, he'd slipped on some ice, and twisted his ankle, hence the limp.

After Roy left, Rob saw a chance to see if Phyllis was serious about letting him hit that one time in the future. "Was you serious about giving me some later on?" he asked.

"Hell no, mutha. I ain't giving you nothing. You can buy some if you got a couple rocks, but you ain't getting nothing free here," Phyllis responded, her hands on her hips, and the cold air condensing her warm breath as she spoke.

"Yeah, that's what I meant. You know I wouldn't play you cheap like that."

"I know. I just don't want no misunderstanding."

"You know, I'm giving you a rock tonight. Do you thing I can just touch it for one second? Just to keep my mind focused on getting some later — you know what I mean?"

"Well…. I guess so. Come on, make it quick, before Roy gets back. Just a quick touch, no fingering, or that's going to cost you more than a rock."

"Thanks Phyllis," Rob said, moving in close to her and reaching under her coat and skirt underneath. He ran his hand up, and was happy to find she wore no underwear. Moving his hand higher he cupped her hairy mound. He could feel himself stir in his pants. His breath came faster. She was the first woman he'd touch in a long while, as he said.

Phyllis jumped at his touch, pushing his hand away.

"Damn, Rob. You got some cold hands. That's enough. Roy might see you."

Rob ignored her protest, and held his hand on her warm mound for a moment longer, and then pulling back, while saying, "um… um… um… I'm definitely coming back for some of that. My hand might be cold, but your twat sure ain't. The next time I gets me a quantity, it's me and you, at Dave's place. Cool?"

"Yeah. Whatever. I might let Dave hit it one time too, if he's got any money. Be cool, here comes Roy. Don't forget about your promise. Two rocks and no less."

"You got it baby," Rob said, turning to see Roy quickly limping back to them.

"I told y'all it wouldn't take long for me to get back,"

Roy said, as he passed Rob and Phyllis, walking fast, and with out stopping. "Come on I'm ready to get high."

Phyllis turned to follow her man, with Rob following. As she walked in front of him, he grabbed a hand full of her large behind. Phyllis looked over her shoulder and smiled back at Rob while thinking, *yeah fool, that's gonna cost you another nickel.*

"I gotta go and pee, don't start without me," Phyllis said, as soon as they entered the garage. She excused her self, and on the run, went to use the toilet in the cold, dark, vacant, house that still smelled of burnt wood, and was a little creepy with the sound of something hanging loose banging in the constant winter wind. She stood, legs spread, and squatted over the cold toilet without her butt touching the broken seat.

Once inside the garage, Rob looked around, and saw the single bulb hanging from a rafter by its cord, and glowing faintly, barely enough to light the space. Seeing the carpet covering the once bare concrete floor, he said, "Damn, Roy, y'all making the place pretty comfortable. Where did you find the carpet?"

"Nice, ain't it? That came out of a vacant house about two blocks over. Would have moved in there but the lights and water was off. There is a nice bed in there too I'm going back and get tomorrow, but forget that, let's see what you got," Roy, impatiently queried, as he unfolded a wooden folding chair, and positioned it next to the old wobbly card table, and took a seat, leaving Rob to find his own seat.

Rob found two empty plastic milk crates, and stacked them top down next to the card table, and sat on top of them. There were many of those crates around the impromptu living space. In one corner, they were stacked on their sides, four high, and four wide, to make a pretty good storage cabinet. "You know what?" he said, still looking around, and seeing the quilt covered mattress on the floor, "if I was you, I'd put some of those crates in the right place, and bring out two doors from inside the house..." He was interrupted by Phyllis, who was returning from the house.

"Hey Phyllis," Rob continued, seeing her returning, "I was just telling Roy here, if y'all brought two doors out of the house, y'all could place them on top of a few of them crates. And if y'all placed the mattress on top of the doors, y'all would have a bed that was off the floor."

Phyllis stopped to listen to what Rob was saying, as she stood looking at the mattress on the floor. When Rob finished, she turned to Roy, saying, "I don't believe this, Roy, why didn't you think of something like that? You know how scared I am when we're on that mattress, and a rat runs across it. Damn good idea, Rob."

"I told you I was going to get the bed from that house we were in, so don't sweat it." Roy defended himself. "Now, lets see what you is got Rob. I'm ready to flame up some good dope."

"Okay, I'm coming. Break the seal on that half-pint and let me take a swig," Rob said, as he pulled the small bag of crack from his pocket.

Roy did as he was told and handed over the opened half-pint of cheap vodka, while his eyes were locked on the small bag of crack Rob was trying to untie. "Nice sack, what you got there, about four or five dimes?" he asked, Rob.

"Yeah, about five," Rob, continued, "I kinda found a laptop computer just laying there on the back seat of this car. It was calling to me — please take me — I'm getting cold, so I took it. Just to keep it from freezing, you understand," Rob, embellished, laughingly.

Both men slapped hands, as they laughed together.

"I took it to Rick's place, and this is what he gave me," Rob finished, as held up the bag of rocks.

Phyllis, seeing the small bag of rocks, left to get another saucer from the kitchen in the abandoned house.

"Wait a minute, you mean to tell me that's all Rick gave you for a laptop computer?" Roy, asked, unbelievingly, and continued, "man, do you know what a laptop is going for?"

"No," responded, Rob, honestly.

"Well, I ain't never owned one, but I understand they goes for about Five-hundred, to around Two-thousand dollars, you dummy. Rick got you good" Roy, admonished.

About this time, Phyllis returned to the garage and took a seat, on the mattress. She held onto the small plate to put her rock on once the split was made, "You ain't split that stuff up yet?" she asked.

"Hey baby, let me tell you how Rick just mugged Rob," Roy said, as he laughed so hard, he could hardly get the words out, and wanting to get back at Rob for the comment about the bed thing, and making him seem kind of stupid in front of his woman.

"Okay, keep it up, and you ain't gonna get none of this. Me and Phyllis is gonna smoke by ourselves." Rob warned, starting to get a little angry.

Roy noticed Rob's annoyance, and shut up.

"Forget him, just give me my part," Phyllis pleaded.

"Give me something to split it up on," Rob said.

"Here use this," Phyllis said, handing Rob the dirty saucer.

After brushing as much of the dirt off the saucer as he could, Rob dumped the contents of the small plastic bag onto the plate. He split off, what he estimated, was a dime apiece, for Phyllis and Roy, and took the rest for himself.

After breaking her dime into small crumbs, Phyllis placed a small piece into her piece of broken TV antenna stem, and getting the lighter form Roy, quickly lit it up. As she burned her rock, her eyes were dancing in her head, shifting from side to side, looking at nothing. She held the lighter to the stem, while she was no longer inhaling. The dope had her geeked. She was able to hold onto the hot metal tube long after it must have gotten unbearably hot. Eventually, she exhaled the breath she was holding, while holding the metal stem up and looking at it.

Roy broke his dime into two smaller pieces. He dropped a piece into a broken glass stem, and taking the hot lighter from Phyllis, lit his piece of stone, and quickly sucked in the thick white smoke. After exhaling through his nose, he got up and began walking around the garage, peeping through any crack in the walls, or garage door, he could find, while stuffing small pieces of newsprint into the cracks. He was paranoid, and afraid someone might be outside peeping in at them. Not only did he peep through any crack he could find, he sometimes put his ear to the wall, as if he could hear something on the other side, all while still holding his stem in his hand.

Rob watched the pair go through their antics as he prepared his dope for smoking. He'd seen their behavior before, and others he'd smoked with, and paid no attention. Using the lighter, which Roy left lying on the card table — he fired up his makeshift pipe made of a plastic half shot liquor bottle, with a small metal tube stuffed in a hole in the side. He smoked his rocks as fast as he could. He didn't want to share anymore with his host. As soon as he exhaled, he put in another good-sized stone and fired it up. He smoked so fast he didn't get the benefit of each hit, wasting most of his. He might have just as well given his companions another small crumb. He'd have enjoyed his dope more. When he smoked it so fast, lighting one stone behind the other, he only got the high from the first hit, the rest not affecting him except to make him a touch more paranoid. It was as if he'd smoked only one stone, giving him one continuous high that fell as soon as he finished his last, hurried, hit. His greed came back to cheat him.

As expected, before he could finish all of his, Roy and Phyllis did beg for another small piece that Rob gave to them. He wanted to smoke in peace, and not have to listen to their begging. It took the trio all of an hour to smoke everything — and about another half-hour to finish pushing their stems.

Long after Roy, and Phyllis had exhausted theirs, Rob, who had more residue was still getting a strong cloud from pushing his pipe with a straightened piece of coat hanger he kept with him. After each push and re-light, he gave the couple, shotguns — the practice of hitting his stem, holding the smoke in for a while, and then blowing the smoke into someone else's mouth. He did that until his stem / pipe, also, held no more residue. Even after he knew the pipe was exhausted, he still sat and looked at it, turning it one way then the next, while hoping for one last hit to magically appear.

After each shotgun from Rob, Phyllis, picked up the edge of the quilt on the mattress, as well as the corner of the mattress, sometimes lifting it half off the concrete floor, and feeling under it, trying to find an imaginary piece of dope she might have hidden there, but hadn't. Eventually, she gave up on looking under the mattress, and began to pick at the folds of the quilt, smoothing it, and staring at it, as if she could will a crumb to miraculously appear.

Finally, her high worn off, and she turned to Rob to try and get another crumb she was sure he'd hidden somewhere. Rob had to explain to her the dope was completely gone, and to stop pestering him, which did little to stop her. Once geeked, she'll continue to beg as long as there was the smallest chance she could get another crumb.

Now thoroughly geeked and tired of listening to

Phyllis beg, and while thinking on how he was going to get more, Rob was ready to leave. It was just getting dark outside, so he thought he'd go out and see what he could steal. As with most thieves, he did his best work under the cover of darkness. He sat, a blank look on his face, trying to figure where his best chance of taking something would be. He'd made his stalking rounds earlier that day, and knew nothing of value was left unprotected, except for the laptop he lucked up on. But he was determined to come up with something, anything, to trade for more rocks.

"I'll be back," is all Rob said, as he got up to exited the garage. As he opened the door, several small pieces of newspaper Roy had jammed into the cracks above and along the sides of the door, fell to the floor. He stopped to look at the shower of paper, looked over his shoulder at the now seated Roy, who was finishing off the Vodka with the bottle turned up while draining the last drop. He shook his head and then slammed the door shut. *Greedy bastards*, he thought, as he stepped into the cold night air, his flimsy jacket doing little to ward off the chill in the winter breeze. He looked up at the darkening sky, and saw ominous clouds, and hoped it didn't snow before he finished his mission.

Rob was still a little pissed at being shortchanged by Rick. He was determined to, somehow, make another big score, and this time Rick would give him what he deserved for his plunder. Maybe a little more to make up for the shortfall.

When he first began his quest, the drug had numbed him against the cold, but eventually wore off. He was now starting to get colder than if he hadn't gotten high. His blood vessels were restricted, causing less warming blood to circulate to his extremities. Crack did that. It's a known fact that smoking the drug can cause the blood vessels to restrict to such a degree the smoker's blood pressure rose high enough to precipitate a stroke, or irregular heart beats, resulting in a heart attack, but it wasn't a heart attack he should be worried about tonight.

He spent several hours looking for a house to break into. He circled block after block, stopping at this home or that house. Sometimes he'd go so far as to sneak into the back yard and inspect his probable target from the rear, only to reject it for one reason or another. One thing was sure, he wasn't going to quit until he'd made a score.

He knew of a home in which a single working woman lived. When he'd walked by it earlier, the lights were still on, and her car still in the driveway. He decided to pay the house another visit. It took him about fifteen minutes to return to the targeted house — this time, finding the house dark, and the woman's car was missing.

Yeah, even if she is home, I could over power her, and take whatever I want, including some hot stank if the situation was right, he thought, as he walked past the house, turned around, and walked past it again.

That's what crack dose to most people. It causes the individual to make bad decisions. Causes them to act without thinking about the consequences, of if they do recognize the wrong — not care. It tricks men into thinking they are horny. In reality, the drug robs the male of the ability to have an erection, therefore, if Rob did attempt to rape the woman, he wouldn't have been able to, unless the affects of the drug had worn off.

On his third approach, Rob crept around to the side of

the house that was in darkness. He was looking for a way in. He found a basement window looking like it wasn't securely fastened. Bending over, and kicking from behind, he gave the window a hard shove with his foot, and just as he'd suspected, the flimsy lock gave way.

Getting down on his stomach, his feet going in first, he wiggled through the small opening. It was a tight fit, but he being no more than skin and bones, was able to squeeze through. His feet hanging down, met with no support, so he decided to drop to the floor. His drop was not as long as he'd anticipated. He landed on top of a clothes dryer, making what seemed to him, a loud hollow sound. He froze for a moment, listening for any indication of someone being frightened out of their sleep. He heard nothing other than his racing heart.

He jumped down off the dryer, landing on a pile of dirty clothes on the floor, almost falling, but able to catch himself, grabbing the back of the dryer. His eyes slowly adjusting to the dark, he looked around for something he could take right then and there, and found nothing more than several cardboard boxes that didn't appear to have anything of value in them. Searching further, he was able to find a door slightly ajar at the top of some stairs, and which led to the kitchen. Going to the stairs, he stood for a moment to listen for any movement in the kitchen. He only heard the sound of the furnace cycling on to blow warm air to the rest of the house, and feeling good on his cold body. After another moment, he began his climb up the stairs. He put his foot on the first tread, and tested it to see if it would squeak — it held solid.

As he slowly climbed, he thought, *how clever I am, climbing these stairs ever so slowly, not making any loose treads squeak. Yeah, as quiet as a cat. Yeah, I'm a cat burglar. The unstoppable, Rob, here to take everything you got. Un-hum, a master burglar on a mission, doing what I do best. I wonder how good her thang' going to be when I dip in it. She probably ain't had no good lovin in a long time. She'll probably love her some good Rob, might want me to move in here with her, and sex her all day, every day,* he thought, the drug perverting his mind.

At the top of the stairs, he paused again. Except for the sound of a battery-operated clock hanging on the kitchen wall, the house was dead silent. Through the door, and slowly into the kitchen, oh so very slowly, he crept further into the house, his eyes adjusting more to the darkness. He jumped as the refrigerator started, causing his heart to thump in his chest.

Damn, Rob, chill out man. You got to be cool if you is going to pull this off, he told himself. He found a knife block with several large knives stuck in their various slits, and a meat cleaver most prominent. Pulling it, it felt heavy in his hand. *Yeah, if the wench gives me any problems, this will change her mind,* he thought, with his heart slowing. He began easing along the wall as he crept further into the house. Through another door and into the dinning room he sneaked, each step carefully placed. He stopped to take note of a shinny, silver looking platter in a glass fronted china cabinet.

Yeah, I'll take that on my way out. It looks expensive. It might be real silver. I bet she's got a DVD and maybe a nice stereo too. Man, I'm going to clean up in here. I bet Roy won't be laughing when I comes back with a whole eight-ball this time. Hell I might go on and get some of Phyllis's hot stank right there in the garage, and make Roy wait outside while I do his woman. Yeah, maybe I'll do her right in front of him. I bet he won't be laughing then.

Through a large archway, he eased into the front room. He made a mental note of what he'd take with him when he left. *I got to remember to bring a blanket back down stairs with me to carry all this good stuff in when I leave, but first I got to get me some middle aged booty, make her holler for more. Even better yet, I could lock the doors and stay here for a week or two, eat her food, and watch her TV,* he thought. *Hell, I might invite Roy and Phyllis over, and Roy can bang him some new stuff, while I gets my thang on with Phyllis in the same bed, right next to him. That would be wild, I bet,* he thought.

As he crept through the house, his mind raced — *this will be a premo score. I ain't doing nothing but busting in houses from now on. Maybe, only single women's houses? I'll be the terror of the neighborhood. Yeah, bust in, bust me out some booty, and take what they got. I'd better start wearing me some kind of disguise. Hell, I might be able to tie them up and rape me some stank any time I wants, and use their place to smoke in. Who knows? I might be able to turn them out, and they might not want me to leave,* he sickly thought? *Rick will be happy to see what I'm going to bring him, maybe another laptop? This time, if Rick don't give me what I deserved for my stuff, I'll take it to Poco's place. Poco will take care of me. The only problem with Poco's dope was the quality ain't as good as Rick's, but I'll get more.*

His thoughts returned to his task at hand as he reached a stairwell leading to the second floor. Still stealthily quiet, he started to climb the stairs to the second level, while expecting to make a killing from the stuff he'd take. *But first, I got to get me some old school stank,* he continued to think.

Here I come, me-lady, coming to give you some young dick. I hope you is ready to be screwed real good, he thought, as he made it to the first landing where the stairs turned to continue up. *Almost there,* he thought.

With the cleaver held low by his leg, and slowly, ever so slowly, he peeped around the corner while looking up at the top of the stairs

He saw the flash, but never heard the mussel blast of the double-barreled shotgun that all but decapitated him.

———

The single woman who lived in the house had, having had a long day, decided to stay home and get some rest. She and her daughter, as they had every year, spent the whole day doing some early Christmas shopping. But, this year, instead of shopping at the mall, the daughter had her mother drive her to a big box store that also had a gun department.

While the mother was off perusing the clothes department, the daughter bought her mother a shotgun. She knew the neighborhood her mother lived in was going downhill fast. She feared for her mother's safety. But she couldn't let her mother see her buy the weapon. The mother would have done every thing she could to stop her from purchasing the weapon.

While loading the car, the mother saw the gift-wrapped weapon, wondered what it was, but didn't pry while thinking it might be a gift for her. Returning home, the daughter presented the odd shaped box to her mother, who was totally surprised by the early gift, but didn't have the slightest idea what it was.

As the mother unwrapped the angular shaped gift, she wondered what could be so heavy. The gun was in a carrying case that gave no hint as to its contents. The mother rested the case on the coffee table and opened it. Her first reaction was to jump back at the first sight of the deadly looking weapon.

"What is this, baby?" The mother asked, "You know I don't want no guns in my house. Besides, I'm scared of them."

"I know, momma. I know you think you don't need this, but please take it anyway to make me feel a little more at ease. You don't have to put it where you can see it. I'll load it for you and you can put it under your bed, and forget about it. Please momma, do it for me. I can't rest thinking about you staying in this house by yourself, and you not having anything to protect yourself. I know you'll never need it, but please take it, just for my peace of mind."

The woman relented and took the gun. The daughter showed the mother how to point and pull the triggers of the two barrels, one at a time. Of course the mother wouldn't touch the weapon, but watched as the daughter, whose husband was on the police force and had shown her how to use a similar weapon she had at home.

The daughter loaded the weapon, placing two buckshot shells in the two chambers and took the firearm upstairs to place it under the mother's bed. It was clear the mother was still a little dubious about having the gun under her bed, but didn't press the issue. She planed to place it in a closet as soon as the daughter was gone. No way was she going to sleep with that thing just below her. *Hell,* she thought, *it might go off or something.* She, in her wildest imagination, thought she'd ever have a reason to use it.

After the gun was concealed under the mother's bed, they discussed going out to get something to eat. It was at that moment, Rob, while looking for somewhere to break into, passed the house and saw the lights on and the car in the driveway.

The mother declined the invitation. She told her daughter to take the car and bring it back tomorrow. They said their good-bys and the daughter left. The mother, totally exhausted, went upstairs to take a nap before getting up to fix herself something to eat later that evening. Fortunately, she wasn't a deep sleeper. A few hours later, when Rob landed on the dryer, she was startled out of her sleep.

When she heard, what she thought was a noise in the basement — her first thought was she might have been dreaming. She sat straight up in the bed, trying to hear over her racing hart. She could hear nothing suspicious. She started to lay back down after hearing nothing else, but changed her mind and decided to check just to make sure. She knew she wouldn't be able to go back to sleep unless she knew for sure everything was all right.

Retrieving the shotgun from under the bed, now happy her daughter had forced it on her, she was glad two shells were already chambered. While barefooted, with no bathrobe, and dressed in only her lightweight nightgown, she eased into the hallway. She listen intently, wondering what she'd do if she did hear something? *Probably drop the shotgun and run back to the bedroom,* she mused. Her daughter had told her all she had to do was point the gun in the general direction she wanted to shoot, hold the weapon tight against her shoulder, and pull the trigger that would fire one barrel. She was told that if she had too, she could pull the second trigger to fire the other barrel. *Yeah, right,* she thought, *the way these things kicks, if I fire one barrel, I'll probably be too busy getting up off the floor to do much of anything else.* But she was still glad she had the heavy shotgun in her shaking hands. *I'll have to thank her later,* she planed, *when I tell her about this episode.* She still didn't think she was in danger, but wasn't taking any chances.

Walking ever so slowly, the shotgun at the ready, she made it to the end of the hall where the stairs began. She was about to take a step down on the first step, when she saw on the wall, a shadow of someone approaching the first landing — the shadow being cast by the glow from a streetlight in front of the house, and which streamed through a crack in the drapes covering the front window.

She jumped back, and brought the shotgun to her shoulder. She peered down the barrel at a point near the wall where the person would be as they came around the corner on to the first landing.

Her breathing rapid — her hart was beating so hard she was sure anyone in the house could hear it. The barrel of the shotgun was shaking, but she stood her ground with her finger on the triggers, ready to fire.

When she saw a head ease into the stairwell, and turn to look up in her direction, she pulled both triggers. She'd planed to pull only one trigger, but she being so excited, and with the adrenaline racing through her veins, pulled both.

The blast from the shotgun knocked her back onto her bottom, as she'd imagined earlier, and causing her shoulder to hurt from the recoil of the powerful big bore weapon.

She sat there until she regained her sight from the blinding flash of the gunpowder. She couldn't hear anything — her ears were ringing. Had she missed? Her vision gradually returning, she could see a large hole in the landing wall, and what looked like black spots around it. She was afraid she'd missed. Her first inclination was to run back to her bedroom, lock the door, and try to reload the shotgun if she could. The problem was, she couldn't remember where her daughter had said she stored the other shotgun shells. She sat there her mind racing while thinking, and listening for any indication someone was still in the house.

No one could have ducked back before I fired, she reasoned. *No way I could have missed.* She decided to inspect the hole in the landing wall, sure whoever was coming up the stairs would have taken off behind the blast. She didn't hear anybody running out, but she wouldn't because of the ringing in her ears.

Staying on her bottom, she slid closer to the end of the stairs, and took a good look at the gaping hole with dark spots all around it. That's when she realized the dark spots were flesh, blood, skull, and bits of brains.

She started screaming, and was still whimpering when the police, who the neighbors had called behind hearing the shotgun blast, forced their way in and found her.

The woman had to spend a week in the hospital. Her

shooting Rob had almost caused her to have a heart attack. She eventually recovered and returned home. She'd remain a nervous wreck for some time to come, but she'd be all right with the passage of time. As traumatized as she was, the shotgun remained under her bed. She was afraid of it, but not that afraid.

As for Rob, let's say he'd never break into another home.

It was the next day and Nancy was in the front room sitting on the couch naked, smoking two rocks Rick had given her for the sex they just had. She was in such a hurry to smoke the rocks she didn't bother to wash or get dressed.

After having sex with Nancy, Rick returned to the bedroom to further investigate his new toy. Earlier, he was lying across the bed tinkering with his newly acquired laptop when he discovered how to open the programs not password protected. He found a lot of insurance stuff, and several pornographic folders. The porn was of the owner of the computer, and some woman. Whatever it was, it turned Rick on, hence the love making session he'd just had with Nancy, who was more than willing to engage in for more dope.

The computer provided Rick with a welcomed diversion from getting high. He spent several hours learning how to work it. The only problem was the battery. The low battery warning light had come on a short while ago. Rick's decision to take the computer from Rob, minus the charger, was coming back to hunt him. If he was going to continue to use it, he'd have to go out and buy a charger. It was early morning and he figured he had enough time to eat a little something, take a short nap, and then pry Nancy's lips from her stem long enough for her to accompany him to the pawn shop first to get a few dollars and then to the electronics store.

Unknown to Rick, a new crack house had opened on his block. The operators of the new dope den were a gang of young, gangster-rap inspired thugs, who were out to make a fast buck, and a reputation. They were loud, and belligerent, and delighted in flashing their handguns, while declaring how they took no crap.

They would stand on the front porch of the abandoned house in which they set up shop, talking loud, playing their music at maximum volume, and making a general nuisance of themselves.

They would yell, "Rocks here," to anyone walking by, even to the youth on the street, as well as to people who it was obvious weren't in the life.

They, sometimes, blocked the street with their chrome wheeled, vintage, whips, and dared anyone to say anything. They, in their youthful exuberance, decided to take over all of the drug distribution in the neighborhood.

They decided to not do a drive-by at Rick's. As they had to another competing dope house on the west side of Detroit before the police put so much pressure on them they had to move east.

They planed to catch Rick outside of his house, or somehow gain entrance and pistol-whip him and his woman with orders to leave the neighborhood. And, maybe in the process, have a little fun with Rick's fine woman.

The first thing Rick did after his short nap was to fire up a 51. Lately it seemed he couldn't do anything without dope in him. The 51 caused Rick to become sluggish, and made him move in what seemed like, slow motion, but he liked playing with the computer so much he was still determined to go out and get the charger.

Nancy was still sitting naked on the couch, and still trying to push her stem when Rick woke up. She'd been in that same spot for several hours. He wondered if she'd sneaked into his stash while he was asleep. But he wasn't too worried about it. He knew she wouldn't take too much if she did. At least not enough where he noticed anything missing when he set up his 51.

He got dressed, and was about to pry Nancy lips off her stem, when he heard a knock at the front door.

"Take your naked ass in the bedroom while I see who this is at the front door," Rick told Nancy, while going to the window next to the door and peeping around the covering bed sheet.

"Who is it?" he asked, the new face.

"JB," came the reply from the stranger. "I got something you might want, as he held up a DVD player for Rick to see. The DVD player peaked Rick's interest. *Maybe I can get it for a tiny dime rock,* Rick thought. "Go around to the side door," Rick instructed, as he pushed the bed sheet back into place, and went to close the bedroom door on his way to the side door.

"Who is it?" asked Nancy, who was lying on the bed with the single cover pulled up nearly covering her head. She was geeked from the many hours smoking the dope, with her own case of paranoia going.

"I don't know, some new guy who wants to pawn a DVD player. Stay in here until I get rid of him," he ordered.

Rick made his way to the side door, and removed the two-by-fours in place to prevent forced entry. Had he not smoked the 51, he'd have never invited the stranger in. He'd have asked some questions, at least find out how he knew about his place, and if the answers weren't right, he'd have made the man go elsewhere. But being high from the 51, his mind was not functioning. Another indication of how the drug only took from the user.

Rick had opened the door a couple inches to make sure the stranger was alone, when two other men, who were standing with their backs against the outside of the house, joined the stranger in pushing Rick back, and forcing entry, their pistols at the ready.

Rick stumbled backwards, and then tripped on the contraband piled on the floor. He fell onto his back — unarmed and high, he was powerless to stop the men from coming in. The stranger, the first in, threw the broken DVD player aside, and pulled a pistol he had tucked in his waste band.

"What? What? Don't move punk, or I'll cap your ass where you're at. Where is your door man?" the stranger, asked, Rick, while pointing his gun at Rick's head, a look in his eyes indicating he wasn't bluffing.

"I ain't got one," Rick said, one hand held up, as if to repel an attack, and his eyes so wide they seemed to glow.

The invaders laughed in unison, while berating Rick for being so stupid.

"A dope house without a shotgun? You talk about dumb. This punk really don't know what he's doing," said the stranger to his companions, relieved that he didn't have to deal with a shotgun man.

"I can't believe this. Nobody on the door?" the first man repeated with his arms out to his side, the pistol in one hand. "Get this idiot of the floor," he ordered.

The men picked Rick off the floor, and were half carrying him towards the front room, when they came face to face with Nancy, who, while still naked, and tweaked out of her mind, came around a corner to check on the disturbance she'd heard.

"Damnnnn," the stranger, a.k.a. JB, and the obviously the leader, uttered, when he caught sight of Nancy's young and curvaceous body.

Nancy was so high she couldn't process what was happening, but she wasn't so high she overlooked the pistols in the hands of the men. She froze in her tracks.

JB walked up to Nancy and raised one of her breast with the cold barrel of his pistol. "Baby, you so fine, you need to dump this looser, and hook up with me. I know how to take care of a fine shortie like you," he said, while pressing himself against her, and reaching for her behind.

Comprehension now setting in, Nancy started to tremble. She turned her head away, and gently tried to push the gun from under her breast. Her turning her head, as if sickened, angered JB. He quickly stepped behind her, wrapped his arm around her neck, and proceeded to pull her toward the bedroom — the pistol to her head.

"Hold up a minute, I'm going to hit this right now," JB said to his posse, "Y'all take that punk and tie him up until I gets through with this fine piece of meat here," he said, as he dragged Nancy into the bedroom, and closed the door.

The men dragged Rick into the livingroom and sat him on the floor in front of the couch, and began looking for something to tie him with.

Rick hadn't said a word until now. Seeing JB take his woman into the bedroom, obviously to rape her, loosened his tongue.

"You ain't gonna to kill us, is you? I ain't got much money, but I got a lot of good stuff you can have, just let me live. Y'all can have a turn with my woman, if you wants. Just let us go when y'all is finished," Rick pleaded.

The man who was standing in front of Rick, gun

pointed at Rick's head, glared down with a smirk on his face, and then kicked Rick in the mouth as hard as he could. "Shut up, punk. All we gonna do is kick your ass, and if you ain't out of dodge by the end of the day, we will be back to cap you and your o-g." (Old- girl) "And I is going to get me some of that sweet ass anyway," the gunman declared.

The other three gunmen echoed his sentiment. "Hell yeah, me too," one said.

"Word," mirrored another, while slapping the hand of the third invader.

Rick knew the men would not let him and his woman live after all of them had raped her. Now, cold sober, tears began to run down his face. He was scared mindless. He began to tremble, uncontrollably. The men, while using Rick's belt to tie him, could hear the sound of the bed banging loudly, and rapidly against the wall in the bedroom.

Rick, hearing the rape of Nancy, began shaking even more. He put his head back — eyes closed, and began weeping openly, the tears streaming down the side of his face and into his ears.

"Oh yeah, hell yeah, damn, that's some good stank," JB seemed to be saying a little louder than normal, as if he were trying to put on a show for his boys, and as the rhythm of the banging bed against the wall increased.

To Rick, it seemed like the sounds of the rape had gone on for an hour. Actually, only a few minutes had passed. Finally the sounds quieted, the door opened, and JB stepped out, gun in hand, while looking back at Nancy, saying, "Don't move."

He left the door open. Nancy could be seen lying on the bed, naked and on her back, her hands covering her face. She was sobbing deeply, her body trembling as she wept.

"Damn, that is some goood stank, tight too, anybody else want some?" JB asked his companions, grinning widely.

Boogieman, who was holding the gun on Rick, volunteered a little too eagerly. "Me next, but I don't want no sloppy seconds, I want some of that sweet back door," he said.

The one called Boogieman deserved his moniker. He had a misshapen head, narrow at the top, and wide at the mouth, with oversized bucked teeth, large lips, and bulbous eyes. His short body was adorned with wide shoulders and thick arms. He'd adopted the nickname after being told by a woman he was one scary looking dude. That he looked like the Boogieman. He, later, felt acting the way he looked detracted from the way he felt about himself. After a while, his violent act became his violent nature. He'd offten say he was the Boogieman and your worse nightmare.

He hated women. They'd rejected and made fun of him all his life. And now that he had the chance, he was going to get even via Nancy. He was going to take revenge for a lifetime of ridicule by women, and make them pay, without impunity, through her.

Rick, who was bleeding from the mouth, started to protest, but said nothing after a long look from Boogieman.

"J, keep an eye on this punk, while I do my thaang," Boogieman, asked, JB. He jammed his pistol into his back pocket as he walked to the open bedroom door. He, while unbuckling his belt, went into the bedroom, and while looking back over his shoulder, a big toothy grin on his misshapen face, closed the door.

A long silence followed — then a loud, angry,

demanding voice, screamed, "suck it! I said suck it, bitch!," the voice could be heard yelling, followed by a louder slap that caused Rick to jump, and with the tears increasing, drop his head while whimpering, his whole body shaking with his sobs.

"Yeah, Yeah, that's good, harder, yeah," the voice continued, "Now roll over and let me see that apple booty," the voice, loudly, demanded.

More silence, and then a muffled scream from Nancy.

The sound of the bed banging the wall started again. Bam... Bam... Bam... Bam, and with every bang, Nancy could be heard screaming. The other men in the front room stopped doing what they were doing, and stared at the closed bedroom door. Even to them, the attack seemed to be a touch more violent than they were prepared for.

The Bed continued to bang against the wall. Bam... Bam... Bam... Non-stop. The screams continued. Rick felt terrified and helpless to stop the assault. He knew his fate was sealed. Especially it Boogie had anything to say about it. *No way were they going to let him go, he being a witness to the violation.*

Bam... Scream... Bam... Scream... Bam... Bam... Scream, the torture continued. All the men in the front room only stared at the closed door, mesmerized, including JB.

All the sudden, everyone in the front room jumped, as someone knocked loudly on the front door. In the bedroom, the banging, and screaming continued, unabated.

JB ordered one of his cohorts to peek, and see who was knocking, and to get rid of them.

One of the subordinate thugs went to the bed sheet covered window, pulled it back, and peered at the person knocking. "We closed," he said to the knocker.

"Let me talk to Rick real quick," the knocker replied.

"I said we closed," responded the thug, and stepped

back from the window.

The tormented screams continued from the bedroom. Whatever Boogie was doing to Nancy in the name of his insane revenge, must have been vicious.

What was once knocking turned into insistent pounding on the front door. "I just want to ask Rick something, it won't take long. Is Nancy there?" the knocker asked loudly, through the closed front door.

"Get rid of that crack-head," JB told the thug, as he looked back at the bedroom door, the banging bed, and the screams.

The thug cracked the front door a couple inches, and asked the knocker what he wanted.

The screams continued...

The knocker pushed the door open a couple more inches, and tried to enter the room. He stopped with a weird look on his face when he caught sight of the gun in the thug's hand. He shifted his gaze to the closed bedroom door as if he heard something emanating from there.

The screams continued...

"Tell you what, I'll come back in about an hour," the knocker said, as he withdrew from the front door a little faster than he should have. The thug, knowing the knocker had heard the screams, tried to stop him — tell him he could come in. But before the thug could utter a word, the knocker was off the porch, and walking away fast, while looking back over his shoulder, a look of utter despair on his face.

"I think he heard the girl," the thug told JB, after closing the door.

The screams continued...

"Damn, why did you let him get away?" JB asked.

"Damn, J, I didn't know he was going to move that fast," responded the thug.

The screaming from the bedroom finally quieted,

although the sound of the bed moving could still be heard.

"We got to finish here, and get the hell out of this place," JB instructed. "D, you go and get Boogie off that wench, while we take care of business out here," JB directed.

D went to the bedroom door, and opened it. What he saw sent chills through his body. Boogieman was still pumping Nancy hard, from the rear. She had a pillow under her stomach, elevating her rear end. Her head was turned toward the door, eyes open, motionless, and staring blankly at D, but not seeing him, as he stepped back from the doorway, while watching the brutal madness, and with his mouth hanging open.

One of Nancy's arms hang limply over the side of the bed and swung back and forth to the motion of her attacker. Her butt was covered with, what looked like a combination of blood and feces.

Boogieman was looking at D, that wide, big tooth, sadistic, grin, on his ugly misshapen face. He seemed to be in a trance, and was not aware of what he was doing.

The odor of feces overpowering, D was about to vomit, as he backed completely out of the bedroom with his nose pinched between his forefinger and thumb. He turned to get JB, "J, I think the crazy mutha done banged that girl to death!" he said, as he backed up a couple more steps. A look of questioning horror on his face.

JB, who was telling Rick why they were going to kick his punk ass, turned to D's summons. "What now?" he said, as he turned to see what D was talking about. "What you talking about, piss brain, you can't kill nobody that way," he said, as he walked past D, entered the bedroom and saw the motionless Nancy — a trickle of blood drying in one corner of her mouth. A golf ball sized bubble of mucus hang from one nostril, not growing or busting, just hand there, probably filled with part of her last breath.

"Aw, snap, what the hell you doing, Boogie? Get your ass off her! I think you done killed the bitch," JB said, as he raised her lifeless arm, and tried to find a pulse — there was none. The fingertips of the hanging hand were dark red, already beginning to fill with lavidity. Nancy was dead. JB moved close to her face, and looked deep into her eyes, which would later prove to be a big mistake. What he saw would hunt him for the rest of his like. They seemed to asking why???

It could have been any one of a number of causes for Nancy death, or a combination of several.

Her heart rate was dangerously elevated due to her last, several hours long, crack binge, and could not withstand the trauma of the vicious rape, of she might have smothered the result of Boogieman's attempt to quiet her screams, by holding her head, face down into the bed, of she may have expired from shock, caused by the pain of her sodomy. Whatever the secondary cause, the primary cause of her death was drugs.

Boogie, who was still pumping, seemed to return to reality, and stopped his insane molestation upon hearing JB's command. He looked down at the bloody mess he was assaulting, and recoiled backwards so hard he flung himself completely off the bed, and into a heap on the floor, against the wall, a look of utter disbelief on his face.

"Aw hell, Boogie. You really done messed up now. How we going to leave this punk ass Rick alive now you done croaked his old lady? Now, we got to cap him too," JB said, as he walked in a circle, eyes closed, his gun held to his head, mussel pointed up.

"Not only that, I done tapped the stank myself, and my DNA is in her. Now we got to burn the place. Man, you is one messed up, sick..." JB stopped talking — he was at a loss for words. He just stood there, looking down on the dead Nancy, and those questioning eyes. Even though he was a hardened criminal, he felt a twinge of compassion for her.

"The hell with this, Boogie," JB said, regaining his voice, "You killed the shortie, you is gonna be the one who caps her old man. You already asshole deep in this mess, ain't no point in us getting caught up in some screwed up crap you did. Get your ass up and take care of your business. Pop that sissy one time in the head," JB continued, as he pointed his gun towards Rick, on the floor. "We ain't got all day. I think one of Rick's crack-head customers might have heard your crazy ass killing that shortie. He might keep his mouth shut, but we can't count on it," JB prompted.

Boogieman got up off the floor, put on his pants, and all in one motion, that crazy grin on his face, retrieved his semi-auto from the bed — walked into the front room — walked over to Rick, who was still sitting on the floor, his eyes closed, and tears streaming down his face. Boogie pointed the pistol between Rick's closed eyes, and pulled the trigger, killing Rick instantly. The report of the large pistol had everyone's ears ringing, and caused everyone to jump at the suddenness. The combined odor of gunpowder and burned hair filled the room.

JB, who watch Boogie kill Rick, as easily as one might spray a roach, without hesitation, or remorse, was wondering what he was doing hooked up with this crazy, psychopathic, psychotic, mutha?

JB knew something about the little man wasn't quite right. He knew that Boogie was a little insane, but not that crazy. JB once liked him, however, because Boogie seemed to be a man of action, and could prove useful to the gang. As a matter of fact, it was Boogie who wielded the MAC 10 auto pistol during the drive-by of the dope house on the west side in which the shotgun doorman was killed. That was some place some guy named, Smokey, owned, and the incident made all the papers. It was then the Mayor declared he was going to clean up the neighborhood, forcing JB to move.

JB didn't have long to ponder his decision of bringing Boogie into the gang — a decision he now regretted. Only a few seconds after the shot that killed Rick, the front door exploded open, banging heavily against the wall, the doorknob embedding.

"Police! Police!" came a loud proclamation, "Get down! Get down! Every one on the floor!" the cops ordered, as they came streaming through the busted door, all screaming at the same time, and weapons at eye level, ready to deal with any resistance they might meet.

JB, and his gang, were caught completely off guard. They were all mesmerized by the sight of the dead Rick and the big splatter of blood behind his head where the bullet exited.

Boogieman was so surprised by the sudden arrival of the police, he turned in their direction, his gun still in his hand. A blast from a cop's shotgun was the last thing he ever saw. The heavy 00 buckshot sent him flying through the air, to hit the floor fatally wounded. The other members of the gang immediately dropped their weapons, and ducked, as they attempted to follow the drug raid team's directives.

The crack-head customer, who'd knocked earlier, looking for Rick, didn't keep his mouth shut after all. He called the, "Stop Crime" hot line, and reported the possible rape of a woman in a crack house and a man with a gun.

Had it been anyone else, besides, Nancy, with whom he was secretly in love, he might not have dropped the dime. The thought of something happening to her, tormented him, but as fortune would have it, he was too little, and too late to help her.

The police hearing of a rape, and in a drug house too, as well as an armed individual, wasted no time arriving on location. They were ready to move on the house as soon as the black raid truck stopped in front.

As the gang was led out of the house in cuffs, the crowd that had gathered cheered and applauded their arrest. Nobody, including the drug addicts, liked any of them. As JB was being stuffed into a marked police cruiser, he had an expression on his face, which seemed to say, *yeah, I'll be back to deal with y'all later.*

JB and his partners in crime, except for Boogieman, who was killed by the blast from the shotgun, were taken into custody, tried, found guilty, and sentenced to natural life in prison, without any chance of parole. The charges of home invasion, felonies with a firearm, gross sexual misconduct including sodomy, and the double murders, would insure that they, except JB, would die behind bars.

JB went insane while waiting on his trial, and spent the rest of his life in a mental ward on suicide watch. He couldn't get the look of Nancy's dead eyes out of his head. They haunted him day and night, awake and asleep. They would stare back at him from inside his closed eyelids — stare back from the darkness of his tormented soul.

He saw them in his food. He saw them in mirrors. He

saw them in the eyes of others. He saw them when he closed his eyes. He saw them when he looked directly into the bright Sun. He tried to pluck out one of his eyes with a sharpened spoon — they were still there.

They were in his head.

They kept asking — why? Why? Why?

Chapter 2

Tiny and a crack-whore.

Damn, I hope this bitch ain't run off with my money, Tiny thought, as he waited for Elisabeth to return from the dope house. He and she'd been smoking rocks earlier, and he was more than a little paranoid. He'd have gone in himself, but was the nervous type. He didn't want to be caught up in a raid while inside the dope house. The problem was that anybody he enlisted to cop for him couldn't be trusted. They were all crack-heads and would rip him off by breaking off a piece of the rocks he ordered, or taking his money and not returning altogether. He knew that most crack smokers can't be trusted. One of the least trustworthy of all crack-heads is the crack-whore, i.e. Elisabeth.

Damn, where the hell is she? I know the cops will come rolling up in a minute, he thought, *come on Elisabeth.* Ten minutes had passed since Elisabeth left his car, an old Tempo with a broken driver's side window that'd been covered with a plastic trash bag, and a heater that hadn't worked since the start of winter. Tiny had been planning to repair the window for some time, but it seemed he could never find the money. Every time he had the cash to fix the broken window and heater, or buy some much needed tires, he could hear the rock talking to him — calling him, the craving soon rising up out of his stomach into his chest and he was off to the races. Sure, at times like that, he only planed to buy just the one rock, but he never stopped at just that one. Before long, he'd gone through his rent, gas, food, and any other money he should be taking care of business with. He knew, but didn't want to admit, the drug always took precedence over everything else, including his car. Deep down, he knew what the real deal was. The drug was slowly and insidiously taking over every aspect of his life — causing him to make bad decisions.

A light snow was falling while being blown by a light breeze and he was getting cold. His drug-induced paranoia had his nerves on edge. The rock he and Elisabeth had shared earlier was working on him, causing his mind to desire sex. That's when she offered him what he wanted in exchange for another hit. He, being under the influence of the drug, and swearing he'd smoke just the "one" rock, made a bad decision. He spent part of his rent money, again. He knew that reality would set in and he'd regret spending the additional money at the exact moment he got his nutt. That is, if he was lucky enough to be able to perform to begin with, and if he was lucky enough to complete without loosing his excitement. The drug had a way of denying those things the drug fooled an individual into thinking he wanted, no, needed, that being sex, or more drugs. But did that stop him? No, and never would, no matter how rational he tried to be. The craving would always override the mind's attempt to do the right thing.

Frig this crap — I'm going in to find her slick ass, he decided, and then thought, *naw I better not. I know she's going to start an argument — better wait. I sure hope she don't smoke so much of the stone we won't have enough left for the both of us,* he thought.

As he watched, several other people had gone in and

come back out of Edward's dope house. *It didn't make no sense it's taking her so long to come out unless she was smoking the dope I paid for,* he thought.

Crap, he thought, *I ain't letting her take no more of my money,* he decided, without much conviction. *She does this every time I sends her in to cop. Damn, where the hell is she?*

The bad thing about it was he'd do the exact same thing the next time they partied together, and deep down he knew it.

Tiny, at thirty-one, lived alone in a small one bedroom apartment, having been kicked out of his mother's home when he was caught doing crack in the bathroom. He had a job as a tire repairman in a small tire repair shop, repairing and replacing tires on customer's cars that happened to drive in. He was short in height, but had broad strong shoulders that helped him at his job. Actually, he was almost as wide as he was tall, giving him a walking pancake appearance. He was a good worker — whenever he bothered to show up, that is. He didn't know his boss was going to fire him if he missed, or was late one more time, and judging by the way he stayed up all night whenever he was smoking, which sapped all his strength, making it impossible to perform the heavy work at his job, that one more time wasn't far in the future.

Because he smoked, and wasn't that attractive, and had broken up with his abusive girl friend, who he knew was using him, she also being a smoker, and who denied him the sex he occasionally wanted, he didn't want another steady woman. He began to party with rock-stars, and crack-whores. He was more comfortable with the addicts because he and they knew the score. He knew they weren't attracted to him, and didn't want to have sex with him, but he also knew they, to get a rock or two, would do just about anything he wanted, and that was all right with him.

Most people thought Tiny got his nickname because of his height, about five-foot-one or two, and that was all right with him, because he really knew why he was called Tiny, and it had nothing to do with his height.

Many years ago, his ex-girlfriend, one day, called him a, no screwing, tiny prick mutha, during an intense argument over some rocks, and in front of everyone in the dope house. A little later, someone had teasingly called him Tiny, and the moniker stuck, eventually, everyone calling him that.

Now that all who were there at the time of the argument have since moved on, and the dope house busted by the cops, he was cool with the innocuous, Tiny, and he was also comfortable with Elisabeth. They'd partied many times before, and in spite of the fact his organ was only about four inches long at its zenith, he knew she'd keep her mouth shut, allowing him to have some unembarrassed fun.

As he sat and waited, a pair of headlights turned onto the street about two blocks away, and was coming in his direction. As the car drew closer, he tried to slide down in his seat, and try to not be so visible. The car came upon him, and then passed. He let out a sigh of relief — it wasn't the police.

He knew if the police stopped to inquire as to what he was doing parked in front of a dope house, at 3 am, and ask to see his driver's license, proof of insurance, and registration, none of which he had, not to mention the fact the plate he had on the car was stolen, he'd go straight to jail. He wouldn't pass go, he wouldn't collect two-hundred-dollars — he'd go straight to jail.

The car having passed, he was even more ready to get

the hell out of there, and now. *Where the hell is this wench*, he thought, again, as he looked over his shoulder to see Elisabeth coming around the side of the dope house. She stopped in front of the house to look up and down the street before coming to his car.

"About time," he said to himself, as he started the old car's loud engine. She opened the squeaky door, and quickly got in. Her lower jaw working from side to side, like a cow chewing its cud, a good indication she'd been smoking.

"What took you so long?" he asked, as she sat down on the passenger seat, and pulled the squeaky car door closed on the second attempt.

"Sorry about that baby, come on... let's go," she replied, as he pulled away from the curb, glad to get away from the busy dope house. "You know how slow Edward can be when he got them crack-head women in his place," Elisabeth offered, while looking over her shoulder through the rear window, searching for any police cars that might be following. She was geeked, and paranoid, especially after breaking off a piece of the rock and smoking it while inside. Tiny knew what she said could be true, but he also knew, by the way she slurred her words, and the action of her lower jaw, she was lying. Besides, Edward didn't hand out the dope, his door/shotgun man did that. Hell, Edward was always to busy freaking with them crack-whores to be bothered with such mundane task. He knew she'd been pinching off the rocks and smoking them in the house. He hoped she hadn't pinched off too much of the stones, and left enough of the two nickels for them to share. He knew that she'd demand the larger portion of what was left when they got back to the apartment, and he had to give it to her to get the sex he wanted. Tiny didn't say anything, although he wanted to. He knew he couldn't prove it, and accusing her would lead to an argument that might mess up the oral sex he was about to receive. They drove back to his apartment in silence.

Except for the noise of the un-muffled engine, the streets were quiet. At this early time of the morning, the streets were almost deserted, causing the noise of the car to echo off buildings as they passed. Fortunately they only had a few blocks to drive and didn't pass a police cruiser.

Both, Tiny and Elisabeth were geeked, and the noise of the engine was getting on their nerves, especially, because they had the dope in the car. The old car's heater was useless. Cold winter air came in around the flapping plastic that was covering the driver's side window, and which added to the noise of the engine. The car was riding on three bald tires and a donut, but all was good. Tiny had a couple nickel rocks, or what was left of them, and a woman who was going to give him sex for one of them, much the same as they'd done many times before.

Elisabeth was still a little wide eyed from pinching off the rocks she was sent to buy for Tiny. He didn't care. If he wanted to make sure he got what he paid for, he should have gone in and bought the drugs himself — of course, he wouldn't do that. Being already geeked, it was hard enough for him to, simply, sit out front and wait on her to come out. He kept promising himself he wouldn't go out to get more dope once he was back inside his apartment and smoking, but he could never resist an opportunity to get busy with Elisabeth, especially if things didn't go as planed when they got busy this time. Sometimes, Elisabeth, after she got started smoking, was slow about giving Tiny the sex he'd paid for. On several occasions, she'd ignore him until his high wore off, and then he'd want to go out again, while hoping she'd do what he paid for that time. The unfortunate thing about his situation was that it would repeat until Tiny was flat broke, and even then Elisabeth would try to get him to get some credit from Edward, credit she couldn't get, because she never paid anything back.

    Back at Tiny's small run down apartment in which he was three months behind in rent, he and Elisabeth went through their usual routine of putting new char in their stems — cutting up and preparing to smoke the dope. The single, smoke covered, twenty-five-watt bulb, he had in the ceiling, cast a golden glow over the whole room, and made it hard to see what they were doing. It was one of only two bulbs in the whole apartment, the other being in the bathroom. I guess you could count the bulb in the empty refrigerator, which held only a half-eaten bowl of molding baked beans, raising the total to three.

    He knew he'd soon be evicted, but because of the way the dope deranged his thinking, he decided to worry about that when it happened. During the few times he was sober and lucid, he made plans to get caught up on his delinquent rent, as well as stock the apartment with something to eat other than the Ramens noodles he constantly dined on. He'd stand outside his car and look at the broken window, deciding to make sure he went to the junkyard and buy a replacement. He'd plan to get that tire and heater fixed, but every time he took one hit from his stem, those plans literally went up in smoke. It wasn't the many rocks he bought after the first, which got him in trouble — it was the first. The first rock was the "one" which demand he buy more. If he could only stop at that one rock, as he planed, he'd be all right, but no matter his good intentions, it was the first rock that warped his thinking and deluded him into thinking he'd do only "one" more, and that "one" would always turn into a series of "one" more, until he was broke, it happened every time, no matter his intentions. The sad thing is it would continue to happen until he was jobless, homeless, and probably car-less. His only glimmer of hope would be when he hit rock bottom, and then, only if he had any vestige of self-respect left, he'd seek help to control his addiction. Maybe then, he'd enroll in a drug treatment program, and hopefully, find the courage to not smoke that "one" first, rock.

Tiny put in half of his few, undersized, pieces, of his smaller share of the two rocks, lit it, and took a long drag on his stem, held his breath as long as he could and then blew out a heavy white cloud of smoke. His mouth began twitching, his chin shifting from side to side, as if he were chewing on something.

He wanted to say something, but could hardly get the words out. It was as if his brain and mouth were disconnected. "C... c... come on, and take care of me," he managed to stutter to Elisabeth, as he slowly took off his pants and well worn boxers, while holding his stem in one hand, his mind racing, all kinds of weird thoughts materializing, and just as quickly, being forgotten.

The drug went straight to the pleasure center of his brain, focusing his thoughts on sex. Elisabeth paid little attention to Tiny. She, in her own stupor, was busy crawling around on the floor on her hands and knees (known as tripping or geeked) picking at anything that remotely looked like a piece of rock. She picked up, and put it into her mouth to taste test, paint chips, crumbs, anything small and white, or near white. Anything, which might be a crumb from a stone, was tested.

Tiny, who was pulling at his little appendage, was getting impatient. "Beth, I said come here, and get busy now, before I lose my high."

"OK baby, in a minute," Elisabeth promised, without looking up.

"Hell no, I said now, woman," Tiny implored.

"I'm coming, right now baby," Elisabeth answered, as she continued her hallucinogenic search for the imaginary piece of rock she was sure she'd dropped.

They went through this same routine every time they smoked and partied together. He'd hit his stone, and demand sex. She'd hit her stone, and begin to look for a dropped piece, while ignoring his demands. If nothing else, crack addicts were creatures of predictable habit.

"Whoe, I said get out of them clothes and get busy, now, or get your ass out of my place. I'm ready to eat some nooky," Tiny demanded, as he put another small piece into his stem.

"OK baby, but can I hit another small piece, before we get down? Just one more small piece, to put me in the mood?" Elisabeth begged.

"Hell no. You do the same thing every time we parties," continued Tiny. "You can hit a piece while I do my thing. Now get your ass on the bed, and gap them legs." He said, now in full perv mode.

"Damn mutha, won't you give a woman a chance to get ready?" Elisabeth retorted, without looking up from a corner of the room, and pushing at the fibers of the dusty carpet.

While crack stimulated the imaginary sex drive of men, it had the opposite effect on women. Elisabeth continued her search, looking under the mattress — in a shoe on the floor, picking it up and shaking it — in her own pubic hairs — in places that a reasonable person would know nothing was there to find, but she was high, and definitely not thinking reasonably.

Eventually, she got up off her knees and stood peeping through the side of the torn window shade, looking for something only her crack-deranged mind could imagine.

"Later on for this crap. Get your sorry, crack-head, ass out of my place, now," Tiny demanded, not really expecting her to leave, but knowing she'd respond to a threat.

Elisabeth, her high wearing off, released her grip on the shade and while looking at the floor, went to the other side of the bed, sat down, and undressed, not bothering to go to the bathroom and washing off.

"I'm ready," She said to Tiny, as she teased him buy playing with her snatch, one leg propped up on the bed.

"Where is the piece you promised, I want to smoke it while you gives me some of that good attention," Elisabeth added, for good measure.

Tiny, now getting turned on while watching her fingering herself, broke up what was left of the last piece into many crumb sized pieces, put a small crumb in her palm.

She looked at the small speck, saw how small it was, but said nothing.

He told her to lie back, as he put a larger piece in his stem, and lit it. She did as she was told. She lit her stem at the same time he did, inhaled deeply, and laid back while opening her legs.

Now under the complete control of the drug, Tiny laid his stem on the ragged night stand next to the bed, rolled over, grabbed her parted legs, and went straight for her with his tongue. The slight fish order of her unwashed snatch, didn't bother him.

Although, he thought he was doing a great job of pleasuring her, he wasn't. The drug would not let him concentrate. He was working to hard, to fast, and sporadically.

She wasn't in the mood in the first place, and was ready to hit another piece. She allowed him to continue for a few more seconds, uttering a fake moan or two, and then asked him to stop. "Umm, baby, that's enough for now, let me hit another piece and I'll do you," Elisabeth said, as she pushed his head away from her, and sat upright.

"Sounds like a winner to me," responded, Tiny. He was ready for another hit himself. As Tiny took his next hit, he stood between her legs, as she sat on the edge of the bed, and serviced him. Although it felt good, her actions didn't have the desired effect. The drug did that to men.

They continued the smoking, and freaking until the dope was gone, and they'd pushed their stems several times.

"Hey baby, let's get one more dime," Elisabeth asked, after getting all she could from her burnt stem.

"I'd love too, but I ain't got no more money. You know where we can get some credit? My bridge card will kick in, in a few days, and I can pay them back," said Tiny.

"You know I can't get a sheet of toilet paper on credit, but I know where I can get about thirty or forty dollars," Elisabeth, said, enthusiastically, and while holding up her stem and inspecting it.

"Are you talking about your tricking ass old men, way on the Westside?" Tiny asked, already knowing the answer.

"Yeah, you know the ones you drove me too before. All those old men want is a little of my good loving. It won't take but a minute for each one," She answered, getting up and beginning to get dressed before he'd agreed to go. She knew him well, and knew he wanted to make the drive as much as she did, but he was one of those types that had to analyze every detail of an action before he made a move. They were going, all right, all she had to do was wait for him to realize it.

"Sounds like a good idea. The only problem is, I don't have enough gas to get us there. Well, maybe I can get us there, but you better be sure you can make some money or else we won't be able to get back," Tiny said, contemplatively. "Not only that, you know my heater don't work," he continued, "how many stops we got to make? I don't want to be sitting in that cold car for too long."

"Tell you what, drive me to the telephone booth, let me make a few collect calls, and we'll know exactly what is what," Elisabeth proposed.

"Let's ride," Tiny responded, his mind already contemplating flaming another rock.

They got dressed in record time, and drove to the gas station where there was a pay phone. Elisabeth was able to set up three dates. She was planing to ask for twenty dollars apiece, but would except ten. It being in the middle of the month, the tricks she was about to see wouldn't have much money. But if they could get a little attention from her at a discounted rate, they'd find a way to raise a few dollars, particularly, if she was coming to them.

———

Elisabeth, a tall, slender, relatively nice looking woman with a close cropped, boyish, hair style, and who wore large, hoop, earrings, to detract from her longish neck, was an excellent lover while applying her expertise, lip service, when she wasn't high.

During her short stay on the Westside of Detroit, she was able to build up a small clientele of older men who loved her specialty. However, as crack-whores were prone to do, she ripped off one of her dates for several hundred dollars after drinking and freaking with him all night long, and putting him to sleep. She knew this elderly man didn't play that game, and would have killed her if he could find her. She knew he always kept a pistol on him — a pistol he wasn't afraid to use. She thought it a good idea if she moved to the eastside and never again go anywhere near where he lived, or hung out. No loss, she had several other tricks to trap, she reasoned.

In the car, Tiny looked at the gas gauge. It was lying on empty. The car had a small engine, but he still wondered if they had enough gas to get them to the Westside. Actually it didn't matter if they did or didn't — they were going.

They hit I-94 heading west in the noisy drafty car. There was no traffic on the freeway and the ride took fifteen minutes to reach the first date's house. A small brick house with a small front and back yard. The most recent snow hadn't been shoveled from the front walk, or the porch steps. A set of footprints led up to, and from the front door, probably the mailman's. The man's car was parked, snow covered, in front of the house. A light could be seen in one of the bedrooms. *He's home,* she thought.

Elisabeth had Tiny park a few houses down from the date's. She went in and was back out in less than ten minutes, grinning like a circus clown. She'd expected to receive only ten or twenty dollars but was paid fifty. The old guy had hit his number, and while saying he was glad that she'd called, felt generous.

She was ready to go back to the Eastside, and cop more dope, but decided to not stand up the other dates she'd promised to visit — a semblance of pride from a crack-head prostitute. But the money was making her anxious, and her heart was no longer in her future dates. She was ready to get another hit right then and there. It was hard for her to not tell Tiny to make a stop at one of the dope houses she knew of on that side of town.

She, reluctantly, completed her dates with the other two, elderly, men, who were not as generous as the first, one giving her fifteen dollars, and the other twenty. The whole adventure took only a half-hour.

They bought gas, returned to the eastside, bought more dope from Edward — this time with her coming out in a few minutes, and going back to Tiny's apartment, they smoked it in less than a couple hours. Other than Tiny pulling on his little pud, no sex this time, the dope was on her and she wasn't about to blow her high while trying to get him off.

As is usual in relationships such as theirs, their sex for drugs arrangement didn't last. Elisabeth, while trying to catch a date on one of Detroit's streets, was killed by a psychopathic serial murderer, who only prayed on prostitutes.

Her death didn't faze Tiny. There were plenty of rock-stars to replace her. Crack-heads don't form close bonds unless they are codependents, anywy. Any relationship a crack-head has is only as valuable as the amount of drugs the other person can assist them in obtaining. And crack can be a cold, unforgiving, and demanding mistress. Eventually, Tiny did loose his job, and was evicted. He managed to secure a half-assed job as a doorman in a new dope house that opened in his neighborhood until it was raided. He was jailed for loitering in a dope house as well as illegally having a firearm he didn't get rid of fast enough when the cops came in the front and back of the house simultaneously. That was the last anyone saw or heard of Tiny. What he did after getting out of jail, no one knows. Hopefully, he enrolled into a drug treatment program. Maybe the judge, during his sentencing, ordered him to seek treatment — maybe?

Chapter 3

James loses to a lesbian.

James and Vera had been together about fourteen years. James, at about 6 feet, and 50 years of age, was a laid off warehouse worker. He was married to a sanctified, self-righteous, church going woman, who found fault with everybody, and everything. In addition, because of her weight, she didn't like herself and loved to argue. James got to the point where he refused to argue with her any more, and began to stop by Spike's after hour place, or Boss's whorehouse, rather than go home after work. During a period he was laid off for a few months, he got up in the morning, and leaving home, would not come back until late that night. And on occasion, by spending the night at a "friends" house, he managed to avoid her all together.

James was absolutely unhappy, and ready to get out of the marriage. The problem was they had three kids together. Three kids who needed his support. But it was better to provide the support from a distance, rather than they see their parents arguing all the time. He went through the process of paying the household's bills, and not much more. Yes, he slept there, but as soon as he got a chance, he was up and out, trying to find somewhere to go, or someone to spend time with. Actually, he wasn't the type who liked being alone, so when Vera, a co-worker, approached him one day after he'd returned to work, and told him she liked his personality, and wanted to hook up, he was all for it. He'd seen Vera around the job several times, but had no idea she was interested.

Vera was short, stocky, attractive, woman of 46, and in spite of her age, and weight, had a classic hourglass figure. She had a peculiar mouth that turned up at each corner, and made her seem to have a permanent smile. She constantly wore her hair in a ponytail, its length enhanced by a tacked on piece. She too, worked at the warehouse, where she and James met, but was later discharged because of her chronic absenteeism.

At the time she and James got together, she had an abusive, cheating, boyfriend, who did nothing to help her after her discharge from the warehouse. Her, then boyfriend, not only provided nothing toward their living expenses, or the drugs they both used, he'd steal any money she might bring in, to buy drugs for himself. In the absence of his aid, she resorted to prostitution to raise money for her habit. However, he was the extremely jealous type, and she had to find ways to take care of her tricks without him finding out.

James was not one of her tricks. He was someone she, actually, liked, and who treated her like a woman. James liked her as well. He liked the way she told him everything when they first met with total honesty, and played no games.

"I have a man right now, and I do drugs, and have several tricks. If you can't handle that, ain't no point in us hooking up," she told James, and James had no problem with her activity. He, instinctively, felt she viewed him as more than another trick, and he didn't have to worry about what she was doing when they weren't together. He knew he wasn't the best lover to walk the streets, and felt she wanted more from their relationship than sex — that being, someone she could be honest with and who would accept her as she was. And James fulfilled both those requirements. Sometimes he'd drive Vera to turn a trick with one of her dates. He'd wait for her to finish, and then she'd pay for a motel room for the two of them. They'd have a good time together, making love, and talking about their cantankerous ex-partners.

James and Vera flirted with the prospect of becoming a couple at some time in the future, providing he left his wife, and she, her no good boyfriend.

Wanting to share her whole life with him, Vera introduced James to crack during the second year they dated. It was in a cheap motel — the same place they often visited.

"Baby," Vera began, "I got to ask you something," she said, as she sat on the bed, fishing through her purse, searching for her works. She was preparing to hit her first rock of the evening.

"Yeah, what's that?" James asked, as he stood in front of the barely working TV trying to find the triple X movie playing on the closed circuit channel. He knew about her smoking, and paid her no attentions as she put a rock in her stem.

"I know you don't mind if I smokes when we're together, but I'm tired of smoking by my self. It's like you ain't having as much fun as I am. I was wondering if you wanted to try a hit — just one hit. If you don't like it, at least I'll feel better about smoking by myself," she lied.

Although what she said held a kernel of truth, her actual motive for wanting him to smoke was more diabolical. It was true she wanted someone to smoke with, but her true desire was to get him to help her purchase the drug. Smoking crack can become a very expensive habit. Although, she was being paid well by her tricks and sugar daddies, her addiction was outpacing her income. She knew how addictive crack can be, and figured if he took one hit, he'd be hooked.

"James turned around to face her, "Baby, I don't know. I've seen how you acts sometimes when you're smoking. It's like you loose all your self-control. I don't want to end up like that."

"I know what you mean, James. But you don't have to worry about loosing control of yourself. You're stronger than that. All I want you to do is try one hit. I promise, I won't ask no more. Try it for me."

"Well all right, I'll try one hit. But I can tell you, judging by the way it smells, I know I ain't going to like it. What you want me to do?"

"Great, baby. Here take this," she said, handing James her works." (The stem used to smoke crack)

James took the stem — put it to his lips, ready to inhale.

Vera told him to tilt his head back so she could light the rock already in it. She lit her lighter, placing the flame near the rock in the end of the stem, and told James to inhale.

As he inhaled, he heard a loud crackling sound as the rock burned. Although James was a smoker, he fought back the desire to cough. The thick white smoke was dense, and strong, going straight to his brain within a few seconds.

He liked the way it seemed to go straight to he groin area, causing him to think freaky thoughts. But what he didn't know, but would soon find out, the thoughts he was having, he wouldn't be able to act on. The affects the drug was having on him were manifestations of the drug working on the pleasure center of his brain, while at the same time, robbing the rest of the body, particularly the groin area of critical blood flow necessary to have an erection.

From that moment on, they bought their drugs and smoked, and freaked, together. From that moment on, and particularly in the circle of people they hung out with, whenever you saw one, you saw the other. Anyone seeing them, and not knowing better, would think they were a long time married couple, and they smoked dope every chance they got. That was twelve years ago, and James was absolutely unprepared for the effect the drug would have on him.

    James, and Vera, after several years of sneaking to the motel to smoke rocks together and have sex, decided to move in together. He dumping his argumentative wife, and taking only his clothes, she shedding her thieving, cheating, jealous, boy friend, and taking what little furniture along with her clothes, they made the move.
    They moved into a single bedroom flat that was located in a less than desirable neighborhood, where the rent was cheap, and the dope was plentiful.
    When they began their cohabitation, things went smoothly, but soon began to decline. As is always the case, the insidious drug was starting to take a toll on their judgment, their ability to handle their business. They lived in the flat less than a year while smoking dope every opportunity they got.
    Their downfall started with Vera. James would give her his share of the rent, and she'd spend it on stones. Not every week, but often enough to get four months behind in rent. James knew what she was doing, but found it hard to really admonish her. Actually he wanted the dope she spent the rent money on as much as she, and used her irresponsibility as an excuse to smoke along with her without recrimination. After all, he'd tell himself, as he sucked in the intoxicating smoke, I gave her the money, and she's the one who messed it up — it ain't my fault if the rent ain't paid. It was only another way the drug forces the mind of a user to justify a wrong decision.

Eventually they were evicted. They moved on to another place, where the same thing happened. They always found a way to rent another place to stay, but for some reason, the pattern seemed to repeat itself — move in — stay for a while — get behind in the rent, and utilities — get evicted, and move on to another place. This course of action happened so frequently both accepted their lack of responsibility as normal — both refusing to accept the truth. Accept the fact the drug had a way of making the abuser find a way to justify any bad decisions made in the interest of buying more dope. It distorts the users thinking — distorts the users sense of reasoning — his ability to distinguish between reality, and fantasy. Neither wanted to face up to the fact the entrapping drug was in control of them, rather than the other way around.

Their frequent moving, having the utilities turned on, and not paying the bills, left them no choice but to split up. They were no longer supporting each other. They could no longer raise the first months, the last months, and the security deposit needed to move into another place.

They got so far behind on the electric bill they would have to either pay off the total bill, or make a large deposit to have their lights turned on at the next place. They could have the lights turned on in someone else's name, but that option was out of the question. Anybody who knew them, and knew about their drug use, would not stick out their necks on their behalf. Would risk having a large, unpaid, light bill in their name. Of course they could have had the lights turned on illegally, but that would only last until the meter reader came around, and they would be in the dark again. Of course, they could have had the lights, illegally, turned on again, but the utility company would eventually turn the lights off at the pole, and take the meter, making it harder to have someone restore the service.

Because James was still attempting to live a more or less normal life, and because of his inability to cope with Vera's total devotion to the drug, the split between the two was inevitable.

She moved in with one of her daughters, and he decided to take a room in a cheap hotel, The Open Arms, that rented on a monthly basis and where the rent was cheap. There, he didn't have to worry about paying an electric bill, and without Vera to influence him to do something stupid, was able to take care of other important business, such as keeping insurance on, and gas in his older car. He continued to smoke, but not nearly as much as he did when he was with Vera.

Vera and he stayed in contact, and it wasn't long before she moved into the hotel with him. Besides, Vera was running out of options. Vera's daughter had no choice but to ask her mother to leave, not being able to cope with her mothers constant drug use, particularly, around the daughter's children.

Once they were together again, James and Vera could buy more drugs. They got along fairly well with each other because they had something in common, the drug use, which was reinforced by the fact they were co-dependents, the only bond two addicts can have.

Although James liked to smoke as much as Vera, and after living alone for a while he discovered he could, with some restraint, take care of business. Vera, on the other hand, being totally bridled by the drug, and who couldn't get enough, sometimes going for days at a time, found a way to get him to spend more money on those few occasions when he refused.

She knew James was like most men who smoked, the drug tended to make him feel freaky, make him want to indulge in some form of sexual activity. Actually James was nothing like that — it was all in his mind, the direct result of the drug's affect on his brain and in that respect, he was no different than most men who indulged. And because Vera and James had an open relationship, she still turning a trick or two, she decided to take advantage of the drugs insidious affect on him.

One evening, during a crack smoking session, and he half-heartedly rambling on about his sexual fantasies, while declaring his intentions to not spend more on drugs, she put her plan into action. She left the room saying she'd be back in a minute. She'd, during their stay in the hotel, befriended a lesbian rock-star and prostitute, Donna. Putting her plan into action, Vera found Donna on the fourth floor of the rundown hotel, which was known as the party floor, and made a proposal to her, and Donna was more than eager to join Vera in the scheme. They'd put their heads together and come up with a plan by which they could squeeze more money out of James.

When Vera returned to the room, she had Donna in tow. They came into the room laughing and talking loud. They found James laying on the bed and pushing his stem. He was watching an adult triple X movie on the VCR, his mind racing with all sorts of lascivious fantasies.
"Hey baby, this is Donna," Vera said, to the surprised James. "She said she'd party with us, if you buy me and her a couple dimes."
"Hey, Donna, is that right?" James asked, not believing his luck. He was about to party with two women as he'd imagined on so many occasions when he was under the influence.
Donna, with one hand on her slender, proportional, hip, responded, "What's up, James? Yeah I'm game, but I

want my rocks before we party."

Donna was medium height woman of about 30. She was what some might call skinny, but well proportioned. Her perky breast complimented her narrow waist, and developed hips.

She wore her hair cut short, which only embellished her beautiful face. She was not long out of the penitentiary, having served her time for drug dealing. During her stay in prison she was turned out, and became bi-sexual, but leaning more towards lesbianism.

She tricked in the building, preferring to date couples, but would take anything she could luck up on. Putting her prostitution skills to good use, she managed to have her rent paid by the middle aged manager, who was her best trick.

"No problem, but did Vera tell you what I like to do when I'm getting high?" James queried.

"Yeah, she said, you like to go down," Donna answered, as she ran her hand over her stomach for dramatic affect.

"You don't have no problem with that? I ain't going to have to beg you to get busy after you take a hit, am I?" James, asked, having been in this situation before, with Vera, and having to plead, beg, and finally demand to do what he wanted to do.

"No, Baby, I don't play no games like that," Donna assured, as she started to take off her clothes.

"Whoa, slow down girl. I got to get the dope first, you want to ride along?" James asked, now getting off the bed and putting on some clothes.

"Hell yeah, you ain't going to leave me here alone!" Donna said, in an excited voice while seeming to get excited about getting some dope.

James was dressed and ready to go in less than a minute. The three of them jumped into his car and drove to the nearest dope house, where James spent fifty dollars he'd not planed to spend. *It's all good,* he thought, as he willingly gave up the money, *I'm going to do me some serious partying tonight.* The drug had him again. Had him making another bad decision.

Back in the room, James was the first to get undressed. The women wanted to take a hit right away to get in the mood to handle James's future demand for sex. James watched them smoke a piece of their rocks before he lit his. The freaky feeling only last for a few seconds, and he didn't want to get ahead of them.

Vera, as usual, after exhaling the thick white smoke, immediately came out of her clothes, and got down on her hands and knees, and began to look for an imaginary rock her drug deranged mind told her she'd dropped.

Donna, after blowing out her smoke, held her glass stem to the exposed light bulb of a shade-less lamp resting on the metal bedside table, looking for who knows what, as she tried to take off her clothes with the other hand.

James watched Donna endlessly stare at her glass stem, and thought, *aw crap, here we go again,* as he prepared to flame up. "Damn, Donna, come on, take off your clothes, I'm ready to get busy," James said, impatiently, after lighting a portion of a stone.

"Okay, okay, okay baby, here I c... c... come," she said, as she continued to glare at her glass stem, turning it, mesmerized by it, trying to find any residue that wasn't covered by the black carbon deposits from the cigarette lighter.

"The hell with this crap, Donna, I said take off your clothes and get your ass on this bed, and gap them legs now. I wants to get down to business," James, who was getting angry for trusting another crack-head, ordered.

Donna, who was in a crack stupor, slowly got up off the side of the bed, laid her stem gently on the scarred metal night stand, and started to strip. To James, it seemed to be taking forever for her to get undressed. He watched her jaw twitch from side to side, much the same as a cow would chew cud. When she did get her blouse off, he liked what he saw. Her angular frame, silky smooth, caramel skin, and perky breast turned him on.

Finally removing the remainder of her clothes, she laid down on the bed, legs bent at the knee and agape, ready to receive the attention she really didn't want.

James, seeing her in the provocative position, lit another piece of a rock. He inhaled deeply, and exhaled the thick smoke. His eyes glassed over. He laid the metal pipe down on the night table, and pushing Donna's legs a little further apart, licked his lips, and went to work on her.

The noises, he made, caused Vera to come up off her hands, and knees beside the bed and watch the erotic activity. She leaned over and gently caressed one of Donna's breasts, before bending over, and kissing an erect nipple. Donna, who was not responding before Vera's attention, grabbed James' head, and gyrating her hips rapidly, uttered a loud moan, as she exploded in an immediate finish.

James, watching Vera attend to Donna's breast, was surprised. After all these years, he had no idea Vera was bi-sexual. He was really getting turned on.

Donna pushed James's head away from her crotch, and told Vera to lie down on the bed. "Get your ass on this bed now wench," Donna told Vera, the lust in her eyes revealing her true nature.

Vera complied, and Donna got on her knees, and went to work on her, giving Vera attention only another woman could. The site of Vera soon completing, like he could never get her to do, was too much for James. He was fully aroused and ready for action in spite of the drugs attempts to keep him flaccid.

He placed another piece of crack in his stem, got behind Donna, inserted his manhood, lit the dope, and without moving, exploded instantly. The drug going to the pleasure center of his brain, and almost causing sensory overload, had him trembling from head to toe as he blew out the smoke breathlessly.

As time went on, the three of them repeated the scenario many more times. Most of the time it involved the two women, while he watched, which was okay with James. He imagined them repeating this scenario many more times in the future, well as much as he could afford, anyway. He still had other things he wanted to pursue.

———

What James didn't see coming, was that Vera, and Donna would fall in love with each other, and move out to get a place of their own. His plea to join them was rejected, mostly by Donna. She wanted Vera and her disability check for her own, and the last thing she wanted was another man to pleasure.

After the move of the women, James, while crestfallen, went on to have sex with any women who would party for a rock, or two. He, eventually, unknowingly, contracted HIV, the results of a lot of unprotected sex with a woman, who, being cross-addicted, mainlined heroin as well as smoked rocks. He continued to smoke, and have unprotected sex with her and any female he could find. He was angry with all women.

It wasn't long before his health rapidly declined, and he eventually died of full-blown AIDS, alone, and bitter, but not before he'd passed on his affliction to many women, who passed it on to others. Had he sought help when he first began showing symptoms something wasn't right, he might have lived for many more years. But his complete lack of concern for himself, caused by his depression, which was the direct result of his drug use, as sure as if he were a train on two steel rails, led him to his ultimate demise.

The drug took his family, his humanity, his pride, and finally, his life, and eventually the lives of several other women whom he had sex with.

Chapter 4

JC meets his match.

JC, a minor street dealer, whistled, as he ran the soft chamois cloth over his shiny new twenty-five-inch custom wheels. He was a young man who liked to dress in the latest fashions and keep his vintage Chevy in pristine condition. He wore his baggy designer jeans low around the bottom of his butt, his underwear showing. His large designer leather jacket was very expensive. The heavy gold chains around his neck, combined with the stylish gym-shoes, hinted at his profession — either a rapper or dope dealer. With the bill of his baseball cap turned sideways and worn over a color-coordinated doo-rag, you could say he looked the part.

He, while rolling his rocks, and having a touch of larceny in his heart, while considering himself clever, didn't have a fixed location from which he worked. He liked to drive around town and solicit his customers, who were entering or leaving liquor stores.

"Got the rock," he, while leaning against the front of the store, would say, as prospective customers passed him. He knew his method of rolling was risky, however, he thought dealing in front of stores with the people traffic, was less dangerous than standing on a corner alone, where he could be easily robbed, or spotted by popo, (police, or Pissed Off Police Officer).

He knew enough to understand once you stake out a location, his customers would look for him at that location all the time. Although, he had to constantly recruit new customers, he figured he had a better chance of avoiding popo by not approaching anyone who was not in work clothes. Most undercover cops and officers off duty, unless they were in deep cover, dressed in casual clothes.

JC had a low overhead. He purchased his rocks from the neighborhood crack houses, split them in half, and resold them. He would, for example, buy a hand full of dime rocks, split them in half, which gave him two nickels for each dime. He'd then sell the $5.00 rocks for $10.00. Most of his customers, who bought his small dimes, complained about the size, but they usually bought them anyway. They always wanted to complete the transaction and move on as fast as possible. That is typical of most crack smokers. They would buy just about anything set out in front of them unless it was absolute garbage. JC knew that fact, and used it to his advantage.

JC was doing very well. The only problem he had was his love for clothes. He sometimes spent a little too much on his wardrobe. He, on occasions, spent so much on his clothes or car he didn't have enough money left to re-up his supply of dope. He didn't sweat it. He dad a little larceny in his hart. Whenever he found himself short of money, he'd buy a bar of soap, or a bag of non-salted peanuts, chop them up into dime size pieces, bag them up so the customer couldn't examine them easily, and sell them for $10.00. He was aware the practice of selling soap or peanuts for crack was very dangerous. He never knew how someone he'd gypped might react, if at some time in the future, they should recognize him. For that reason, he couldn't hang around any location too long. He also had to remember where he sold the bogus dope — hard to do after doing it so often. He was afraid his gypped customers might demand their money back, which he was not prepared to do. Even worse, they might try to do him bodily harm, which he though he was prepared to handle, having the small pistol tucked in his waistband, at his back. He'll soon find his fears would prove valid.

It had been a good day for JC. His practice selling the small rocks had made him a nice profit for a few hours work. He'd made enough cheddar to go shopping for that new leather jacket he wanted. As soon as he sold these last few stones, he was heading for the clothing store. He'd slowed the practice of selling small pieces of soap or peanuts for dope. He was finding he was getting a little carried away with the subterfuge and it might backfire on him. With him covering, primarily, the same liquor stores, there was a good chance he might run into someone he'd previously burned.

It was getting late, the clothing store closing soon. He decided it was time he make tracks for his favorite couturier. On the way to the young man's fashion store, he decided to check out one last location, where he'd previously sold the real and bogus rocks.

As JC approached the half-rundown store on the near Eastside of Detroit, there seemed to be a steady stream of customers entering and exiting the outlet. He thought he'd stop and see how many of the liquor store's customers he could turn into his customers. *Roll these last few stones*, he thought, and then off to the clothing store. *Zing, bam, in and out, my pockets full of money*, he imagined.

There weren't many familiar faces in the parking lot, but because he knew this neighborhood was known as a high drug use area, one of the reasons he picked this store in the first place, he was confident the sales would be there.

After parking his car on the far end of the parking lot, JC went inside the store to buy a can of orange soda. Back outside, he took up a position in front of the store not far from the entrance, and leaned back with one foot propped against the wall while sipping his pop, and trying to look casual. There was a partly cloudy sky overhead, and a warm, gentle, breeze blowing, making for a perfect early summer afternoon.

"Rocks here," JC repeated in a whisper as the liquor store customers passed in front of him. A few people gave him strange looks or ignored him all together, but there were those who stopped to see what he had. When he showed them the small dime rocks, they moved on. As he worked, he marveled at some of the people who stopped to see what he had. They were the not so obvious, undercover, drug abusers, while not, at all, appearing like an addict. But the sales weren't there.

It's going to be a slow day, JC thought, as several more people walked passed him while giving him sidelong glances. He was about to finish his drink and find another location to peddle his dope when an older woman, who looked as if she might be a smoker, staggered slightly as she approached.

"Rocks here," JC said to the middle-aged woman, who looked to be more than slightly intoxicated.

"Yeah baaaby, what you selling?" the older woman asked, while breathing hard as she stopped in front of him, her uncombed hair blowing in the light summer breeze. She was dressed in a dirty blue jogging suite with a stained, once white, T-shirt underneath the jacket. Two rusty ankles topped her soiled sneakers with the shoestrings untied. A hint of a stain in the crotch of her pants indicated she might have urinated on herself at some time.

"I've got some nice dimes, how many you want?" JC asked the woman.

The woman weaved a touch and stood looking at JC

as if trying to get her thoughts together, and then began searching her pockets for money. "Let me see how much money I got, baby. I know I got it here somewhere," she responded, as she reached into her baggy sweatpants pocket, and pulled out a few crumpled dollars, and continued to search for change.

JC was beginning to regret stopping her. She was taking too long to get her money together, and he felt he was missing chances to sell to other customers who were passing.

"Come on lady, I can't wait on you all night, you costing me money," JC urged, as he watched another customer pass him on the way into the store.

"Here, sweetie, give me one dime," the woman said, while holding out a hand full of crumpled singles and a few cents in change.

"What the hell? How much you got here? I don't take change anyway," JC protested, as he took the cash from the woman, and counted all $7.37 of it.

"Hell no, I don't go short, and I don't take change," JC said, as he attempted to give back the money.

"Aw, don't be that way baby, I ain't but a little short. I'll take care of you the next time I see you. Besides, sweetie, your dimes is kind of small. Why don't you let me go for five, so I can buy me a half-shot?" the beleaguered woman persisted while not accepting the return of the money.

―――――

Unknown to JC, as he was negotiating with the woman, he was being watched by two men in an old car parked in the lot across from him.

"Hey Benny, I think that's the mutha who sold me those peanuts about a week ago," Willie told his buddy while sitting his half-cup of gin on the dash. "Hold on a minute, I'm going to get my money back from that punk."

"Taking the gun?" asked, Benny, while reaching under his seat to retrieve the deadly pistol the men had been riding around all day with while, unconsciously, looking for a reason to use it.

"No, I'll be back for it, if he gives me any crap," Willie said, while climbing out of the ancient vehicle.

Willie, a small man in his late twenties, had a chip on his shoulder — he being five-five, and self-conscious about his height, and having the Napolean Complex. He was always trying to prove how much of a man he was. Trying to show he took no crap from anyone. Having the gun in his possession, combined with the mind numbing gin, made him even more belligerent. Factor in his Little Guy Syndrome with his quick temper, and he was a very dangerous individual to cross.

Willie got out of the car, crossed the lot, and approached JC. He had to hold up his baggy jeans with one hand and walked wide legged to keep them from dropping lower than they already were.

"Member me, I bought them dimes from you bout a week ago. They was peanuts. I wants my money back, all fifty dollars of it," Willie demanded, as he stepped up to JC while interrupting his conversation with the older woman.

JC, after sizing up Willie, and knowing he had his snub nosed Smith & Wesson .38 tucked in the small of his back, told the smaller man, "I don't know who the hell you are, and I don't sell peanuts. You best to get the hell out of my grill."

"Word, playa" Willie responded, as he turned to go back to his car, and the gun. He was livid, and wasn't about to let this punk mutha talk to him that way. *This mutha don't know who he's talking to,* he thought.

JC knew there was a good chance something like this could happen. He was a little shaken. This was the first time anyone he'd gypped had confronted him. He couldn't remember Willie, but knew the man was probably not lying. He'd sold bogus rocks to so many people there was no way he could remember all of them.

The old woman, who was trying to buy from him, and who heard the exchange between JC and Willie, decided to take her money and leave. JC thought it a good idea if he did the same. He began to walk toward his car he now regretted parking on the far end of the lot. As he walked, he watched Willie return to his vehicle and get in on the passenger side. The old car's misfiring engine started with the muffler a little louder than normal, and a faint blast of white smoke coming from the tailpipe.

JC, while looking back over his shoulder, still had a distance to go before he reached his vehicle. And by the way the shorter man walked away without an argument, JC knew the man wasn't finished with the subject.

The car, with Benny driving, eased out of the parking space, and came in JC's direction. JC watched as the vehicle approached him, but kept walking. He thought about running the remainder of the distance, and probably could have made it, or at least found cover if he made his move now, but something in JC wouldn't let him show fear. He stopped and turned to face the car as it came. He reached behind himself, and put his hand on the small pistol. The car continued towards JC, rolling slowly, its engine rumbling.

Willie had the window down and was staring at JC with a frown on his face, and determination in his eyes. As the car moved slowly toward JC, he and Willie almost abreast of each other, they locked eyes, both watching mutually. It was obvious some real bad crap was about to happen.

JC, seeing the look on the man's face, knew he might have made a tactical error. The man in the car had a slight advantage because JC couldn't see his hands.

———

To the men, what was about to happen seemed to take several minutes, but actually took less than a few seconds. It's funny how in a crisis, time seems to slow down.

———

JC began to panic, his mind racing, but not able to make a decision. *Should I pull my gun now and start blasting before we gets next to each other — or should I wait to find out what they're going to do — or should I duck behind another car like a scared punk — or should I stand my ground, show these sissies I don't play?* All those thoughts passed through his mind in a flash. His hand on the small pistol at his back made his decision for him.

I ain't running. Come on... Come on, mutha, he thought, *I got a surprise for you.* He was thinking they might get out of the car, rough him up a little, and try to rob him. He was wrong.

Knowing he was at a disadvantage, JC began to make his move as the men came abreast each other. His hand tightened on the grip of the small pistol, and he began to pull it from his waistband.

Willie saw JC with his hand behind him, and observed the small motion indicating his intentions. Willie raised his cocked pistol from below the window, pointed it towards JC's chest, and squeezed off two rounds from the stolen Glock .45 autoloader, a powerful firearm. The blast from the pistol was louder than he expected, causing his ears to ring.

JC had no chance. It all happened before he could clear the barrel of his pistol from the waistband of his pants. He was sent flying backward from the impact of the two hollow pointed slugs. The two bullets hammering JC's chest with a combined weight of close to four-hundred-pounds apiece, knocking the wind out of him and ripping two holes in his lungs. He hit the pavement on his back, more dead than alive, and with his hand still behind his back. A third shot missed his head by inches and ricocheted off the concrete, making a high-pitched whirling sound, and lodged in the side of a parked car. Willie was going to fire a fourth, but didn't have a chance. As soon as he began shooting, Benny panicked, and stepped on the accelerator and the car while belching white smoke, sped away, leaving the parking lot almost on two wheels, the tires screaming as it turned onto the street.

JC, while looking up at the partly cloudy blue sky, his hand still behind his back, was circling the drain. During the last few tics of his short pathetic life, several thoughts went through his mind...

This don't hurt too bad...

Tic...

Sure wish I could breath, though...

Toc...

Mom sure was right... she said something like this was going to happen before she kicked me out of the house after trying to get me straighten up. I sure wish I'd listened to her... Ha, too late now... When I get out of the hospital, I'm going to find that mutha and shoot him between the eyes...

Tic...

Damn, I sure wish I could breathe...

Toc...

I know, I'll get some sleep, and when I wake up, I should be able to breathe better...

Tic...

JC closed his eyes and rattled his last half breath.

Toc.

JC's rock rolling days were over.

Many people saw, and heard the shooting. Everybody in the lot ducked behind cars, or anything that might provide cover, and didn't get the plate number of the car. All they could do was provide a general description of it and its occupants, and how it had a busted muffler, and smoked as it sped away.

As fate would have it, a man who'd ducked behind a telephone poll at the far end of the lot when the shooting started, got a good look at the car, the plate, and occupants, when the car passed him. He gave the information to the police, who arrived on the location in a few minutes, and in force. They immediately sealed off the paring lot with yellow tape, no one was allowed in, or out.

An ambulance arrived, and after a preliminary check of JC, confirming he was dead. The ME was called along with several detectives and the crime scene investigator. The Medical Examiner officially pronounced JC dead at the scene, bagged and tagged him and hauled him away. The shell casings from Willie's gun were retrieved, and bagged to be sent to the crime lab.

JC was dead, but as fait would have it, his murderers didn't get away. The two men were caught later that day, thanks to the observation of a rookie officer, who was trying to make his bones with the department. He, while trying to show he'd be a good cop, was paying particular attention to everything around him. He spotted the plate of the shooter's vehicle as It was parked in another liquor store parking lot not too far from the shooting location.

The two men were drunk and still drinking while talking about how they dealt with that cheating punk. They still had the gun in their possession. The front of Willie's pants was still wet from when Benny sped away, spilling the cup of gin resting on the cars dash.

At the trial, the evidence was overwhelming against Willie, and Benny. They tried to use self-defense as an excuse for the shooting, claming JC had a gun on him, and was about to shoot at them. The fact JC never had a chance to brandish his weapon rendered that line of defense out of the question. The jury only deliberated a couple hours before coming to a verdict.

Both men were found guilty of second-degree murder and sentenced to twenty years in The St. Louis Correctional Facility located in ST Louis, Michigan. Occasionally, justice was swift.

Even though JC was a low-life, cheating, street dealer, he didn't deserve to die like that. But crack is an evil, jealous, demanding, drug, and will extract its due from all who are fool enough to partake of it, or be associated with anyone who does. And in one way or another, it will take your self-esteem, your time, your job, your money, your family, and eventually, and sometimes, your life.

Chapter 5

T and Jam get jammed.

The wind was howling in brief burst, placing its icy fingers on any exposed skin. It seamed to be coming from all directions at the same time. The light, powdery, snow was picked up, and raced along the ground, sometimes swirling in little tornadoes when it was caught in a corner or crevice. When the dry snow hit something solid, it raised into the air and became little ice cubes that got into any opening in your clothing. The normally bright sun was no more than a fuzzy ball in the overcast sky, and promised no future relief from the cold weather.

It was not a day to be outside standing in one spot, but that's exactly what T and Jam were doing. They were street dealers. They could have broken into an abandoned house, and set up shop, but they loved being in public, so on the street they stayed. They'd been rolling from their street corner location since they went into business the past summer. Both being young, around 19, they liked their location because they loved to holler at the girls who happened by. Every now and then, one or the other would luck up and get a sweet young thing' telephone number, but rarely had time to capitalize because they were always on the street rolling their rocks. Actually, collecting digits was more a competition between the two, and something to do between sales.

T, short for Terrence, and Jam, short for Jamie, were both intelligent young men, and were like so many other young unemployed men in Detroit. They both had the ability to work a 9 to 5, but were unable to find productive work that paid more than minimum wages. They had a lot in common, probably the reason they could work together so well. They both had a rebellious streak, having come from broken homes. The custodial parents in both cases happen to be the mothers, and were both into the drug life, and provided very little guidance to their children.

Both boys dropped out of school as soon as they reached the drop out age of sixteen. Jam was the second of five siblings. Of the five, only the oldest, his sister, Shamika, had completed the basic education of high school, and was working in a beauty supply store. His two younger sisters, and one brother, all under him, were not doing well.

T, the middle child of two other brothers, was headed down the same road his older brother, Clay, had taken. Clay was in prison, having been arrested for car jacking, and armed robbery. It was just a matter of time before T would be joining his brother in the gray bar hotel if he continued to do what he was doing.

T and Jam were brought together as a direct result of their drug using mothers. The two boys' mothers were smoking partners. When one of the mothers had something to smoke, they both did. They usually smoked their dope at T' mother's house because she had an extra bedroom, and fewer children running around the place.

Jam would constantly have to chase his mother down at T' mother's house, to get her to return home because of a problem there. Because he was frequently at the other boy's house, and because they were about the same age, and because they both were sick and tired of the mothers using drugs, T, and Jam, bonded, and became good friends, and began to share, and discuss their anger. In a way, they became each other's counselor and confidante — probably preventing them from becoming angrier than they already were. From then on, when you saw one, you saw the other. They became closer than their own siblings — so it became natural that when one tried a venture, they both did.

Neither could see themselves working in a fast food restaurant. To make a few dollars, and because jobs were scarce in Detroit, they tried selling illegal DVD recordings of the latest movies as they came out. That venture failed because of intense competition drove the price of a DVD down, from $5.00 a DVD, too 3 for $10.00, and eventually 2 for $5.00. Carrying the ponderous disk around, and making the copies, as well as maintaining their customers became burdensome. They decided the little money they made was not worth the effort, and gave it up. In the mean time they watched the two mother's drug dealer pull up in his vintage car with the big shinny wheels, and loud boom box in the trunk, and they envied him. He was obviously making some nice cheddar. So one day, when the dealer was making a delivery to his mother, T asked if he could have a word with him. The slightly older dealer, who happen to like T, and unknown to T, was occasionally having sex with his mother in exchange for drugs, granted the young man a conference.

T told the dealer about how he was always broke and about how there weren't any jobs anywhere. He asked the pusher if he could hook him up with some product — get him started in the trade? At first, the dealer was reluctant — not wanting to anger T's mother who was one of his best customers, and they had that sex thing going on, too. But T was persistent in his request.

The dealer eventually relented, and gave T a quantity on co-signment, and at twice the price he normally charged for his drugs. T knew the price was exorbitant, but was so happy to have his own bag he didn't care.

The first thing T did, after getting his bag, was to bring in his friend, Jam. Together they figured a way to make a profit from their overpriced dope. Jam suggested they split the rocks in half, and sell them to their mothers. Jam knew the mothers would protest at first, but if caught at the right time, the mothers would buy the tiny rocks. Jam also knew the convenience of having the stones readily at hand would be a great incentive for the mothers to buy, and he was right.

Once they got started smoking, the two mothers, not caring where they got their next rocks from, within a week bought everything the boys had. The boys kept chipping the rocks smaller, and smaller, until they were getting the equivalent of three times their worth. The boys made enough money to pay off their bill to the pusher, and buy their own stash at the going price.

They continued to sell to the mothers, cutting the size of the rocks the whole time. This continued until the mothers having spent the aid checks, and any money they could get from their bridge cards, started asking for credit. Credit they refused to pay back. The mothers would say they'd raised and fed the boys, and given them a home for the first nineteen years of their lives, and they shouldn't have to pay back their own sons, and they didn't. Of course T and Jam gave their mothers as much "credit" as they could afford, but weren't able to withstand the constant barrage of begging. The boys decided to get away from their begging mothers, and hit the streets. Being, inexperienced, and lacking street savvy, they would sell on the street corners, near bus stops.

Their decision to push from a bus stop gave them a reason to be standing in one spot. PoPo would roll by occasionally, give them the once-over, and keep going. Of course the police knew what they were doing, but as long as they didn't receive a complaint from someone, it really wasn't worth their time to bust the two minor dealers. Another reason the cops didn't bust the young men right away was because a big drug sweep had just gone down on the West Side, and the jail was full. They figured they would be back later to arrest them when the time was right, and space was abundant, if that should ever happen, or, of course, if they got a complaint.

Because the police never hassled them, T and Jam had a false sense of security. They really thought they were putting something over on the cops — no such luck.

"911, what is the nature of your emergency?" the operator asked.

"Hello, my name is Raymond Watts, I want to report two punks who are dealing drugs in front of my business."

"I'm sorry Mr. Watts, 911 is for emergencies only, you'll have to call your prescient to report your problem." the operator informed Ray.

Raymond thanked the operator, and then placed the call to his prescient. He was totally at his wits end. His business was suffering because of the two men planted in front of his business. He'd tried to get them to move, and was almost assaulted because of his efforts. Calling the police was his last resort, when it, he now realized, should have been his first choice.

It took a while for him to reach the right department, but he was patient. Finally, he was connected with someone who could help him. He told the detective about the trouble he was having with the two dope dealers harassing the young ladies who came into his business. How they were disturbing the peace with their loud cat calls, profanity, and laughter. He described the unwanted dope traffic interfering with his legitimate customers who visited his cleaners. The detective thanked Mr. Watts for the call, and told him he'd assign a narcotics team to take care of the situation.

T and Jam weren't dressed as warm as they should. Neither wanted to appear square, so they had to wear the less than proper clothing for the weather. It was a cold day, and a sporadic wind blew in from the west, and the leather jacket Jam wore, with a throwback jersey underneath, and a white tee-shirt under that, did little to keep the cold from his body. His designer jeans would have been okay if he were moving in and out of warm place, but without thermos underneath, they allowed his legs to feel the low temperature. T, who was dressed similarly, was doing no better in his efforts to stay warm. Both men would have fared better with heavy winter parkas with insulated hoods, instead of the lightweight baseball caps they wore.

In spite of the cold wind, the boys stayed at their location, rolling their rocks. An old car pulled over to the curb in front of the two young pushers. Jam motioned for the driver to move down a little, out of the bus stop. He ran over to the car's passenger side, and motioned for the driver to open the door. Normally, he wouldn't get into the car, so the driver rolled down the window instead, and watched as Jam danced around in the cold. The driver expected the young man to tell him he was out, and when to come back. Instead, Jam told the driver to open the door. The driver apologized, and unlocked the door.

Jam jumped in, put the window up, and cursed, "Dammmmn, it's cold out there. Yeah, I know I don't usually get in, but it's cold and windy, and I wanted a little heat."

Besides, he knew the driver, one of their long time customers. T went into lookout mode while his partner was in the car. If he saw the police coming, he'd whistle to warn Jam.

"Sho yo right, J. I don't know how you do it. Aint no way in hell I'd be out in this kind of weather," the driver responded.

"Aint got no choice, got to make them duckets," Jam defended, "What you need homey, got some nice twenties?" Jam said, as he looked through the rear window, keeping an eye out for the police.

The driver laughed. "Come on, J, you know it's the middle of the week, I ain't got that kind of money. Just give me a couple nicks."

"I hear you, playa," Jam answered, as he reached for his pant zipper, pulled it down, and reached inside where he had his stash in a pouch he had tied around his waist, while saying, "Ain't nobody got no money in the middle of the week, and month. It's dead out here."

Jam pulled out a larger bag of crack rocks that were bagged in their, tiny, individual, packs, poured some of the contents into his hand, and picked through them, to find two $5.00 pieces. Finding them, he inspected them thoroughly, before handing them to the driver, not wanting to give him a dime by mistake.

The driver handed Jam two five-dollar bills, as he took the two smaller rocks.

"Okay dude, catch you again as soon as I get some cash."

"Word, playa, catch you on the flip," Jam said to the driver, as he replaced the bag back into his pants, zipped up and got out of the warm car.

A cold blast of winter wind caught him as he got out, and almost knocked him off his feet. *Damn, it's cold out here,* he thought, pulling up his collar, trying to keep the snow from getting down his neck. As he stuck his gloved hands into his pocket, he noticed Mom, a middle-aged customer, in T's face.

While Jam was doing his transaction inside the car, a middle-aged woman came around the corner, and approached T. She was dressed in an olive green army jacket. The collar turned up around the back of her head. With each step, her flimsy black jogging pants flapped in the wind. She was walking fast in her lightweight gym shoes, and no socks. She turned her head against the strong wind that carried a fine, crystalline, snow. Anyone could see she was not dressed for the weather, but that didn't stop her, she was on a mission.

T, upon seeing her coming, rolled his eyes skyward. *Aw damn, what does this old lady want,* he thought, as she drew near, her gym shoes flapping against her naked heals. He knew from experience that at this time of the month she probably didn't have any money, and probably wanted some credit. She always paid, but sometimes was a little slow about it, especially if she got started smoking before she took care of her bills.

"Heyyy T, how you doing?" she asked, in a slurred, slow, voice, before she reached him.

"Wha-up Mom?" T responded, looking past her, indifferently.

"Hey T, can you do me a small fav..." T interrupted her before she could finish.

"I knew it, you want some credit?" T said, as he began to turn away.

"Yeah, but just one nick, you know I always pay, come on, help me out, I got you covered, soon as I get my disability check I'll give you ten, I promise, just one nick, you no I ain't lying," Mom said, in rapid fire staccato, almost in one breath, and while holding her coat tight around her, her uncombed hair flapping in the wind.

"I can't help you this time, I don't have any to spare," retorted T, while recovering from another blast of wind, and looking up the street, hopping another customer would drive up so he could get in the car and enjoy a moments warmth, as well as get away from this begging woman.

"All man, come on, I know you got it," Mom continued to beg. "I told you I'll pay interest.

"I just told you, I can't help you. Now go on about your business, old lady," T said, starting to loose his patients. He turned and started to walk towards Jam, who was getting out of the car. The woman scampered around T, and took up a position between T and Jam, walking backwards.

She was geeked, (high, and not listing to reason) and was not taking no for an answer. "I'll bring your money back in one hour, just one nick," the old woman, persisted.

By this time Jam was standing besides them, listing to the exchange. Jam was not so patient, and didn't like the attention the conversation was attracting.

"Well, come back in an hour, when you got the money, now get the hell on bout your business," Jam said, as he pusher her on a bony shoulder.

The disappointed woman stumbled a little, stopped her begging, gave Jam a look that would kill a charging elephant, pulled her coat tightly around her frail body, brushed back her shaggy hair, and without another word, flip-flopped her gym shoes back around the corner, obviously angry, and not looking back. A gust of wind caught her in mid step, knocking her off balance again. She pulled her coat tighter, and determined, continued her quest.

She'd try another dope place before going home. The only other place she knew of was five blocks away. It would be a long, cold, walk. At least the wind would be at her back while going, but coming back she'd nearly freeze. And all to see if she could get one more small rock on credit. A rock she was not sure she could get to begin with, but was going to try. She wanted another hit real bad.

T and Jam looked at each other, laughed, and slapped gloved hands. They then, took up their usual positions, looking for their next customer, while trying to stay warm. Not many people were out walking in the cold weather, which made for a long day, and possibly night. But they had invested most of their money in their bag and had to make some sales. Another car approached them from the other direction, made a quick U-turn, and pulled into the bus stop.

It was T's turn to get in the car and the warmth. He walked swiftly toward the prospective customer, leaning against the wind, anticipating a moment's comfort in the heated car.

Narcotics Officers Bates, and Terns, who were assigned the Watts complaint, cruised by the corner where T, and Jam were doing their thing. They were driving the surveillance U-Haul cube van. To the un-informed, it looked like any U-Haul rental truck. It had one way windows on all sides of the box, which were painted over with a special one way paint to match the color scheme of the exterior, much the same as the advertising on the sides of the city's busses. The boys paid the truck absolutely no attention as it rolled slowly by.

"Let's go down a couple of blocks, and you get in the back with the camera," Kevin Bates told Otis, his partner, "I'll park the truck across the street from them. You take whatever evidence pictures you can, while I go in to talk to Mr. Watts."

"Now, you know you ain't right. You're going to walk right pass them, bold as all get out, and interview the very person who reported them," Otis said, to his partner, as they both laughed at the private gag.

"It is kind of ironic, now that you mentioned it," Kevin said, still laughing, as he looked down at the complaint to make sure he had the right address.

Coming around the corner again, the officers put their plan into action. They parked across the street from the pushers. Officer Bates got out of the truck, and crossed the street on his way to Mr. Watts' business. He walked within a couple of feet of T, who was acting as lookout for Jam, who, right out in the open, was handing something to a customer, and receiving what was obviously money. The Boys were really getting bold with their act.

As Officer Bates passed them, his plain clothes concealing his identity, the boys gave him the once-over, and not a second glance.

Mr. Watts, while coming from a back room, welcomed the prospective customer who'd just entered his cleaners, "Good evening sir, how can I help you?"

Looking quickly over his shoulder, Kelvin said, "Hello Mr. Watts, I'm one of the narcotics officers who've been assigned to clear up the nuisance you have in front of your business. My name is Officer Bates, my partner, Officer Terns, is out side gathering evidence. Just wanted to let you know we're on the job. We plan to observe for a while, and then attempt to make an undercover buy, followed by their arrest. So you can relax, your problem will be gone by the end of the day, and thank you for your call. We need the help of the citizens to get a handle on the drug trade in Detroit. Thanks again," Kevin finished, and shook Mr. Watts hand before exiting the store.

Mr. Watts thanked Officer Bates for responding to his

problem so quickly, and offered to grant free dry cleaning for he, and his partner, anytime they wished.

Kevin thanked Mr. Bates for the offer, and told him he might take him up on the offer, after discussing it with his partner, but, also, told him such a gratuity was really not necessary, and left the store.

On the way out, he decided to try and set up the undercover buy. *Hey, you never know,* he thought. Judging by the way these boys were rolling out in the open, Kevin figured they might feel secure, and assured enough of themselves to sell to a complete stranger. As he passed T, on his way back to the U-Haul, Kevin called T over.

"Hey mellow, whose got the rock?" he asked.

"What the hell you talking about, I don't know you," T responded, looking Kevin up, and down, as he reached inside of his jacket.

"Whoa," Kevin said, holding his hands out in front of him, "I didn't mean no harm, I just moved to this neighborhood and I wanted a little something-something to smoke. I'm looking to cop about ten nickels, or five dimes," Kevin added, for a little extra incentive. T seemed to relax a little and removed his hand from the gun he most assuredly had concealed under his jacket.

"You got the cash on you now? I don't deal in credit," T, asked, the undercover officer.

This is the point where the buy would be boom or bust — depending on the answer Kevin gave T.

"Now? No, I wasn't ready to cop right now, but you tell me where I can find an ATM and I can get the money and be back in five minutes" Kevin, an experienced officer, responded correctly. If Kevin had produced the cash immediately, T might have suspected him for the nark he was.

"What's your name," T asked.

"George," Kevin said.

"Okay, George. You see that gas station down the street? They got an ATM," T directed.

"Thanks a lot, my man. I'll be right back, don't go anywhere. By the way, what do I call you?" Kevin asked T, as he started across the street.

"Just call me T."

"Right on T. Give me ten minutes," Kevin requested, while backing towards the street.

"Word, playa," T said, now looking at the U-haul parked across the street.

Kevin crossed the street, and climbed into the truck.

"Did you get some good pictures?" Kevin asked Otis.

"Sure did, what the hell were you talking about with that punk?" Otis asked, while remaining in the back of the truck.

"You ain't going to believe this, but I just set up a buy with the dumb asshole," Kevin answered, as he started the truck and pulled away from the curb, and seeing T watching his every move.

"Aw no you didn't? You mean to tell me he's going to sell to a complete stranger? This is too easy. Where we going now?"

"I told him, his alias is T by the way, that I didn't have the money on me, so we're supposed to be going to an ATM," Kevin explained.

"What are we going to do about marking the money, we don't have an invisible ink marker with us?" Otis asked, now moving to sit in the passenger seat.

"Think man, think. We don't need to mark the money, have you forgotten the fact you'll capture the transaction on film? Better than marking the bills. Pictures will stand up better in court," Kevin reminded.

"You're right, but remember to not turn your back to

me. I need a clear shot of the drugs, and money changing hands, with your face clearly in the frame," Otis reminded Kevin. "Other than that, we're ready to roll. Let's do this," Otis encouraged.

They called the prescient, as they drove, and requested four marked cars to be on stand-by a couple blocks from the transaction site. The marked cars would move in on officer Terns' command.

"When we send in the arresting officers, we have to remember to tell them the one named T might be packing," Kevin, informed, Otis, "And please don't forget to remind me, to put in the report I'm making this buy with my money. I'll need to fill out a voucher," Kevin pleaded.

"Better yet, why don't you write down the serial numbers to the bills you'll use? That will assure the return of your money after the trial," Otis suggested.

"Damn good idea, what would I do without you, except get my share of the donuts we're given," teased Kevin.

"Ookayy, that will be the last time I look out for you. You better watch your back, smart ass," Otis, teased back.

The officers headed for the gas station they were directed too. Just in case T was watching them, the officers drove into the station. They sat in the gas station about five minutes, using the time to write down the serial numbers of the two twenties, and the one ten they would use to make the buy. They returned to the boys to make the buy. Otis had already moved to the back of the back.

The U-Haul, parked in a good location, Officer Terns in the back watching through the one-way Plexiglas window, and manning the camera. Officer Bates exited, and walked towards the two dealers. Apparently, the boys were watching him. As he exited the truck, they put their heads together, and whispered something to each other. I wonder if those two fools are thinking about trying to rob me, Bates wondered.

He continued across the street, and approached the two thugs. He kept a weary eye on T, who had the gun. If T made one false move, he'd give him a personal invitation to meet his maker. He knew you never underestimate these crazy fools, who sold drugs on the streets. They would not hesitate to take you out if given the slightest provocation.

"Sorry it took so long. There were two people waiting to use the ATM in front of me, but I got the cash. The deal still on?" Kevin asked, as he approached the thugs, walking toward T.

"You cool, you cool. How many did you say you wanted?" T asked, looking up and down the street, and at the U-Haul. He seemed to be more cautious, but was ready to go through with the deal anyway.

"I only need five dimes right now, but when I get paid, I want to cop a ball, can you handle that?" Kevin asked T.

"Hey dude I can handle anything you want. Looks like we're going to have a good relationship. However, remember, when I deliver a Ball, I like to bring it to your house. You moving near hear?" T probed, as he looked at the truck again. His intuition was on full tilt. He thought about asking to consummate the transaction inside the truck, but didn't listen to his instincts.

Had T asked to get into the truck, Kevin would have been caught completely off guard. He hadn't thought about that possibility. However, the request for his address, although not expected, was easy to handle.

Bates knew he could make up a fake address — the dealer wouldn't have a chance to check it anyway. As soon as the transaction went down, the arrest team would be on their way.

"Yeah cuz. I'm just around the corner, two blocks down, third house off the alley on the left," Kevin pointed in the general direction.

"Word? Let me give you my cell phone number. Give me a call when you ready," T said, while handing Kevin a business card. The capital letter T, and a phone number on it, "After you've moved in, just call me and give me the address. I'll be by within the hour. Cool?"

Bates took the card, gripping it on its edges. He knew the boy's fingerprints were on the card, and it might be presented as evidence during the trial. He gingerly stuffed it in his breast pocket.

"Right on, bro." Kevin said, as he took the card, and the five-dime rocks T was handing him, which were rapped in used lotto ticket paper.

Otis, who was photographing the exchange, picked up his service radio, and called in the arrest team as soon as the money was exchanged and before Officer Bates could turn around and come back to the U-Haul.

Kevin turned to go back to the truck, waving buy to the boys, knowing the arrest team was already on the way. By the time he opened the door to the truck, four marked cruisers, two coming from one direction, and two from the other, came roaring up, and came to a tire screaming stop in front of the two dealers, with the cherries and blues turned on. Eight officers, two from each car, were out of the interceptors as soon as the cars came to a stop. The officers had their guns drawn, and were ordering the two thugs to lie down on the cold ground, face down, and hands behind their heads. T and Jam, taken completely by surprise, had no choice but to comply.

Mr. Watts was watching the whole thing through the big front window of his cleaners. He was grinning from ear to ear. His problem had been solved in less than three hours. *I should have placed the call to the cops much earlier,* he thought.

The officers moved in, and handcuffed the two,

searched them, and found the drugs along with the 9-mil pistol T had in his waistband.

Officers Kevin Bates, and Otis Terns, started up the surveillance U-Haul, and left the scene after the boys were stuffed into separate cars. Two more pushers and a handgun were removed from the streets.

At their separate trials, Terrence and Jamie, the boy's real names, had literally no defenses. The photos, the drugs, and gun assured them a nice, lengthy, visit to the gray bar hotel.

The claim of entrapment offered by T, who said Officer Kevin Bates had approached him first, was thrown out because of the pictures of him selling to other customers while Officer Bates was inside the store talking to Mr. Watts. T also received the automatic, mandatory, extra two-years of time for committing a felony while in possession of a firearm.

Chapter 6

Jeff, Quick, and Amos, looking for trouble.

"Damn, man, you doing it wrong," Jeff said, in a whisper, to Amos.

"Shut the hell up. I done this enough times to know what I is doing" Amos retorted. "This is a big lock, just takes a little longer."

"That's what I'm talking about, why are you messing with the lock? Just put the bar into the loop on the hasp, and then snatch, and twist at the same time. That part of the door is not as strong as the lock. I thought I taught you something the last time we did this," Jeff admonished, as he pointed to where Amos should place the pry bar.

Amos relented, and did as he was told. The loop into which the lock was inserted, cracked with just a little force, and the door to the tire shop partially opened. Everyone froze for just a second, as they listened for the sound of an alarm. No alarm, but they already knew that. They'd cased the place earlier, and decided the back alley door was the best way to get in without being detected.

―――――

When Detroit went to curb side trash pickup, and made most of the alleys easements, lighting in the alleys hadn't been maintained. There was a very dark spot right behind the tire repair shop, just waiting for some crook to take advantage of.

Jeff called Quick, who was acting as lookout, and the three of them entered the shop and pushed the door closed.

Jeff, Amos, and Quick were life long friends of about the same age. When you saw one, you saw the other two. They'd grown up in the neighborhood together, attended school together, until, as a group, they decided at the age of 16, to drop out. They got into a life of crime, having no support from their young parents who were either on drugs or in jail — much the same as T and Jam. It's surprising how many kids on the streets come from similar backgrounds. If one of the boys didn't want to work for a living, none did, and none having gotten into the drug scene, yet, they resorted to other forms of crime to get a few dollars. They were very dependent on each other. So far they'd managed to avoid arrest. However, with their frequent acts of vandalism, and break-ins, prison or death would not be long in their futures.

Once inside, they searched the shop for any money or power tools they could sell. Not having flashlights, they had to rely on the faint glow coming from the streetlight out in front of the business. There were corners where they could barely see what was in front of them, but by striking a cigarette lighter, they managed to pretty much cover the whole shop.

What they didn't know was the owner never left money in his shop after closing. He also took all valuable tools with him in his old pick-up when he closed down for the night. Anything else of value was bolted to the floor. He was no fool. He knew his shop was vulnerable to a break-in, and chose to take valuables with him, rather than rely on locks or alarms — alarms the police were slow to respond to on occasions, they being overworked and undermanned.

"Damn, ain't nothing in here worth anything," Jeff hissed quietly to no one in particular, as he peered in a dark corner.

"You're right, ain't nothing here but these old, used up, hammers, and bars, and air hoses with no fittings and tape around them to seal the leaks," Quick agreed.

Amos, who was returning from a back room, joined in, "I found a compressor in the back room, but it's bolted down and nasty as hell, and I ain't getting dirty trying to carry that heavy mutha."

"Forget this, let's get the hell out of here, ain't nothing we can sell," Amos finished.

"Damn right man, let's go," agreed Jeff.

The three men left the tire shop the way they came in, and left the back door standing wide open.

Back on the street, Quick whined, "what we gonna do now, I need a drink, and something to eat?"

"Quick, you're always hungry," Jeff teased.

"I know. It ain't my fault," Quick defended. The doctor said it was a gland thing, or something like that."

"Well, if I was you, I'd have that gland removed

before you explode," Jeff continued.

"Yeah, funny, Jeff. Real funny," Quick, came back, "You so funny you needs to be working in one of those comedy clubs downtown."

Quick, at about five-five, and who weighed in at about 300 lbs., which was carried on two short stubby bowed, legs, was anything but quick. He got his nickname, not because of his speed of action, but because of how fast he could make food disappear. He was not the smartest of the trio, and happy they let him tag alone with them. Unlike his running mates, he had an aunt, who would take him in any time he wanted to move in with her. He thought about staying with her for a while, but never did, fearing the loss of contact with his only friends. His aunt told him if he decided to live with her, he'd have to buckle down and get back in school, follow her rules, and wouldn't be allowed outside after ten at night. Deep down, he was a good boy, and really wasn't inclined to do some of the stuff his two friends got him into, but what was he supposed to do? Not living with his aunt, not having to go to school, and not having a job, his life would be one boring day after the other if he didn't have them to follow. So follow them he did, all the while wondering how long they would continue to get away with some of the crap they tried.

"I got an idea, but it's a little risky," Jeff said, halfheartedly, as the boys walked down the street, their heads down, and hands in their pockets, bolstered against the cold breeze blowing in their faces.

"I knew you would come up with something, you

always do," praised Amos.

"What you got?" asked Quick, while wondering, what now?

"Okay, check this out. You know this new dope house that just opened in the hood, called Double D's?" Jeff asked his companions.

"Yeah, you're talking about the place a few blocks over," Amos answered.

"Yeah, that's the place," Jeff continued, "Big Bertha took me by there about a week ago. You remember, that time I told you I'd be right back. She wanted somebody to walk with her. That's one scary woman. Besides, I think she likes me. Well, anyway, while I was in the place, I checked it out. You ain't going to believe how this dude is running the joint. First, Double let me in without asking any questions. He didn't ask Bertha who I was either. Kind of sloppy if you ask me. He ain't got anybody looking out, nobody on shotgun, no bracing on the doors, nothing. Now, you really ain't going to believe this," Jeff continued, laughingly, "he keeps his money, and his dope in a cigar box, right there in the front room, like he thinks he's some kind of invulnerable king of the hill, and no one would dare touch him…"

Amos interrupted, "you got to be kidding, Jeff. You mean to tell me he don't stash his stones and money in another room. Some place where everybody who comes in won't know where its at?"

"That's right. Right there in a cigar box in his hand the whole time I was there. Crazy if you ask me. This dummy looks a little on the young side, and inexperienced. Like he ain't never been robbed before. Like he don't have a clue. He's just asking to be knocked over if you ask me. We could take him no sweat. Maybe get a few hundred apiece — counting the rocks and money together. Hell, if we don't get him, somebody else will. What you think?" Jeff, asked, not looking at the other men as they walked.

The three men walked in silence after hearing Jeff's proposal. Quick and Amos understood what Jeff was suggesting they do. Neither of them wanted to admit embarking on such an adventure was a little scary, especially, to Quick. He didn't like half the stuff the others got him into, and this was the most dangerous they would try.

They were minor hoods. All of their previous crimes were acts of vandalism, or breaking into homes and businesses in which no one was around. The thought of robbing someone face to face, let alone a dope dealer, was just a little out of their comfort zone. Just because Double-D was young, didn't stop him from being a mean, revengeful, mutha, who would not rest until he retaliated on those who robbed him. Yes, it was a risky proposition any way you looked at it, and they all knew it.

After walking for a few blocks, no one saying anything, Amos had a question, "Do you think we can get away with it?"

"Sure we can," answered Jeff, while trying to appear confident, when actually, he was a little dubious about the idea himself. "That place is just asking to be hit. If we plan it right, we can hit it and quit it in no time," he said, still trying to convince himself, "We can keep the money, and sell the dope."

"Okay, I'm in. There sure is enough rock-heads around here," said Amos, quietly, after a short pause, he still wasn't excited about the idea.

"Me to, I guess," echoed, Quick. He'd follow his companions to the gates of hell in his oversized boxers, if they decided to go there.

"Word," Jeff said, enthusiastically.

Now that they agreed, Jeff felt a bit better, although, secretly, he was hoping the other boys would talk him out of the extreme move, but he knew once he proposed the robbery it was as good as done. They had no choice. None of the young men had the fortitude to say they shouldn't do a certain thing, or so much as say they were apprehensive about something. None wanted to appear weak to his companions, especially, Quick. So they all acquiesced to the half-baked plan, good or bad.

As they walked, they were concentrating so hard on the task ahead of them they weren't focusing on how cold it was. A strong gust of wind changed that.

"Damn, its cold out hear, lets go to my place, and make some plans," Jeff, suggested. "My mother is probably getting high, and we might be able to steal something to eat."

"That sounds real good to me!" Quick said, a little too enthusiastically. Everybody had to laugh.

They followed Jeff to his mother's house in silence, each thinking of the robbery, and worried about the consequences. This was their first robbery, and neither knew what to expect. They all knew most people who got into rolling were a little crazy, and sometimes vicious. Nevertheless, they belayed their fears by hoping Double-D, being so young, might be the exception to that rule.

Jeff, Amos, and Quick, walked around to the rear of Jeff' mother's building. She lived on the first floor in the rear or the deteriorating, two storied, building, which still held remnants of its once grandeur with a yard light out front that had the building's address hanging from an arm, and a large gravel parking plaza in the rear. Jeff wasn't aloud to keep a key to the building. His mother didn't trust him, so he had to knock on the window to be let in. His first knocks got no response. He knocked louder, and more persistently.

Finally, he could hear his mother's voice, loudly asking, through the covered window, "Who the hell is it?"

"It's me, mom. Can I come in for a minute, and get

warm?" Jeff responded.

"Boy, are you crazy? You know better than to come knocking on my window at this time of night. You alone?"

"Naw, mom, Amos and Quick are with me. Come on, let us in for just one minute. We won't stay long. We just want to warm up a little."

"All right, hold on for a second," Jeff's mother relented. She was naked, and retreated to the bedroom to get her bathrobe.

That second turned into five minutes. Jeff was about to knock again, but heard his mother's apartment door open. The back door to the building soon opened. They followed Jeff's, bathrobe, and flapping house shoes wearing mother back to the small, one bedroom apartment.

As they followed, his mother was mumbling, obviously irritated, "Don't do this again. You know I have company at this time of night."

Jeff's mother, at forty-two, and who was a little on the thin side, at about five-seven and one-hundred-thirty-pounds. Her brown complexion, and full lips, adorned an attractive face featuring two, large, bright eyes needing no makeup, and she wore none.

Besides, the dates she serviced could care less about her make-up. Their only concern being what she had between her legs and that was fine with her. Had she decided to settle down, and get into a relationship with a single individual, she could have. Several of her dates liked her and had tried to convince her to do so, but that wasn't what she wanted. She liked having multiple partners as much as she liked smoking rocks, and she knew any men who wanted to make her their own, and even if they said she could continue doing her thing, would change their minds once they were hooked up. Besides, she still loved Jeff's father, and secretly hoped he'd return, and they would be a couple again.

He, like her, smoked crack, and they got alone fairly well, until she began pressing him to spend more money, that is. He had a job, and a car, and bills to pay, and wasn't about to get flat broke every time they smoked together. One night they got into a heated argument, and he left, while vowing to never return. He packed his clothes into garbage bags, and told her to have a good life — he was through.

As it happens, there was an older fellow who lived down the hall, and heard the couple arguing. When this secret admirer knocked on her door, and offered her a hundred dollars to come down to his room for a while, she being angry and high, as well a geeked, accepted. She didn't expect Jeff's father to return, so when she was coming out of the trick's room, while pulling her housecoat around her naked body, and finding her boyfriend standing in the hall, while wondering where she went, she knew she was busted.

Jeff's farther only stood and watched her come back to their apartment while she not saying anything. He knew what was up. He'd seen how the older dude looked at her, and knew he wanted his woman.

Just as she was about to go through her apartment's door, the older fella poked his head out, and was about to ask her when he could see her again, but when he saw her boyfriend, Jeff's farther, standing in the hall, he quickly ducked back inside and slammed his door.

Her boyfriend didn't say a word. His intentions of returning, and making up with his woman, vanished. He, while giving her a hurt look, turned and left. She never saw him again. He didn't so much as return to gather the rest of his belongings. To this day she still doesn't know where he moved too. She'd heard through the grapevine he'd moved into a hotel on the southwest side of Detroit, but she never followed up on the gossip. Just like that, a fifteen-year relationship was over.

She and her neighbor continued to trick for a while until he got tired of her, and began bringing in younger women. She didn't mind. Now that she was into the tricking trade, she didn't have any problems find willing dates. One way or another, she was going to get her dope.

Once inside the apartment, Jeff's mother, without another word, went straight into the bedroom while closing and locking the door. A short while later, The three boys could hear some rhythm and blues music come on in the bedroom, sounding kind of tinny, coming from the small clock radio. This wasn't the first time they'd been in the apartment with Jeff while she was entertaining. All three boys knew what she was doing in there — knew she had a date, and was tricking while getting high.

Now in the warmth of the apartment, the boys went about making themselves at home. Amos went to the bathroom. Quick, as usual, went straight to the kitchen, opened the fridge, and found an opened, half-eaten, pack of almost stale bologna. Taking a couple slices, and two slices of bread, with nothing to dress the sandwich, he made a dry sandwich, and returned to the livingroom. He wanted a glass of water, but found nothing to drink out of. He figured he'd use his cupped hands to drink from the faucet later. Jeff cleared a pile of dirty clothes from the threadbare couch, and laid down on it, putting his feet up, without taking off his shoes.

The couch, a 19-inch, black and white TV resting on a milk crate, and a rickety card table with a crack in the middle, and two folding chairs, was the only furniture in the front room. The large front window was covered with a bed sheet. Not just any sheet, a sheet with Superman printed on it, while in that classic pose, he was flying around the Earth, in outer space, one arm extended in front of him. It was probably a hold over from when Jeff was a toddler, but he couldn't remember the sheet from his past.

The lighting in the room was poor, a single sixty-watt bulb hanging nakedly from the ceiling fixture in the dinning area, being the only source of illumination. There were no pictures on the walls, and a well-worn carpet covered the floor. A single centipede crawled up one wall, which was unusual because they usually stayed under the carpet where they ate the padding. Yeah, it was sparsely furnished, but it was shelter, and most importantly, warm.

Jeff's mother had long ago given up on pretense, her drug habit becoming the most important thing in her life. Her only child, Jeff, was grown, and able to care for himself, leaving her free to indulge in her addiction as much as tricks, and money, would allow.

After the boys attended to their immediate needs, they sat down on the couch, making Jeff move his feet, and began putting together plans on how they were going to rob Double-D.

"Okay, this is how we're going to do it," Jeff began, "I'll get my gun, (a Saturday night special, .25 automatic) from Dave's. Like I said earlier, when I was in the house, I noticed he didn't have shotgun protection, and bars across the doors. Double has seen me before — I should be able to get in without any problem. After I get in, Quick, you go to the back, tell anyone coming Double is sold out, and will be back up in an hour. Amos, you take the front, and do the same. After I make sure me and Double are alone, I'll pull my gatt, and tie him up, we don't wont to hurt anybody, unless it's necessary. I'll grab the box, and come out the back door. Amos you listen for me to whistle. When you hear me whistle, you come around to the back, and we'll leave down the alley. The fences are high on that alley, so no one will see us."

"What will we do if somebody is in there?" asked Quick, while taking the last bite of his sandwich and wishing he had another.

"Hell I don't know. Let's see… Oh I got it — fist, I'll tell Double I wants to talk to him in private about buying a nickel or dime, whatever he sells. I'll tell him I don't like doing business with someone watching me. I'll ask if we can wait for his last customer to leave, and then after he sends his last customer out, I'll go to work," answered, Jeff.

"Sounds like a plan, to me," said Quick, his mind still on another dry bologna sandwich.

"Yep," is all Amos said. He still wasn't convinced this armed robbery thing was a good idea. Nevertheless, as they'd done since they were pre-teens, what one did, all did. Kind of like the three musketeers, he envisioned them.

"Word," Jeff said. "Okay, today is Friday — we'll hit him tomorrow when he might have more money from his Friday sales. Cool? Sound good to you guys?"

No one answered Jeff's last question. Their silence spoke volumes. But the key thing was neither of them protested. The boys were about to find out how quickly things can go sideways…

———

Quick, Amos and Jeff spent the night at Jeff's mother' apartment. Quick and Amos slept on the front room floor, while Jeff took the old couch. Nobody got much sleep. Jeff's mother and her date were on missions (dope runs) in and out the remainder of the night. On occasion, Jeff could hear his mother moaning quietly. Other times he could hear the loud squeaking of the bedsprings, as she, and her date engaged in intercourse. Jeff was accustomed to those noises. His mother had been on drugs for some time, at least since he was seven or so, and after his father left, she'd taken up tricking to support her habit. At that age, he didn't know what the noises meant, but by the time he understood, it was no big thing to him. Besides, by the time he was in his early teens, he'd begun hanging in the streets whenever a date showed up.

It was around day brake when his mother's date finally left the apartment, probably ran out of money. Things quieted enough for the boys to get some sleep. Their only disturbance being the periodical passing of a fire trucks, their loud siren blaring. The firehouse was only two blocks down the street, and it seemed the firemen never got much rest.

On one occasion, after being woke up, Jeff could hear the persistent clicking of a cigarette lighter coming from his mother's bedroom. Apparently his mother was still busy pushing her stem. Quick got up to go to bathroom, making loud grunts while he was in there. *Damn, don't that boy know how to crap in silence,* Jeff thought.

Later, Jeff was the first to wake up, still sleepy and hungry, he shook his friends awake. It was late afternoon.

"Damn, I'm hungry," slurred Quick, still half-asleep.

"Yeah, me too, but you can't get anything else from my mother's fridge, she won't let me in again if I let you eat what she has left. After we hit Double's, we will graze at the Coney," assured Jeff.

Amos, after being roused awake, just sat up and gaped, blankly, as he tried to figure out where the hell he was. He wiped the drool from the corner of his mouth, and stretched. He wanted to lay back down and get a few more moments of slumber, but Jeff wouldn't let him, softly kicking him in the side every time he closed his eyes. Eventually, the boys got themselves together, and bundled against the cold, left the apartment. Jeff's mother, completely exhausted, was finally asleep when the boys left.

"Do y'all still remember the plan?" asked Jeff, as they walked in the cold afternoon air. There was a bright sun in the sky, but dark clouds were moving in from the northwest, promising more snow.

"Yeah we got it," retorted Amos, as he looked at the sky, thinking, it's going to snow — that's all we need right now.

"Yeah, I got it too, but damn it's cold out here," added Quick, his short, fat, legs, pumping to keep up with his fast walking companions.

"Damn, man, you always complaining. Will you please shut up, and get your mind on what we're about to do, for a change," Jeff, fired back to Quick, with a half laugh. "Okay, here's what we're going to do. You two go over to Quick's auntie' house, and wait for me to get my gun from Dave's. I'll pick you up there and we'll go over to Double-D's, and get us some money."

Quick and Amos did as they were told, which was all right with Quick. Maybe he could get something to eat at his aunt's house. She always had something good in the icebox. Jeff took off in another direction, walking fast, on his way to Dave's, to get his little pistol.

When first arriving at Dave's small, rented, house, Jeff thought Dave might not be home. That would put a serious crimp in his robbery plan — he not having a gun. Not accepting Dave wasn't home, he knocked repeatedly, not only on the front door, but all the windows around the house, and the back door. To his relief, Dave finally answered the knocks, and let him in.

"Damn, boy, why you knocking on my door this early?" Dave asked, still in his boxers.

"Sorry Dave, but I need my gatt. Had a good time last night, huh?"

"Yeah, well, a brothers' got to get his rocks off every now and then. Damn broad tried to kill me last night, took all night to put her horny butt to sleep. She's in the back, don't know how I'm going to get ride of her. She acts like she wants to move in here or something, and you and I both know that ain't happening. I like variety, and ain't ready to settle down with no one stank."

Dave was a slightly older gangster friend of Jeff's, who was an ex-con, and could be trusted to hold on to the weapon.

"But, before I let you have the burner," Dave continued, "And I know I ain't your big brother or anything like that, but I was wondering why you wants your gun. You ain't thinking about trying to rob no store or nothing, is you?"

"Naw, Dave. I just like having it in my pocket sometimes," Jeff, Lied, "But, damn, Dave, you going to question me every time I comes to get it, because if you is, I won't bring it here no more? I don't know where I'll keep it. I don't want to walk around all the time with the heat on me, but I can't keep it at my mother's, that's for sure. But I'll find some place."

"Whoa, little brother. Naw, dude, I ain't your mother. I just don't want you to make the same mistakes I made when I was your age," Dave said, going back to the bedroom to get the gun, and returning, "Here, player, take your heat, but please keep in mind it can get you into trouble real quick, cool?"

"I feel you, Dave. Thanks for keeping it for me, but I'm cool. Catch you later, Bye,"

"Okay, Jeff, stay cool, see-ya," Dave said, locking the

door behind Jeff as he left. He stood at the door watching Jeff through the window at the top of the door, until he was out of sight. *I know that little thug is up to something. He ain't fooling me,* Dave thought, as he went to the bathroom to take a leak.

After retrieving his little pistol, Jeff walked back to Quick's auntie' house, to gather his partners in crime. The boys walked, not saying much. Quick was eating the first of two ham sandwiches he'd made, this time with every accouterment his aunt had in the fridge. Amos kept looking back over his shoulder as if someone was following him. Jeff just walked, head down and occasionally patting the pistol in his pocket as if he were mentally rehearsing his future actions.

The boys arrived at Double-D's dope house, and put their plan into action. Quick, still eating the second sandwich, took up his position in the rear of the dope house, and Amos did the same in the front. Jeff climbed the front steps, and knocked on the door. Double immediately answered and let him in.

In the back of the house there was waist high weeds with a single path worn through them, and a half-fallen, six-foot, privacy fence, half the slats missing, marking the boundary. A customer confronted Quick as soon as he got to his position. It was a young lady. She came around the fence, and appeared in the yard somewhat suddenly, startling Quick in mid bite of his sandwich.

He took his bite, and swallowed in a hurry, almost without chewing — that, he was good at.

"Sorry, foxy, Double is out right now, but he'll be back up in about an hour, why don't you come back then," Quick told the customer, with as much of an honest face as he could muster. He then added, "Be sure you come back, they gonna be big," trying to legitimize his performance.

The customer, a young woman, with oversized, heavy looking, earrings, stretching her ear lobes, stopped, and looked at Quick. She had her head tilted a little. One earring trying it's best to pull out of the hole in the woman's ear, stretching the lobe to the point it had to hurt.

"Who the hell is you, I ain't never seen you around here before?" she, asked, Quick.

The question caught Quick off guard. He hadn't planed to answer any questions, and had to think fast to keep up the guise.

"I'm D's new door man and look out, who the hell is you? What's your name?" Quick countered, in a stern voice, trying to act confident, and hoping his question would put the woman on the defensive.

"I'm Duchess, and I been coming here about a week, ask D, he'll tell you." She replied, in a softer voice. Quick's counter attack seeming to work.

"Okay, Duchess, D said to not let anyone in, until he's back up in about an hour, come back then. That's all I can tell you right now, but to be honest with you, I think he's in there knocking boots with that last customer, a fine young thing," Quick said, gaining more confidence.

"Forget this, you say an hour, but it'll be more like two hours before you is back up. I'm going over to Edward's," the young woman retorted, as she turned and walked back through the opening in the fence. She turned to give Quick one last glance before disappearing behind the fence, while thinking, where did D find that fat pig?

Quick had begun to sweat a little. Now the danger of discovery had passed, the cold he'd not felt during the conversation with the woman was now assaulting his body with a vengeance. He was starting to shiver. *Damn, I hope this don't take much longer,* he thought, as he walked to the fence and looked up, and down the alley for anyone else approaching and saw only more weed trees nearly blocking the path. In the distance he could see an obviously stolen car with no wheels, and the hood raised. It was covered with dust as if it had been there a long time. He returned to the back of the house, and looked for somewhere to sit down, and seeing only the bird crap covered rear steps, decided to stand.

In the front of the house, Amos was having a much easier time turning away the prospective customers. As the junkies turned to go up the stairs, while giving him a weary eye, all he said was "out" and held out his hand with the thumb turned down. The customers, not wanting to hang around in front of the dope house, usually turned and walked away without saying a word. He was practicing his break dance steps as if he didn't have a care in the world. He was actually nervous, and cold. The dancing helped him to relax, and keep warm at the same time. He, like Quick, wanted this thing to be over as soon as possible. He kept looking toward the door of the house, trying to imagine what was happening inside. A police cruiser rolled slowly by, the officers giving him a long stare, but kept rolling. His heart nearly jumped through his mouth. After he thought about it, the only thing he had to worry about was not having any ID on him. After all, he wasn't going into the house, and damn sure didn't have any drugs on him. But he was still relieved they didn't stop. He took another look at the house. *Come on Jeff,* he thought.

Now inside the crack house, Jeff was beginning to feel his nerves, something he wasn't expecting. He hadn't planed on having to wait out five crack-heads before he put his scheme into action. They were smoking their rocks in the livingroom. No one spoke, the only sound being the clicking of disposable lighters as they flamed up their rocks. Everyone seemed to be in various stages of intoxication, and no one paid him any attention. *This could take forever,* Jeff thought.

D, who'd finished serving one of his customers, turned to Jeff, "I don't remember your name. You came in with Bertha the last time you were here, right?"

"Yeah, D. you ain't never served me before, but I'm cool."

"Word player. What do you need?" D asked, as he opened the cigar box, containing the drugs, and money. Jeff eyes went down to the opened box. From what he could see, there wasn't a lot of money in it, just several twenties, and a few tens, five's and several singles. The box seemed to contain about twenty or thirty small bags of crack. He started to call the whole operation off right then and there. His plan of asking to talk to D after the last customer left, would not work with so many people in the house, and it didn't look like there was enough money in the box to take a chance on.

"Just give me a nickel," Jeff, replied, as he reached into his pocket, and felt the reassuring cold metal of the small pistol, and no money.

"I only sell dimes, and I don't except change," D, informed.

Jeff's hand resting on the pistol in his pocket seemed to circumvent his common sense.

"Oh, okay, can I have a word with you in the other room, I ain't comfortable handling my business in front of all these people." Jeff responded, deciding to go through with his ill-planed robbery.

"Word, brother, but let me tell you right now, I don't give no credit," D, said, as he closed the cigar box, and turned to lead Jeff to the kitchen. As they passed the customer D had just served, the man who was sitting on a blue plastic milk crate, blew out a heavy cloud of white smoke, the odor, which Jeff would never forget, having smelled it so many times in his mother's apartment — a very distinctive order, much like the odor of weed. Once you smelled it, you'd know exactly what it was. Jeff gave the smoker a glance, and as he followed D to the kitchen, watched the man hold his stem up in front of him as he examined it. He didn't smoke and wondered what it was about crack that was so addictive. He only shook his head and kept going.

Everything happening after that moment seemed to happen in slow motion to Jeff. In the kitchen, and before D could turn around to face him, Jeff pulled the little .25 caliber, semi-automatic, out of his pocket, and tilted on it's side at shoulder height, pointed it a Double-D's head. When D turned around and saw the pistol pointed at his head, he dropped the cigar box, and extended his hands out to his side.

"Whoa, my man, you can have it, just don't shoot me, I won't give you any troub…"

"Shut the hell up," Jeff ordered D, in a hushed voice, as he glanced down to the floor, and back up to D's face.

Jeff bent over to pick up the box, while watching D and keeping the pistol trained on his head, but couldn't locate the box. He stood up and glanced down again in an effort to take note of the exact location of the box.

D was waiting on just such an opportunity. As Jeff looked down the second time, D quickly stepped forward, and slapped the gun still pointed at his head.

Had, Double known anything about those cheap, Saturday night special hand guns so prevalent on the streets today, he'd have known those particular weapons were an accident waiting to happen. Besides having, gritty, temperamental, triggers, they didn't have any safety features of any kind. Once they were cocked, the slightest jar would set them off. Several people had shot themselves with the cheap pistols, after cocking them, and attempting to stick the guns in their waistbands. One individual lost a very important appendage through such an, unfortunate, accident.

As D slapped the gun, it discharged. It was only a small caliber and should not have been instantly fatal, unless it was aimed at a vital part of the body, such as the head. Had the pistol been pointed anywhere but D's forehead, the single shot may not have killed him. However, the gun "was" pointed at his forehead.

When D slapped it in an attempt to knock it out of Jeff's hand, and a fraction of a second before the gun discharged, it was redirected from his forehead, to his left eye. The full metal-jacked bullet entered the left eye of D, made a slight turn, and severed his spinal cord, near the base of his skull. D, and the small pistol that jumped out of Jeff's hand upon firing, hit the floor almost simultaneously.

It took Jeff several seconds to comprehend what'd just happened. When the gun fired, he instinctively ducked, not being familiar with firearms. Although, the autoloader was of small caliber, in the small kitchen the shot sounded like a cannon going off. Jeff's ears were ringing from the mussel blast. He looked down at the dead D, and seeing a trickle of blood oozing from the man's left eye, his stomach began to churn. Now panicking, he picked up the cigar box and headed for the back door. He was half way to the door when he remembered the pistol left behind on the kitchen floor. Jeff hurried back to retrieved his pistol, and then made a beeline for the back door, not bothering to look back to see if anyone was following.

He had to fumble with the unfamiliar door lock before

he could open the door. His heart was beating so fast it hurt. The panic had a full nelson grip on his brain that refused to function. *Damn, what's wrong with this thing, it won't open,* he thought, as he fumbled with the stubborn lock.

He stepped back and planted a foot against the door. He couldn't think of anything else to do. The door stood solid, blocking his path. Trying the lock one more time, it turned easily — he was out. He looked back over his shoulder just before leaving, wondering if anyone was standing in the kitchen door watching him. So far no one from the front room had come to check out the noise.

Actually, Jeff had nothing to worry about. The people in the front room, who were getting high, and even though hearing the shot, were in no shape to do any thing about it. When the shot was heard, everyone froze. Their harts already racing from the drugs, and their minds shrouded in a drug-induced haze, were not functioning. All they could do was sit where they were, and stare at each other, trying to understand what the hell was going on in the kitchen.

Outside, Quick and Amos heard the shot. It was not very loud, but gun fire just the same, and they knew it. Amos ran to the back where Quick was standing, looking at the back door, hoping it was not what it sounded like. The two of them heard someone fidgeting with the lock on the back door, and then hearing someone kick the door, they looked at each other, and almost took off running. Eventually, the door suddenly opened, and they saw it was Jeff.

Jeff, after opening the door, came out running. He took the four steps in a single bound, bolting through the fence gate, and headed down the alley with Quick and Amos close on his heels.

As they ran, Amos asked Jeff, "What happened?"

"I'll tell you later. It went bad. Just keep moving."

Overweight Quick, because of adrenaline, was able to

do just that, his short fat legs moving faster than any other time he could remember. They ran for what seemed like ten miles to Quick, all through the alleys, but was actually only a few blocks before they slowed to a fast walk.

At that moment, no one felt the cold. Quick was out of breath, and about to give up. Amos, looking back, and seeing no one behind them, also wanted to slow down. Thankfully, Jeff, seeing his partners falling behind, decided they'd run far enough, and slowed to a walk.

The three boys had run several blocks, zigzagging from one alley to another just in case someone was after them. They were headed to Dave's place to catch their breaths, and figure what to do next. They, eventually, entered an alley, which had several abandoned houses with, open, empty, garages, behind them. The heavy metal doors of the garages had been removed by the scrap metal hounds, while leaving the alley looking like a big mouth with many teeth missing.

Like the abandoned homes, some of the garages that once had aluminum siding on them, had been stripped by the same metal hounds. The same with any copper plumbing inside the homes, along with any heavy electrical wiring. They could take the precious scrap to a dealer and clean up. The dealers took the contraband, knowing it was stolen, but didn't care.

The City Counsel had made an attempt to construct a city ordinance outlawing the acceptance of any materials, which might have come from an abandoned, vandalized, house, but for some reason, couldn't seem to get the votes needed to send it to the judicial department for enforcement.

The boys ducked into one of the garages to catch their breaths.

Quick came in a little behind them. "Damn, did you have to run so far?" he complained.

"Always complaining," teased Amos, "it ain't our fault you can't keep up. Besides you need the exercise, anyway, blimp butt."

"What the hell happened back there? I thought I heard a gun shot?" Quick asked, Jeff, after he got his wind back.

"It was... It was an accident, I swear. The dumb mutha tried to slap the gun out of my hand, and it went off," Jeff defended, "Shot him in the eye. Killed him."

"You did what!?" yelled, Quick.

"I told you, it was an accident, besides, I don't think anyone in the dope house could finger me. They were so busy getting high, and hiding their faces, they didn't get a good look at me," Jeff, defended, further.

"Ain't this about a mutha-frigging-blip? Maybe no one can identify you," Quick continued, "but while I was in the back, I had an argument with this rock-star Duchess, and she might be able to identify me," he finished, as he walked around flapping his arms like a bird, and shaking his head. His pants down around his big thighs making him look somewhat like a big penguin.

"Do you know her? Had she ever seen you before?" Jeff, asked, Quick.

"No," replied Quick, stopping his pacing to look at Jeff.

"Well what the hell you worried about?" Jeff explained, "for one thing, ain't no crack-head going to come forward, and admit they was trying to get into a dope house. And second, think man, the cops ain't going to spend too much time trying to find a dope house dealer's hit man. So calm down, we'll be all right as long as we lay low for a while."

"Well, I guess you're right, at least I hope so," Quick said, not quite sure Jeff was correct, but at least he was not as agitated, but his hunger had returned.

"Did anyone see you in the front?" Jeff asked, Amos.

"A couple of people started towards the house, but they turned around without giving me a second glance when I told them Double was out," Amos, confirmed.

"We cool, we cool. Let's split up, and meet at Dave's to split up the loot," Jeff, suggested.

"Whoa," Amos said, "open the box and let me see what we got."

"Damn, man, don't you trust me?" Jeff, asked.

"Yeah I trust you. Cut the crap. You know that. I just want to see if it was worth the trouble we went through," Amos explained.

"Okay, take a look, make it quick, I want to get back to my mom's house to chill for a couple days," explained, Jeff.

The three boys gathered around to check out the contents of the cigar box. Jeff opened the box. He took out the money and counted it, "91, 92, 93, damn it ain't even a hundred dollars in here, that no dealing mutha didn't have a hundred dollars. Can you believe that?" Jeff, asked, incredulously. "Could be he was just starting a new bag. Let's see how many rocks he has here," Jeff continued, as he pushed the rocks from one side of the box to the other, counting them. "I count 27 rocks, but I can't tell if these is nickels or dimes. What they look like to you Amos?" Jeff asked.

"I don't know, they're too big to be nickels, and too small to be dimes, let's call them dimes," Amos, advised.

"This ain't enough to split up at Dave's," Jeff pointed out. "Let's split it up here. The way I figure, we gets 9 rocks apiece, and I'm going to give you each..." he paused to do some mental calculations, "Thirty-dollars," he finally said, "I'm going to take thirty-three dollars because I did the hard part, and my ass could be up for murder. That'll give us about one-hundred and twenty-dollars apiece, all right?" said Jeff.

"Word," replied, Amos, while slapping Quick's outstretched hand.

The boys split up the dope, and money, and went their separate ways.

Jeff took his share of the dope back to his mother's house where he could sell it to his mother's tricks, after giving her a couple rocks for letting him stay there for a couple days. Quick and Amos sold their share of the drugs to a neighborhood dope dealer for three dollars a rock.

Jeff was right about the murder investigation. The crack-heads, who were smoking in the front room of the house at the time of double-D's murder, ransacked the house after finding the dead D. They were trying to find more dope, and didn't bother to report the shooting when they left, nobody wanting to admit they were in the place. The police were informed of a dead body, weeks later, only after a resident of the area reported a strange order coming from the house. By then the rats had been feeding on the body, including the face. The bullet hole in D's eye was not so obvious.

Just as Jeff predicted, the police didn't bother to perform an autopsy, and chalked the killing up to a drug war, or dope house robbery. The spent cigarette lighters, broken stems, and empty crack bags littering the rooms in the house, indicated the place was a dope den. And the small .25 caliber shell casing found on the kitchen floor hinted at the type of murder weapon, but with no family coming forward, the police did no further investigation. One less crack house and crack dealer they had to contend with, they said in private.

It wasn't long after the death of D the house was burned to the ground. It's speculated the house was burned by the police to make sure they wouldn't have to return there again, but that is absolute speculation never to be proven. Be it as it may, it's strange many dope houses ended up in flames after a violent situation had occurred in them. In any event, we'll let the evidence speak for itself.

Chapter 7

Big-D on the scene.

Big-D drove, aimlessly. He and his two women, Candy and Shirley, had slept the better part of the day away. Now early evening, he thought he might take a ride around Belle Isle, a Detroit park that is also an island, but decided against it. Not much to see during the winter other than the hungry, crapping, sea gulls making a beeline for anything looking like food, while depositing bird crap on his trucks windshield — crap hard to get off.

Maybe, I'll take the girls to get something to eat, he thought. *Or head over to Boss's whorehouse, where there was something going on most of the time. Maybe, get in a card game, or shoot a little craps,* he contemplated. *Maybe watch Lady, Boss's woman, put on a freak show with one of the working girls. What the hell,* he thought, *the first thing I'm going to do is get this truck washed before the car wash closes,* he finally decided.

While about to make an illegal U-turn in the middle of Jefferson street, turning around to head for the car wash, his cell phone rang. "Hello," he answered, as he looked over his shoulder at the girls in the back seat to make sure they were behaving themselves — make sure they weren't feeling each other up while they were in public and he couldn't watch. They were looking back at him with those funny grins on their faces. Grins telling him he couldn't trust them to keep their hands off each other.

"Hey, Big, this is Slow," the caller, said.

"Hey, Slow, what's cooking?"

"That's the problem, nothing's cooking — I'm out of product. When do you think you can swing by, and drop off a couple balls, (8 balls) or some powder?" Slow, asked.

"Word, give me about an hour to pick up some weight. I know the cheddar is right, ain't it?"

"Come... come... come on Big, ain't I always right with the mon... mon... money?" Slow said, insulted, and stuttering, as he tended to do when excited.

"Sho you right, Slow. It's just at this time of the month, these crackhead deadbeats are always asking for credit. Sorry Slow, I forgot who I was talking to," Big said, apologetically, "I'll get by there as soon as possible," he said, and he hung up, while glancing over his shoulder one last time. "Y'all ain't doing nothing back there is y'all?" He asked, the still grinning women, "I know how y'all likes doing freaky stuff in public."

"Naw, daddy. We know you likes to watch us. We're being nice," Shirley replied, giving Candy a quick glance, and still grinning.

"All right, now. Keep it that way until we gets home," Big warned, as he pulled away from the stoplight.

"We promise, daddy, we will," Candy replied, while holding up both hands for Big to see, but still grinning.

Okay, Big thought, *first, I got to get to the apartment to pick up some weight. This should kill, at least, a couple hours...*

———

It was one of those slow, mid-week, middle of the month days. The bridge cards (the same as food stamps) were spent, the pension, and social security checks cashed and gone. There was little hustle money flowing. The temperature was about twenty-eight-bone-chilling-degrees. A heavily clouded sky remained behind the snow that had fallen overnight, and caused the streets to be covered with puddles of salty water. The ominous clouds, promised a chance of more snow to come, but Big could care less about the weather other than keeping his expensive, fully equipped, SUV clean.

Big-D, who was called Big most of the time, (a lot of the dealers use the letter D as their name — the D standing for DOPE or DEALER), was a well known mid level drug dealer/supplier on the East Side of Detroit. He was a huge barrel of a man, at about 6'3" and 350 lbs.

He loved fancy vehicles, beautiful women, flashy bling, (jewelry) and, of course, eating good food. He didn't use, and didn't put down those who did, unless they were beggars. He hated beggars — hated to be pressured into having to repeatedly say no, especially, when the beggar wouldn't listen, and promise to repay when they and he knew they didn't have a chance in hell of coming up with the money. He felt they thought they were putting something over on him whenever he did allow credit, and then the individual would disappear or dodge him because they couldn't repay.

He was an even-tempered, no bullcrap type of dude who loved to laugh and mingle, and have a good time. He was also a good manager, and organizer. He drove a fully equipped, Burnt Orange, Navigator, with 25-inch spinner wheels, the kind that made the SUV's wheels seam to be stationary while the truck was moving. The cream interior was of the softest leather, with plenty of wood grain trimmings. It had a combination TV and DVD screen in the headrest, satellite radio, 20 disk CD player, GPS navigation system, On Star, possitraction differential, 4 wheeled drive, automatic load leveling, run flat tires, automatic climate control and windshield wipers, ten speakers, and much more. If there was a new fangled gadget that could be installed on his truck, he had it installed.

Big-D was never seen without his two live in, as well as riding companions, Candy and Shirley, both beautiful, bi-sexual, his sex partners, and casual rock smokers.

Even though, Shirley, a stunning woman, of thirty, and Candy, not quiet as fine as Shirley, but still beautiful, at twenty-eight, liked him, they were not attracted to him, but thought they had him convinced they were. They stayed with him because he supported them, and their habit.

They put up with having sex with him only because it was easier than working to support themselves and their habits, by turning tricks on the streets, or dancing in some strip club — a regular nine to five job being out of the question. Besides, he was a quick shooter whenever he did attempt to have sex with them. They also liked the sense of adventure they felt when they were with him.

He'd watch them make love to each other, something they liked doing in his presents. They both had a touch of exhibitionism in them and enjoyed being watched. They, after putting on a show for him, would let him "try" to make love to either of them, (he being a borderline diabetic, had bouts of EDS) and bang, he was through in a few seconds. The quicker the better, as far as they were concerned.

What they didn't know was Big was no fool. He knew they weren't attracted to him. He could care less as long as they let him do his due. He let them think they were playing him. He went along with the farce for two reasons, and it wasn't because he couldn't get all the loving he could handle. Especially from some of his rock-star customers, who were always throwing themselves at him — they offering to service him for a dime, or use their hands on him, which he occasionally thought about doing.

He didn't go for any of the available sex with other women, and maintained his two bi-sexual women, because of two reasons. The first reason was because he was once scared, witless, after catching gonorrhea from a very attractive woman, whom no one would guess had an STD. *It could have been HIV,* he later thought. Consequently, he made Candy and Shirley take blood test before he made them his permanent companions, and wouldn't allow them to consort with other men. It was okay if they partied with Boss's girls every now and then, but never with any other males.

The second reason was he was comfortable with his two bi-sexual companions. He knew he was overweight, and having Erectile Dysfunction Syndrome, made him insecure with other women, particularly straight women. He also knew when he got a little too excited, he had a tendency to reach orgasm quickly, leaving him feeling inadequate, something he didn't have to worry about with his gay companions.

He knew they were glad he finished as quickly as he did. He could enjoy sex without feeling less than a stud — no guilt or self-recrimination. Having sex is not a dignified act, and is best enjoyed with someone with whom one is comfortable, and he was comfortable with his two girls.

His specialty was crack, but he also sold pills, of any kind, Weed, Blow (Heroin), Viagra, powdered Cocaine, "You name it, I got it," he'd always say. He had several small dope houses, run by others doing fairly well, all of which he supplied. Although he didn't have to sell in person, he continued to do so because he loved the contact with his customers, and because he didn't have to stay in one spot, waiting for his customers to come to him, he also had a lot of free time. Free time he was finding harder to fill.

His frequent trips to the casinos had lost their allure. Having sex with his two traveling companions, and watching them freak each other was not as exciting as it once was. He enjoyed the streets, meeting people, and flashing his bling-bling, and that's what he found himself doing more often. And of course, he liked taking his two fine women to a nice restaurant, front, and have a nice meal — always a good time killer.

He knew the police were aware of his supplying, but he wasn't worried because his Navigator had several hidden compartments he paid several thousand to have installed. He'd be safe from a street search unless they brought in the dogs. To further keep under the radar, and keep a low profile, he made it a practice of delivering to his customers, and dope houses, only after they ordered by phone, and then after setting up a location where what he was doing, wouldn't be so obvious.

He wasn't always into to drug pushing. He quit his job as security / bouncer in one of Detroit's more popular blind pigs, and got into drug pushing after spending a week with his cousin, Jarow, in Chicago.

"Couz, you too sharp to be working for someone else," Jarow, a tall, thin, failed pimp, would tell him, while smiling, his single gold tooth flashing. "I can set you up with the right people in Detroit, and teach you the ropes to rolling. Look at me, man, I got the cash, I got the women, hell Big, money practically jumps into my pocket," Jarow persisted.

The first few times Jarow tried to get him into the business, Big turned him down. But Jarow was persistent, and persuasive. Big, after listening to the man tout his success time and time again, and watching the women who came through Jarow's place, and how they would do anything to please him, always giving Jarow his props, even letting Big have some fun with them if Jarow asked them to, finally gave in and let Jarow set him up.

What neither, Jarow, nor Big, could know, was a

month later, Jarow would be shot and killed by rival dealers over territory. Jarow's murderers were particularly vicious. They shot him in the head five times with a .22 long, and then dumped his naked body into Lake Michigan. His murderers were never found and brought to justice, probably because the homicide was drug related, and the police, knowing who Jarow was, chalked it up, saying, "One less dealer on the streets."

After hanging up his pre-paid cell phone that couldn't be traced, Big made the illegal U-turn on Jefferson, and instead of stopping at the car wash, headed towards the Lodge Freeway to catch I-94 heading west. He was on his way to where he kept his supply of drugs — a nice apartment on the West Side of the city, in a well-kept middle classed neighborhood.

As he drove, he decided to call several other dope houses he supplied. *Might as well bring enough product with me to stock all my places that might need it*, he thought, as he made a call. He used the speed dial, and waited for an answer...

"Hello," the voice on the other end, answered.

"Hey, Edward," Big responded, "What's cooking, are you straight?"

"My man, Big," the voice greeted, "Yeah, I'm okay for a while, but I could use a couple marbles in about an hour, if you're coming this way."

"Got you. I'm on my way to re-up now, should be there in about an hour, hour and a half, be looking out for me," Big, instructed.

"Hear you, D, I'll be watching out."

"You ain't freaking with one of them women are you?"

"Naw Big, not right now, but you know me. If one of them wants some credit, the freak is on. You know what I mean?"

"Yeah Edward, I know what you mean, but, will you try to hold off long enough for me to get by there before you gets started. I don't want to see that crap every time I come by your place. Cool?"

"Yeah Big, I follow you, but don't take too long. You know all it takes is for one of those sack-chasers to hit on me, and I take a hit, and there I go again. Talk to you in a minute. Now come on. Don't be messing around. Okay?"

"I feel you Ed. Just sit tight, I'll be there in two shakes," Big said, and hung up. *That Edward' going to catch something one day that's going to cause his stuff to fall off if he keeps messing around with them crack-whores,* he thought, as he drove, while smiling to himself.

A half-hour latter, Big arrived at his fashionable Westside apartment. He told Candy and Shirley to wait for him in the SUV. As usual, he warned the girls to keep their hands off each other when he wasn't around to watch. He knew they sometimes got a little frisky while he was away. They would try to turn each other on, so they could get him excited, later. They figured once they got him excited, he'd take them home where he'd give them a rock or two, apiece, so he could get busy with them. The problem was, they sometimes got carried away and began getting serious with their dallying, on several occasions, continuing on to completion. Both of them had a touch of exhibitionism in them, and freaking in public seemed to turn them on. He'd come back to the truck and find them naked in the back seat, going at each other, and he missing it all — that he didn't like. If they were going to get down, he wanted to watch. Hell, he needed to watch their shows to get excited himself, and didn't want them wasting any extra activity when alone. After the warning, they promised to be good, while giving him a sly smile, a smile saying they couldn't be trusted.

"All right now, girls," he told them again, if I come back here and y'all is getting busy. I ain't going to give y'all nothing until you repeats for me, and you better not be faking it, understand?"

"Yeah, daddy, we promise to be good — promise." Shirley said, while giving him a sly grin, and running one hand up Candy's thigh.

"Okay, I'll be back in a minute. We won't be out much longer. It's getting late, and after I make these last deliveries, we can stop and get something to eat and take it home with us. Cool?"

"That sounds good, daddy," Candy said, reaching over to cup one of Shirley's breast, "But you know what we want. We will get a little something-something later, won't we?"

"Come on Candy. Don't I always take care of you two? You know you ain't got to worry about nothing like that. Now behave yourselves while I'm gone. Be back in a minute. Okay?"

"Okay, baby," Shirley said, now looking toward the apartment building. "Now go on and take care of your business. We're ready to go home. We've been ridding around in the back of this truck long enough. Hurry up, will you?"

"Gone," he said, heading for the building's entrance.

He looked up and down the street to make sure he wasn't being watched. *No one knew about this place, but you never know,* he often thought.

He didn't live in the apartment, but had someone else staying there, rent-free, to keep away the burglars, and to cook up the dope he supplied. Only he, the two women, and the live-in knew about the stash. He made a stop by the apartment at least once a day to drop off any money he'd made that day, and to re-up for new deliveries. He only went to the apartment during the day, and never took the girls with him upstairs. He didn't want any of his neighbors in the building thinking anything strange was going on there. And so far, he managed to maintain the façade of an upstanding renter and neighbor.

He climbed the stairs to the second floor front apartment, getting slightly winded as he treaded. Unlocking the door and going in, he found his cooker sitting on the couch, eating and watching a small TV resting on an old coffee table. "Hey, Jesse. Everything been quiet?" he greeted his live-in.

"Hey, Big. Yeah, everything's cool. How you doing?"

"I'm great, Jess. You need anything?"

"No, Big, I just finished cooking something to eat, and I have plenty to drink. Thanks anyway."

"Okay. Don't hesitate to call me if you need anything. Word?"

"Word, Big. Got a big order to fill?"

"Naw Jess. Just the usual," Big replied, as he went to the, concealed, bolted down, safe, in the closet. After removing the bag of rocks on top of the safe, and going swiftly through the combination, he removed what he thought would be enough dope to handle the days transactions, and put in the past nights profit. He then closed, and locked the safe, giving it an extra tug to make sure it was locked. Not that he didn't trust Jesse you understand, just cautious.

"How's the powder holding out?" he asked Jesse, before leaving.

"I got enough to cook up maybe three or four more

balls," Jesse said, and continued, "By it being the middle of the month, you probably won't have to re-up for a couple more days."

"Yeah, it's slow ain't it. Not much call for the blow either. And I ain't had nobody ask for any pills. I guess the rock thing done took over. Well, anyway, keep up the good work. I'll call if anything changes — catch you later," Big said, closing and locking the door as he left.

Jesse got up off the couch, and went to look out the front window to see if he could catch a glimpse of the two freaks Big always had with him. No such luck, Big was parked too far down the street. *I sure would like to freak with them two dikes, just one time,* he thought, as he settled back on the couch and changed the channel on the small TV while trying to find anything halfway interesting.

Back at the truck, Big hid the contraband in one of the concealed compartments and then stepped back to make sure everything was in place before closing the tailgate and getting back behind the wheel. He set the radio to a hip-hop station, and taking one last glance over his shoulder to make sure the girls were behaving, he headed back to the Eastside. He could never tell what they'd been up to during his absence. They always had those funny grins on their faces. He sometimes suspected more was going on than meets the eye.

Oh well, no point in worry about it. Let's see, he thought, as he drove, *first, I'll drop off the dope, then I'll get the truck washed, and then I'll take the girls to get something nice to eat, followed by a nice card, or dice game, at Boss's. Sounds like a plan to me,* he imagined, forgetting he promised to take the girls home to give them some dope to smoke. He had nothing to worry about, though. They would follow him wherever he went without complaining too much. They knew on which side their bread was buttered.

Boss-man, more commonly known as, Boss, ran a whore / gambling house / blind-pig, on the east side of Detroit. There, a patron could buy the attention of any one of several prostitutes of his choice — gamble his money away playing cards, or craps, and get drunk, all in the same location. He also sold a few rocks to a select few. It was a very popular, Eastside, after-hour hangout, and Big liked hanging out there. He liked prancing in with his two women on his arms, while receiving accolades from the other customers. And he particularly liked watching Boss-lady put on her freak shows that always put him in the mood to take his girls home and party with them.

Big-D was feeling good — on top of the world — not a thing to worry about. He couldn't be more mistaken...

Chapter 8

Edward and his dope house.

The persistent and demanding banging at the back door continued as Joe stood in the doorway to the freak room, watching Darlene as she serviced Edward.

"Damn, Joe, you gonna get that?" Edward asked his doorman, while looking up from the action on the mattress on the floor in front of him.

"Oh, yeah, I got that. Sorry bout that." Joe said, as he went to answer the door, but not wanting to leave. He liked watching the women get freaky with each other on the mattress, and was hoping Edward would reward him with some sex from one of them, as he sometimes did.

Edward was sitting in a chair in his dinning room he'd converted to a freak room. A single 30-watt bulb rested at a precarious angle in a lamp in one corner, and provided the sole illumination. Besides the dresser with a cracked mirror, and all the drawers missing, the dirty, stained, bare, mattress on the floor, and the rickety, squeaking, chair he sat in, there was no other furniture in the room. The scuffed hardwood floor was littered with cigarette butts and hadn't seen a broom since Edward moved into the place about a year ago. One huge female roach with a large egg case hanging off its rear crawled up the far wall on legs barely able to carry its weight.

Edward was in a hurry, he'd just ordered more dope from Big-D, his supplier, and was trying to finish being serviced before the big man arrived. Big had already told him he didn't want to see his activities with the women. But hell, this was my place, and if Big didn't want to watch, frig him, Edward had already decided. Like he'd told Big, if one of the women offered him some fun, and he took a hit, he was going to get down, and the hell with everybody else.

His legs were spread open. In between his legs was Darlene, almost choking, as she worked vigorously on him. Every time she tried to withdraw a little, Edward put his hands on her head and pushed her back down, as his hips gyrated rhythmically. Every so often, he'd suck in air between his clenched teeth as the combination of drugs and dope had him in ecstasy.

On the old scared dresser, a small 19" TV had a XXX movie playing — he wasn't watching. His attention alternated between the dresser mirror angled so he could watch Darlene do her thing, and Joyce, who had her head buried between V's legs.

Darlene, V, and Joyce were crack-whores. They hung around Edward's hoping to pick up tricks, or not lucking up on one, putting on freak shows for Edward in exchange for dope. They were ever-present fixtures — very rarely leaving Edward's while fearing some other sack-chaser would weasel there way in, and replace them.

Joe, after locking the back door, returned with the customer. After giving the man his two rocks, he put the money in the cigar box on the dresser.

The customer, a smallish dude named, Terry, was ushered by Joe to the smoking room up front. Terry pretended to not pay any attention to the sex in the freak room, but still took a few clandestine glances at the women on the mattress. If he'd had any extra money, he might have tried one of the girls himself.

Terry went through a doorway covered by a torn,

filthy, bed sheet, and which served as a makeshift partition between the dinning room, better described as the freak room, and the living room, where several other people in various states of intoxication were smoking their rocks.

None of the dope-fiends in the living room paid any attention to what was going on in the provisional freak room. They'd all seen it many times before, and were concentrating on hitting their stems one more time. The only sounds heard in the living room were the clicking of the cheap lighters, and the sounds of sex, coming from the freak room. No one spoke, nor wanted too.

As one might imagine, Edward's was a popular dope den, he allowing people to not only purchase their dope, but also smoke it there. The occasional knock at the back door was answered by Joe, a rather large, ex-con, and house shotgun. He was a simple man who lacked any ambition. Having the power to reject or allow customers entrance to the dope house was all he desired. Wielding the 12-gauge shotgun also gave him a sense of control and power, things he needed in his life, and which he'd never find outside the dope house, but was actually an illusion. Edward held the true control over who was served or let in.

Another benefit of Joe's position was the free sex he was sometimes granted by Edward. Edward, while being serviced, and seeing Joe stroking himself through his pants as he watched, would sometimes, order one of the crack-whores to take care of him while paying them with a rock. For that, Joe was extremely grateful.

The smell of burning crack permeated the entire house. The smoke hovered in the air, and was like a heavy fog. The whole scene was reminiscent of the Opium dens of the past. The only light in the living room came from a single, shade-less lamp resting on the floor in one corner. The windows were covered with old newspapers, and allowed no daylight or prying eyes to penetrate. The front door was covered by several planks nailed in place to prevent unwanted entry. The only way in, or out, was through the back door covered by Joe, and which also had several removable two-by-fours across it.

    The only furniture in the front room consisted of several plastic milk crates, placed along the paint peeling walls. Most people sat, or laid on the uncarpeted, filthy, empty crack bag, littered, floor. They were happy to have somewhere to smoke, and that's all that mattered. They were glad Edward liked to have many people around him, and let them to smoke in his place, not a lot of dealers would allow that.

    Once inside, most of the heads would not leave Edward's until they were broke, and then only long enough to, somehow, go out to get more money. Edward didn't accept stolen property for his rocks, so whoever wanted to buy from him had to have cash or be a female who was willing to party with him. Those that could raise more money would return to join the other people in the living room, who were pushing their stems with what is called a pusher. That's the practice where the small wad of Chore-Boy is pushed the length of the stem, using a nail, a piece of coat hanger, or anything stiff enough to not bend. Repeated pushing, sometimes, would cause whatever residue left behind inside the stem after the first burning of the rock, to be scraped off the wall of the stem, and then could be burned and smoked again. In the right situation, the user would "ress" his stem or pipe. (Rinsing the stem or pipe with alcohol, set the rinse afire to burn off the trash and alcohol. The residue or (ress) is then scraped up, and smoked again) Not as good as smoking a fresh rock, but would do in a tight situation where they'd spent all of their money, and couldn't get credit Edward only gave to women who would freak with him.

Sometimes, if the dope was really good, the stem could be pushed several times. Most addicts, in drug induced stupor's, usually continued to push their stems long after all residue has been smoked — their minds telling them, somehow, they would get another hit from the depleted stem, but rarely did.

Edward was a thin wiry guy of thirty-two, and around six-foot-tall, had a gaunt look about him. His dark skinned face was heavily pockmarked, the results of a childhood skin condition. He had a learning disability, but wasn't what you would call dumb, just a little slow.

He'd been using since he, at the age of sixteen, seeing his mother smoke rocks, sneaked a crumb she'd dropped, while trying to understand why she was so crazy over the drug — sometimes smoking for days on end. It didn't take long for him to get hooked, and wanting more. He'd break into houses, stealing anything he could sell for more rocks. Not being very clever, he was always being caught by the police. The police from his precinct knew him on sight. They would stop and search him constantly, violating his rights, but he was to dumb to know it. They figured he was responsible for a lot of the crime in his neighborhood, and they were not far from right. On many occasions, they found dope on him, and consequently, always repeating the same mistakes, he'd been in jail more times than he could remember.

After his last stint in prison, and after being educated in the gray bar college, he decided to stay off the streets, and open his own crack house. To get the money, he robbed a Family Dollar Store, and used the cash to buy his first bag. After finding an abandoned house, (most crack houses were set up in abandoned houses) he pried off the protective plywood put there to keep out people like him, and moved in. He then had someone come in and, illegally, turn on the electricity, the water, having, never been shut off, and bringing in a few electric heaters, Edward was in business.

He still wanted to use, but had a problem. He was one of those individuals who became extremely paranoid when he smoked alone. On top of that, the drug also made him horny, as it did many men, only in his case, more so. He found a solution to both problems. He'd invite any of the neighborhood crack-whores, who came to him to cop, to stay, and smoke with him. He knew they very rarely had much money, and would soon want more dope, and would soon be asking for credit. When they did, he was always willing to give them a little something in exchange for sex. Because of his many visits to prison, he was not bashful, and would do his thing in front of anyone — hence the freaky activity in the converted dining room.

There was a real bedroom in the house, but he reserved it for when he wanted to get some rest away from the activity of the rest of the house. It was also where he kept his stash, only occasionally having sex in it, and then only if the woman was on the shy side.

Word soon got around Edward would let anyone smoke in his place, and his joint soon became the busiest in the area. His place was open 24-7, and always had someone in the livingroom getting high — and he loved it. The heavy dope-fiend traffic not only provided him with income, but, also, the company as well as the sex he craved, would, also, lead to a chain of events that proving to be his downfall...

Chapter 9

Officers Drake and Johnson on the job.

The slide on Officer Drake's Glock slid forward into battery with an reassuring click, chambering a .45 hollow point round. Safety on, he holstered his weapon, laid the 12-gauge shotgun in the trunk of the cruiser, and turned to see what was taking his partner, Officer Johnson, so long to come out of the station house.

The parking lot was abuzz with activity. It was shift change, and officers were coming and leaving. It had been a good day's service — no officer had been killed in the performance of his duty — a good day indeed. Now, if they could get through the next shift while serving and protecting without being attacked by some nutt-case who would rather take a life than stand up and take his punishment, the day would be perfect.

As Drake turned to look for his partner, he saw two other officers escorting a huge black dude with a bald head into the station house. This guy had on a shirt half torn off his body, exposing bulging prison muscles. His hands were cuffed behind him, and it was obvious the guy wasn't happy about being arrested. *Damn, I'm glad I wasn't the one who had to tackle that big mutha,* Drake thought. *I wonder what he did?*

The angry man was pulling from side to side, trying to snatch his arms free of the officer's grip, making it hard for the them to maintain control of him. Although, not small men, they appeared exhausted with their uniforms slightly disheveled and dirty. But eventually they got him inside. Drake knew once they got the oversized man inside the building, there would be other officers to assist them. *Hell, if it were me I'd have had them come out to the car from jump street, and help me get him inside,* he thought.

No sooner had the two struggling officers disappear inside, than his partner came out walking toward him, looking back toward the giant man in cuffs he must have passed.

"Hey, pard, sorry I took so long to get out of there. Did you see that big dude they just brought in?"

"Hell yeah, I saw him. I was just thinking I was glad it wasn't us who had to put them cuffs on the big musta."

"Partner, no truer words have ever been spoken," Officer Johnson said, as he approached the cruiser and tossed his equipment bag into the trunk. "But listen to this, the lieutenant gave me information on a spot that has neighbors complaining."

"I was beginning to wonder where you were. For a minute I thought you were trying to wolf down some more donuts, ha, ha, you get it, cops and donuts, it's a police joke," Drake, replied, jokingly.

Officer Johnson didn't laugh with Drake. He just looked at him and shook his head. The men got into the car, checked the temperamental computer to make sure it worked, and pulled out of their parking space. "It's a good thing you're a cop, because you sure as hell ain't no comedian," Johnson said, after they got onto the street.

"Aw, man, you ain't got no sense of humor, Mr. Stiff pants," Drake responded, "But what did the lieutenant give you we don't already know about?" he asked, as they made a left at the next corner, heading for their beat.

"You remember the place we shut down over in the Six Mile and Gratiot area?" asked, Johnson.

"Yeah, the place we busted a while back," answered, Drake.

"Well, it's open again, and drawing a lot of attention from the straights on the block. Seems they're having a problem with the heads cutting through their yards to get to the back door of this place. The lieutenant said he received a report from a black and white that patrolled the neighborhood, and reported the people were coming and going from this place like they was going to a department store or something." Johnson added.

"Really? You know what we're going to have to do to shut that place down for good, don't you?" Drake said.

"Yeah, I know, but don't say it. Let's hope we don't have to go there. But, anyway, he said there was an elderly couple, who were afraid to stand on their porch, let alone come outside, and take a walk. He said they, the old couple, were afraid the heads would either break into their house or car?"

"I don't blame them. Some of them heads can get pretty desperate sometimes."

"You got that right. That's why the lieutenant wants us to pick up the U-haul at the 10th and take some pictures, and do some surveillance. Get what we need to get an air tight case on the place and its operators, and get a warrant for another raid," Officer Johnson finished.

Drake said nothing while knowing what was ahead of them — many long hours in the back of the cold cub van.

"Okay," Robert said, "we're off to see the wizard. Onward and upward. To the 10th," he continued. He was the joker of the two. He liked to keep things on the lighthearted side. "Man you get too serious about this job and next thing you know, you're eating a bullet lunch," he'd say. And there were those in his ranks, who agreed with him.

They made a U-turn and headed back toward the

West Side, where the 10th Precinct was located. It would be nice if all the precincts had a surveillance van, but the city' finances being as they were, they were lucky to have the one truck to clandestinely watch the dope houses, which blanketed the city in greater numbers than could be patrolled by the police, let alone shut down. Maybe, one day, the city council would be able to rob some other program to give the police the equipment they needed to properly do their jobs, maybe. In the mean time they did the best with what they had, which wasn't a whole lot.

Officer Robert Drake and Officer Raymond (Ray for short) Johnson were long time partners of the 9th Precinct's narcotics squad. They'd worked the nark division about five years. They knew of every drug house in their district, and most of the addicts as well. They were plain-clothes officers. To just look at them, you'd have no idea they were cops, especially, Officer Johnson, who wore a long, unkempt, black beard, and dreadlocked cornrows in his hair.

They patrolled their area in all makes, and models of vehicles. They particularly liked the older cars that didn't draw much attention. When they really wanted to remain anonymous, they used an old U-haul truck equipped with a special camera with a long-range lens could take perfect pictures from blocks away. The truck had small windows on all sides of the box painted over with one way paint to match the color scheme of the truck, a lot like the advertising you might see on the sides of city busses. They could park the truck a block away from the drug house and watch the customers come and go. Depending on how much film they brought with them, and depending on how much evidence they wanted to gather, or if they were looking for a particular individual, for example, the supplier, they could take pictures for as long as they wished, sometimes all day and night, and they'd done so on several occasions.

They rarely bothered arresting the crack-heads unless they wanted an informant, or someone to make a marked money buy, or the addict was caught up in a raid. The jails were to full of users, and arresting them had little affect on the trafficking.

Whenever they went in on a raid, to hide their identity, they wore ski mask. They let the raid team do most of the work, but it mattered little as far as the danger was concerned. Raiding a dope house was dangerous to all involved.

Usually they didn't raid a dope house unless there were complaints from the "straights" or decent people in the neighborhood. There is just too many dope houses, and they didn't have the manpower to keep all the places closed.

They both loved their jobs, but they knew it was mostly for show. Without cutting off the supply at the top, there is absolutely no way they could stop the sale of drugs. Everybody involved in drug enforcement knew this, but it would never be stated in public.

———

Robert and Ray pulled into the parking lot of the 10th Precinct. The parking lot was a beehive of activity — cars coming in, and going out into the city to serve and protect. They grabbed the first available parking space they could find. The station house lots were never large enough to accommodate all the traffic during shift transitions. Robert got out of the cruiser to talk to a fellow officer with whom he was partnered when he was doing street patrols as a rookie cop, and then saying bye, going into the prescient house.

While Robert went inside to get the keys to the U-haul, Ray stayed in the black interceptor, and reviewed the folder containing the information regarding dope house they were going to watch. The folder didn't contain much information. It included the address of the suspected dope house, or in this case, the known dope house, and the name of the suspected operator, the names, and address of the complainants. No big deal, they'd begun an operation with much less, besides, they knew this house and its operator.

Robert came out of the station house with the keys to the truck. He went to and opened the trunk of the cruiser. Ray heard Robert and joined him at the rear of the car. They gathered their equipment, and dodging the lot traffic, went to the old truck parked in a corner of the lot. As they approached, they could see some careless officer had parked his private vehicle almost blocking in the truck. They decided they could back the surveillance truck out, but it would be close.

To look at it, it appeared no different than any other U-Haul moving van, maybe a little aging, but just as it was supposed to appear. The only thing wrong with it was it didn't have a heater in the box, and the front heater was not powerful enough to heat the entire truck. It could get pretty cold back there in the winter. Come to think about it, it could get awfully hot in the summer, also. Yes, it had over two-hundred thousand mile on it, but it ran fairly well, thanks to the diligent attention of the motor pool.

Whatever shape the truck was in, Drake and Johnson would put it to good use tonight. And actually, when the good and bad points about the truck were totaled, it was better than watching a location from a car. At least a cot could be brought along allowing the officer to stretch his legs. Not only that — when inside the back of the truck, an officer wasn't constantly looking around checking to see if they were made, as they would in a car. Say what you want about the "Camera Box" as it was sometimes called, it really wasn't that bad. Robert slid into the driver's seat, and started the truck, while Ray climbed into the box to check the equipment stored there.

"Damn!" Robert, cursed, loudly.

"What's up?" Ray asked, through the door to the box.

"These assholes parked the damn thing without any gas in it," Robert, complained, "I hope they don't think I'm going to fill the tank out of my pocket," he continued, "You remember the last time we tried to get gas we had a hell of a time finding the guy with the keys to the pumps, and we had to put in gas from a public pump. I ain't doing it again. It took the city months to refund my money."

"I know you're right about that," Ray, agreed. "Let me go inside and see if I can get the keys. I'll be right back. While I'm in there, I'm going to look at the log and see who left it like this. Maybe I can have the station commander say something to him. The hell with this crap, this is the second time we had to fill the tank of this thing. Be back in a minute."

"Okay, but hurry up, it's cold out hear." Robert said, as he laid back into the driver's seat, disgusted. *I hope they remembered to fill the camera with film,* he thought, as he waited. *Should have told Ray to bring a couple rolls of film back with him. Running out of film was no excuse for not getting the required surveillance footage.*

Ray returned with the pump keys, "Yeah, I talked to the commander and he said this would be the last time the truck would be left in this condition. He said everyone who uses the truck is supposed to take it to the motor pool, and have it checked out. And guess what? He said that also applied to us. Ain't that a blip? I complain about how the truck is left, and he gets on my case. The old fart, he alta retire, if you ask me," Ray said.

"Forget him, let's get the truck filled, and get out of here. Damn it's cold and I'm ready to get moving."

"Roger that, pard," Ray said, giving the key to Robert.

The truck started easily, except for the empty tank, it seemed to be in order. As Ray guided, Robert eased the truck around the blocking car, and drove it over to the gas pumps where they filled the tank, filled out the record book stating how many gallons they put in the tank, completed the equipment check, and headed back to the Eastside to start their surveillance.

As they drove, they saw a dope transaction taking place on the streets right out in the open. The pusher, after looking around to make sure no cops was around, walked up to a car and leaned in. He could be seen going to his pocket and pulling out a small package, then putting the money into his pocket while returning to his spot on the street corner.

"Did you see that?" Ray asked.

"Yeah, I saw it. We could bust him right now if we wanted too. He doesn't have any idea we're cops inside this truck," Robert said. "I bet he'd crap his pants if we decided to jump out and tell him to hit the ground. But we've got our assigned project to take care of, and I don't think the Lieutenant would be happy if we spent several hours booking a dealer that didn't have anything to do with our case."

"Yeah, I know, and agree, pard," Ray said. "We can't patrol the whole city, but I'm not letting this go."

"Oh yeah, what do you have in mind?"

"When we get back to the 10th, I'm going to report this character to the commander, and let him assign his team to watching the punk. I don't know, but it kind of rubs me the wrong way when they sling drugs right out in the open, and don't give a damn about us. It's almost as if they're saying frig the cops."

"You're right, Ray, but they don't worry about being

caught, why should they? Hell we just don't have the manpower to bust everybody."

"Maybe not, but I'm going to make sure this mutha get his day in court, if I have anything to say about it."

"Fine with me, pard. I'll put my name on the report with you."

"Yeah, whatever," Ray said, and rode the rest of the way in silence. It was obvious he was feeling a little frustrated.

Back on the eastside street of the offending drug house, Officers Drake, and Johnson looked for an abandoned house in front of which they could park and take their clandestine pictures. They didn't want to park in front of a law-abiding citizen's home, and they had to park a least one half-block away from the house being watched because of the angles involved, even though the camera was capable of much longer ranged photography.

Except for the streetlights in front of the dope house that had been shot out by the dope dealers with a pellet gun, the street was fairly well lit.

Because Ray and Robert were using the U-haul cube van for their surveillance, they were not worried about the lighting. The only problem they felt could be an annoyance was on this particular street, there weren't many vacant homes to park in front of. They had to park within a two-block distance, to allow the night vision camera to work properly. The telephoto lens on the camera would work well beyond that distance, but they were ordered to take pictures in preparation for the raid. And night vision pictures became grainier the farther away the camera was from the subject, and they still had those annoying angles to deal with.

They eventually found the right location, and posted

up about three-quarters of a block away in front of a vacant field next to an occupied home. After setting up the camera, and radioing their prescient house to warn them to keep the marked cruisers away from the area, they settled in for the night. They would take turns looking through the camera at half-hour intervals. Peering through a lens for any length of time could be hard on the eyes.

Two hours passed and not a single person was seen approaching the drug house — not one, which was not normal.

"This isn't working. Someone should have went in by now," Robert said, as he yawned, and stretched, and looked at his watch, for the tenth time. "The lieutenant said there would be a lot of traffic. Where the hell is it?"

"Yeah, I've been thinking the same thing," Ray responded, and continued, "the report did say something about the heads trespassing while going to the back door, let's see if we can set up in the rear of the house. Maybe the heads are approaching and going in from the back?"

"Okay, let me take the camera off the tripod first," answered, Robert.

Ray started the truck and drove to an alley running behind the crack house. After checking out the alley, they couldn't find a spot where they would have a clear view of the back of the dope den — too many garages. Besides, the alley was too narrow to part the truck and not block traffic of the legal residences. They did notice directly across the alley from the rear of the dope house was a fenced in vacant lot. Apparently the lot was used to garden in. They could park on the next street over, and in line with the rear of the dope house, and take all the pictures they wanted.

Even as they were scouting the new location, they could see several people going towards the dope den's back door. They couldn't set up fast enough. The rear door to the drug house was constantly being opened, letting the crackheads in, and closed again.

"Either this guy thinks he is untouchable, or he is extremely stupid, setting up his house in a nice neighborhood like this, and directly across from a vacant lot where he could be easily watched. I've used up a half roll of film, and they still come. This place is doing a bang up business," Ray said, with a chuckle. "I have several pictures of the shotgun man on the door, but haven't got a shot of the house operator yet. I bet you a stake dinner it's our friend Edward back at the helm. I'd better hold off taking any more pictures until I can get a clear shot of the operator, or the supplier. We don't want to run out of film."

"No bet there partner. I agree with you. One thing is for sure, we won't be here all night. We only brought one roll of film. I hope we can get the money shot soon. I don't want to come back again. It's getting cold in here." Robert interjected.

"A-men to that. Next time we bring the... Hold on, hooold on. Guess what just pulled up in the alley?" Ray said, a little excited, as he peered through the lens of the camera, "A big, fancy, Burnt Orange, Navigator. Can you believe this? I think we hit the jackpot — the mid level supplier caught in the act. As many times as we've watched dope houses, how many times have we been lucky enough to catch the big boy on film? Not many, I can remember. But here he is, going into the house as bold as he could be, and I'm going to make him the featured character on candid camera, tonight," Ray said, taking pictures two and three at a time, "But, I can't get a shot of his truck's plate. You jump out, and circle around, and see if you can see it. Go through the yard next door if you have too."

"Okay, did you get a shot of the driver?" Robert asked.

"Yeah, I got him — he looked right at us, as he got out

of the truck. Some woman got out of the back seat, and moved to the front, can't get a shot of her," Ray answered. "He's going to the rear of his truck, now. I'll bet he's retrieving the dope back there," I'll get him again when he comes out of the house," Ray continued, as he held down the shutter button, the camera clicking off several frames, the motor drive advancing the film with a whine. "I'll be taking down the camera so we'll be ready to go when you get back," Ray, finished, not taking his eye away from the viewfinder on the camera.

Robert eased through the yard next door to where they were parked, peeped around a garage, and got a clear view of the plate of the SUV. He had to be careful. There was still a lot of traffic going to the dope house. Several people went in, but only a couple came out. *They must be smoking inside,* thought Robert, as he with no flash, clicked off two pictures of the SUV's plate with a small digital camera, and headed back to the U-hall.

"Did you get your second shot of the big man yet?" Robert, asked, Ray, getting back into the U-hall, while checking his camera to see if the picture of the plate turned out right.

"No, not yet, but you know it won't be long. Those guys never stay in there very long," Ray informed. "Here he comes. He's looking right at us again," Ray said in a whisper, as he held down the shutter button on the camera, and the automatic drive clicking off several more pictures.

Several of the pictures were perfect full-faced shots of the supplier, as he looked, what seemed like, directly into the camera lens. He was more than likely checking out the truck, looking for exactly what was happening to him at that very moment. Checking to see if he was being watched. Officers, Raymond Johnson, and Robert Drake had their money shot.

"Got him," Ray continued, as he started to disassemble

the equipment and turned around to high five his partner. "Let's go find someplace warm, and get something to eat."

As it would happen, the officers would soon discover they had a lot more work in front of them...

Chapter 10

Slow gets laid.

Slow, one of Big-D's dope house operators, was sitting by the front window while waiting for his delivery of product from Big. He hated waiting on anything, let alone having to sit by the window watching for someone. Big told him he'd come through within an hour. Two hours had passed, and it was getting dark, and Big hadn't come yet. He thought about giving Big another call, but decided against it while knowing Big disliked being rushed as much as he hated waiting. *No, best to stay here by the window and wait for him to show up,* thought Slow.

Normally, he'd assign this menial task to Smoky, his shotgun man, but Smoky was busy serving people at the back door, and it wouldn't be long before he ran out of product. *I'll give Big one more hour, and then call him whether he likes it or not,* Slow resolved. *I'll use the fact I'm about to run out of product as an excuse to make Big bring his slow butt on. The hell with this crap, I got to start keeping more dope in the house. Big messes around to much for me.*

He thought about going out on the front porch, but changed his mind. He didn't like being out in public. "Come on Big. Where you at?" He said, aloud, to himself.

"Damn, where the hell he at?" Asked Smoky, as he came along side Slow, while pulling the bed sheet further back, and looking through the dirty window. "We only got enough rock for, maybe, another half hour. He better come on. I want to keep our reputation of always having stone, and always being open... Come on big!" Smoky said, before returning to the back door to answer another knock, another request for their product, the largest rocks, and most potent crack in the area.

"I fe... fe... feel you, Smoke," agreed Slow, as he pulled the sheet even further back, and standing, looked as far up the street as he could. He too was starting to get a little nervous about running out of product.

Slow was not a native Detroiter. He moved to Detroit from Jackson Mississippi, thinking he could find a high paying job. He had no idea the employment situation was as bad in Detroit as it was in Jackson, maybe worse. He tried to find legitimate work, but his searches went unfulfilled. For one thing, he had a felony record, the result of he attacking and nearly killing a man who tried to make him move off a cot he'd staked out in a homeless shelter, the record following him from his home state, preventing him from finding employment in Detroit as well as there. He probably could have found a way around that problem — after all, some might have called his aggression, self-defense. If he'd been able to hire a good lawyer, and was of a different persuasion, he might have gotten an innocent verdict, who knows, but, anyway, he had other limitations hampering his employment prospects.

The one thing working against him more than his criminal record was he was mentally slow, hence his nickname. He spoke very slowly, as if he had to measure each word. His inability to read beyond the 3rd grade level hindered his ability to fill out an application as well as hindered his ability to obtain a driver's license. Of course, he insisted on driving whenever he had the chance, and would always get caught, ending up in jail again and again, which, also, didn't help.

But as luck would have it, Slow, with the aid of a friend, Andrew, a fellow he met during one of his short stays in jail, was able to find a job at a car wash. Unfortunately, his stay at that job was cut short. His leaving the car wash had nothing to do with his job performance, or his illiteracy.

As an employee, Slow was excellent, sometimes paying to much attention to detail. All the car wash customers were happy with the job he did for them, and tipped him generously, no problems there. He had to leave because he, speaking so slowly, and at times, seeming to be a little retarded, the other employees made fun of him. He couldn't take it, so he quit. But, before quitting, he got into a fight with Cash, the ringleader of the tormentors. Even though Slow was much shorter than the 6' 2" Cash, he was a ferocious fighter. He, being quiet, seemed to harbor an inner rage that once released, became uncontrollable.

He got Cash down on the wet concrete floor of the car wash, and was hammering Cash so severely, it took four other men to pull him off the beaten man. They were afraid Slow was going to beat the big-mouthed bully to death, and he would have, hadn't he been stopped.

The other employees discovered Slow was not one to mess with. Andrew, because he, also, had his own imperfections, liked Slow. Andrew had one leg almost an inch shorter than the other. He too, was teased by Cash and his followers, and was cheering for Slow — was yelling for Slow to hit him again — was applauding every blow — was wishing he was the one who delivered the well-deserved recompense.

Another employee of the car wash, Smoky, who was as black as midnight in a sealed box, and who, like Slow and Andrew, was the focus of the teasers, was also happy about the ass kicking. After Slow was pulled up from the well-vanquished tormentor, Andrew and Smoky both congratulated him on the way he stood up to the insensitive idiot. From that point on, the three men began to hang together on a regular basis. They had things about themselves they were self-conscious about, and seemed to comfort each other. None of them could get a girl friend, but as long as they had each other, they were less conscious of the fact, and knew neither would tease the other.

Andrew, "Drew" for short, happen to be a crack addict, his reason for being in jail where they met, but wasn't frowned upon by Smoky and Slow. Actually, practically, all the men who worked at the car wash, except Slow and Smoky, were either drug addicts, or alcoholics.

Slow got into drug dealing in a sort of off-handed way, through Andrew. He found a job with Big-D as the shotgun man in one Big's houses. Slow's introduction to the drug industry happened when he told Drew he was going to find another job at a different car wash. Drew, who knew Slow was a no crap kind of guy, and who stayed to himself, would be perfect as a shotgun man in a dope house that had lost their previous door / shotgun man. The other doorman, who was an ex-convict, was in jail, having been arrested for having a concealed weapon on him when he was searched by the police during a drug house raid.

Of course the drug house reopened shortly after the raid, but had no one to handle the door. Drew suggested to Big-D, the supplier and owner of the house, he knew someone who would be perfect for the position. Drew told Big Slow was someone who was not afraid to mix it up, and was someone who was not on drugs, and was someone who liked to stay to himself, and was honest. Big, while knowing a good man when he heard of one, accepted Drew's suggestion, and gave Slow the job.

Big liked the way Slow kept to himself, didn't talk too much, and didn't get to friendly with the crack-heads patronizing the house. If a doorman got too friendly with the patrons, it's possible he, the doorman, and the patron, could put their heads together and set up the house to be hit, so it was best the shotgun / doorman only deal with the customers on a business level. Slow being the way he was, had no problem with that protocol. The fact Slow didn't use, also, made him a prime candidate for drug house operator.

When one of Big's other houses was raided, and then later burned down, and the operator as well as the doorman locked up, it left a position open for someone wanting to get into the game. To keep the money coming in, Big decided he'd give Slow a chance to run his own house. Big told Slow if he could find a place to roll from, he'd front him with a small bag to get started. Big-D was that kind of guy, he did like people, but he liked money more.

Excited about running his own house, Slow quit his job as shotgun, and immediately went searching for a suitable vacant house in which to set up shop. Slow, being as meticulous, as he was, took almost a week to find a house. He, Drew, and Smoky, who would later become Slow's shotgun man, walked for hours, inspecting house after house, all abandoned. Drew, who, with his bad legs, grew tired of walking. He'd tell Slow time after time, as they inspected what looked like the perfect house, this is the one.

Slow would only look around for a second or two, and then say, "Nope, not the one."

Slow passed on house after house, all potentially good locations. He was looking for something, but he wasn't quite sure what it was until he came across a abandoned house standing alone on a block of vacant lots — all the other housed on the street being torn down. The house Slow liked, although abandoned, was in pretty good shape. All the windows were intact, and the lights and water were still on.

Even though Andrew was tired of walking, and ready to settle on just about anything, tried to tell Slow that most pushers wouldn't choose such a house in such a location. Too much attention would be drawn to an apparently vacant house out in the middle of nowhere with people going to the door, and then leaving shortly afterward. He tried to explain it was obvious the house was a dope house, and would probably be raided within a month.

But Slow didn't listen. "This is what I been looking for," he stubbornly responded. He didn't know why he liked the place so much, in spite of what Andrew tried to tell him, but this would be the house. Maybe, because of his subconscious desire to be alone. Even though there was a clear line of sight completely around the entire place, this was the one, and that was that.

Big gave Slow two balls, and told him good luck. He explained to Slow how to contact him when he ran out while giving him a prepaid cell phone with his number stored in it. And above all, he warned Slow about messing with the money, as if Slow needed to be told that.

As soon as Slow opened, it was clear he wouldn't do business as usual. Most drug houses let their customers inside the house to serve them if the customer was visible from the street, not Slow. Right from the beginning, Slow's customers had to go to the back door, knock, ask for what they wanted through a small hole in the door, stick their money through the hole, and receive their product through the same hole, and it didn't matter his customers could be seen from the street. He did, however, on occasion, allow a fine young lady in to receive her product. Not that he was a womanizer, he was still a virgin, however, he did like to look at them every now and then. Most of Slows customers liked the way he delivered his product through the hole in the door. It was quicker. The customer could get his dope, and get away from the dope house in a few seconds.

As time passed, and word got around a new dope house had opened in the area selling quantity, and quality, his operation started to do fairly well. Slow didn't try to play his customers cheap, and like most of the dope houses in the area, try to sell the customer as small a rock as they could get away with, and it paid off. Slow might have been slow reading, and speaking, but he was a good businessman. In the beginning, every dime he made went to buying more product. Eventually he became one of Big's best selling houses. And, later, every dime he made over his overhead, he saved.

―――――

Big, finally, pulled up in front of Slows. Giving his horn a toot, he drove down a few feet, not wanting to be seen in front of the house. He looked back at the single building in the middle of what amounted to a vacant field, which made the structure stand out more. He could clearly see someone approaching the house from the other side, on their way to the back door. Why Slow would pick a location such as that, made no sense to Big, *but it was Slow's choice, and so far it was working,* Big thought.

Slow told Smoky, who was serving another customer, he was going out to meet Big, and would be back in a minute, as he left through the front door.

Big, while usually arranging a delivery away from the houses he served, sometimes went into the house to drop off product, but not often, and he really felt a little uneasy going into Slow's. He felt Slow didn't mind having to come out to meet him, at least if he did, he never hinted at not wanting to come out, so he wasn't about to change the way they did business. Slow came out, his head on a swivel, watching for popo as he got into Big's truck.

"My man Slow, damn your business is really picking up, ain't it?" Big said, jovially, as he drove away. He was careful to not mention anything about money. He remembered how slow was offended when he said something about money before.

"Yeah, Big, I'm doing okay," Slow responded, as he looked over his shoulder, and saw Shirley, and Candy, in the back seat. "H... h... hey, ladies," Slow, greeted the two women, who were gazing at him, with funny smiles on their faces, and making him a little nervous.

Candy had her legs spread apart, and Shirley had her arm up to her elbow under Candy's skirt. Candy was gyrating her hips slowly. They got a kick out of teasing Slow.

Slow snapped his head around so fast he almost gave himself whiplash. "He... he... he... here's th... th... th... the m... m... money. Ho... how m... much did you bring me?" Slow, asked Big, nervously, and stuttering.

"I brought you what you asked for, two balls, right?" Big, inquired, as he handed Slow the package.

"Yeah, Big, that's what I wanted" Slow said, as he handed Big the money. He could have gotten more, but didn't like keeping too much dope in the house, just in case the place was raided. "You ca... ca... ca... can take m... m... m... me b... back n... now," Slow instructed, still nervous about the two women just behind his head, doing who knows what.

Big, understanding how Slow is, made a few turns back onto Slow's street. He'd put the money into his jacket pocket without counting it. He knew Slow would have counted it ten times before he got there, and Slow was never short. He dropped Slow off at his house, and proceeded to his next stop, no small talk. Slow couldn't get out of the truck fast enough, not saying bye or anything. Just slammed the door and left.

As he drove, Big wondered what Slow was doing with the money he was making. He sure wasn't spending it on anything, as far as he could tell, particularly clothes. Slow wore the same white T-shirt, well worn matching jeans and jacket, run down sneakers, and no hat. The same clothes he'd seen him wear since they met. *Strange dude, but a good roller,* Big thought.

Slow was not spending his money, for what seemed like a good reason to him. His great ambition in life was to buy a limo, and hire someone to drive him around in it. Slow wasn't a flashy type of guy, only he would understand why he wanted that. Probably because he couldn't drive — who knows? For whatever the reason he was saving his money, Slow was doing too well. As life would have it, there were those who wanted to end his success.

The line of crack-heads waiting to be served at Slows dope house grew longer as time passed. His insistence of providing quantity, and quality, was really paying off. As word spread of his operation, people came from far and wide. His became the place to cop from. His orders of product from Big-D had grown from his starting quantity of two Balls, to his present output of three or more 8-Balls a day.

The neighborhood police patrols could not help but

notice all the traffic coming and going from what apparently was an abandoned house in the middle of several vacant lots. The isolation of Slows house is the main reason the police left Slow alone. They didn't even bother to hassle the drug addicts, who were coming and going from Slow's.

The police department had undergone an extreme cut in manpower due to a lack of property taxes being collected from homeowners, the results of many people relocating outside of the city because of crime, and deteriorating neighborhoods. It seemed to be a self-perpetuating, downward, spiral. Where it began, is still being debated. It's a chicken or the egg type of situation. Some say ineffective policing, which caused the crime rate to increase, is what got the city's self-destructive spiral moving. As the crime rate increased, more people began moving away from the city. As more residence moved, the lower the tax base dropped. With less money in the coffers, the city was forced to cut many critical services, the police department being one of many. The cuts in the police manpower caused the crime rate to increase even more, causing more residence to move out of the city — and so it progressed.

Others say it began with the riots of '67, which caused many white families to move from the city. Whatever the cause, there were many neighborhoods that looked like a war zone, the deteriorating abandoned houses and vacant lots outnumbering occupied homes.

The raids of dope houses were limited too only those generating complaints from the neighborhood. Because of the location of Slow's dope den, no complaints were filed. So, as long as the police received no complaints from the other people in the neighborhood, and because the jails were full, and because they were short handed, they would leave the crack-heads alone to kill themselves. Hell, what's the point anyway — if they raided Slow's place, it would be back up and running within a few days with a different operator, anyway.

"Come on Slow, you got to get me some help. I ain't been able to take a break in the last four hours," Smoky, pleaded, as he served another customer, Juice, with more people milling around outside, waiting to be served. It seemed as if the knocking on the door would never stop. People were coming day and night, not giving the men time to rest, let alone get some sleep.

"I hear you. Have you got someone in mind?" Slow asked, heading back to the bedroom to get more product for his most recent barrage of buyers.

"Hold on, let me take care of my man Juice" Smoky said to Slow, "What up, Juice, what you need?" Smoky asked, as he laid his shotgun against the wall, near the door.

Juice was a frail, older man, long time customer, and one of a few men Smoky could let into the house.

"Hey, Smoky, will you ask Slow if I can go two dollars short on a dime?" Juice asked, "I'll bring the rest, when I get my paycheck."

"Sure, you a regular," Smoky responded, "You always pay on time. Hey Slow! Juice needs one, two short, okay?" Smoky yelled to Slow, who was still in the bedroom.

"Yeah, he's cool," came the response from Slow, now returning to the kitchen.

"Thanks, Slow, I promise I'll bring the rest as soon as I get my check," Juice told Slow, gratefully.

"I know you will, you always on time, my man, catch you later."

As Smoky opened the door to let Juice out, two women were waiting to come in. Grandma, a elderly regular of 60, and a younger woman, who'd never been there before, came into the house, and boldly proceeded to the front room, grandma trying to switch with her old frail body, with Slow following.

Grandma was an aging prostitute, who once worked 12th street years ago, a prominent stroll during it's hay-day before the '67 riots. She was one individual who didn't want to accept the fact she was growing older. She was something else, and wasn't above turning a trick if she could find a willing customer.

"Whoes this?" Slow asked Grandma, of the young woman following her to the front room.

"This is Cocoa. She wants to know if she..." Grandma started, and was cut off by Cocoa.

"I can speak for my self," Cocoa, interrupted, as she opened her coat to reveal her body. "Hey Slow, you don't know me, I just moved to this neighborhood," Cocoa, continued, "I was just wondering if I could give you some good loving for a dime or two? I'm real good. I'll have you busting those big nutts in no time. If you don't like me, you don't have to pay me," She finished, while shifting her weight to one side, and putting her hands on her hips, and smiling.

―――――

In any other situation, Cocoa could be considered attractive. She was about twenty-five, five-foot-two, brown skinned with a medium build. She had well formed shapely legs and wide hips. Her, slightly large breast for her build, were straining at the flimsy sweater she wore under her coat. Her hair was slicked down in a boyish fashion, with bangs framing her chocolate, complexed, face.

Like she'd said, she'd followed her ex dope smoking boyfriend to the Eastside, from the Westside of Detroit.

They'd moved east having been evicted from their second floor flat. Both their habits consumed all the available money leaving nothing for rent.

They made the move east when they heard of a cheap, deteriorating, apartment building on the Eastside, which was one inspection from being condemned, and which didn't require a security deposit or first months rent in advance. Once in the building, Cocoa's begging became more insistent. Her boyfriend got tired of listening to her constant request for more dope, and hightailed it back to the Westside, leaving her to her own devices.

Cocoa, her real name being, Celestine, began tricking in the building, but once she had a customer, she'd constantly beg until he no longer wanted to have anything to do with her. Grandma was also a tenant in the building, and they kind of hit it off. Grandma told Cocoa about Slow, and here they were.

Slow, because he had a big head with a large, flat, nose, and being slightly retarded, and speaking slowly, sometimes with a stutter, and being a virgin, was primed to be taken advantage of by the right person. It wasn't like he hadn't received any offers. Other women had attempted to have sex with him for drugs, but he always rejected them. For one reason or another, he felt uncomfortable with them.

This girl, for some unexplainable reason, put him at ease. He felt a little twinge in his pants as he stood there, looking at her, and trying to decide what he should do. Although he wanted her, He was about to turn down her offer, partly because of his inexperience, and shyness. He was afraid he wouldn't know what to do in an intimate situation.

Slow opened his mouth to reject her, as he had other offers, when Smoky spoke up.

"Go on dog, get you some this fine thang. If you don't, I will, and pay for it out of what you owe me."

Grandma, chimed in, "Yeah Slow, get you some good booty, boy. Maybe you can give me a dime for setting you up. I'd knock you out my self, if you'd let me, but I know you don't want no old woman like me."

The encouragement of Smoky and Grandma was what Slow needed to make up his mind. Besides, if things went wrong, it wasn't his fault, he reasoned. He was about to turn the woman's offer down before they talked him into trying her out, he reasoned. "Th... th... the hell with it. C... come on," Slow said to Cocoa, as he turned and headed towards the bedroom, and becoming more nervous by the moment.

Cocoa looked over her shoulder and smiled back at Grandma as she entered the bedroom, and started to closed the door.

Grandma yelled at Slow just before the door was closed, "Hey, Slow, can I get my rock now?"

"Give h... her one, Smoky," came the reply. "But you know you can't smoke it h... h... here, Grandma."

"I know, I know," responded Grandma, as she exited the back door, one rock in her hot little hand, and a grin on her face. Her mind was already in plotting mode. Hell, I can't find me a trick, but if Slow likes this girl, I can bring him others, and get me a rock every time. Yeah, I'll be a halfway Madam, she imagined.

In the bedroom, Cocoa wasted no time getting undressed from the waist up. She wanted to do what she had to do, get her rocks or money, and get out of there. *This Slow guy sure ain't no beauty, but he got what I want, might as well get on with it,* she thought, as she undressed.

Slow stood with his back to the door and watched, not sure what he should be doing, or saying. Actually, this being his first time, he was a little apprehensive, and wanted to change his mind, but was afraid to do so, not wanting to appear like a wimp.

Cocoa walked over to him and took both of his hands in hers, and pressed them to her naked breast. She was hoping to get him as excited as possible to save her work later when she got busy giving him lip service.

Slow began to breathe heavily, his touch becoming pressing, and frantic. He could feel his manhood grow in his pants. Cocoa reached down to fondle him through his bulging pants. She stopped and took a step back when she felt him. He was already larger than she thought he might be, and still growing. Cocoa realized she might have taken on a little more than she could handle. There was no way she'd be able to handle a man of his girth. This would have to be an intercourse only job. Something she didn't like doing, too messy, and she didn't have a condom. "Do you have any rubbers, and something I can grease that thing with?" Cocoa asked, still staring at his oversized bulge. She was not excited, and didn't want to take him on while not lubricated.

"Ain't go... go... go... got no ru... rubber, but I got some gr... grease under th... th... the bed," Slow answered, nervously, excited, and while still trying to reach her bare breast.

"Well, get out or those pants, and get the grease," Cocoa ordered, and continued, "We gonna have to screw, and you know I is going to have to charge you a little more?"

"I'm okay with th... that, I'll give you five, or te... ten rocks, whatever, no more ta... talk, where we going to do this?" Slow asked, impatiently, as he reached under the bed to retrieve the petroleum jelly, his heavy manhood now hanging loose, and he gaining confidence.

Cocoa took the jar of grease from Slow, dug out a good sized glob, and began to apply it to Slow.

"Whoooooa woman! That feels good, you better stop before I shoot my load," Slow warned, his stutter now gone.

"That's okay, baby, go ahead and finish, I don't mind." Cocoa urged, hoping to get out of the intercourse.

"Hell no, I can do myself, I wants to knock some boots, and I want it now," Slow, who was gaining courage, demanded. He took her by her shoulders and turned her around facing the bed, told her to bend over, and tried to insert into the wrong orifice.

"Hey, baby, what you trying to do, that's the wrong hole. I don't go that way," Cocoa, protested, as she stood up, and faced Slow.

"Sorry, I wasn't trying to hurt you, where you want me to put it?" Slow apologized.

"Okay, let's try this again, I'll guide you this time," Cocoa said, softly, not wanting to make him angry.

She turned back around, spread her legs, and bent over, resting her arms on the bed and sticking her butt into the air. As he approached her, she grabbed his throbbing appendage to guide it to the correct location. She managed to get him started when he in one thrust, tried to jam all of himself in, causing both of them to fall onto the bed. This felt better than anything he'd experienced before while doing himself. He erupted before they hit the bed. He let out a loud curse/moan and convulsed several times, as he kept erupting. He thought back to all the times in the past when he'd turned down the many offers of sex. If he knew it felt this good, he'd have been doing it a long time ago.

Cocoa brought him back to the present, "Come on big boy, you got to get up, I can't stay here all day. Where is the bathroom so I can wash up?"

"Sorry, I didn't mean to put all my weight on you. The bathroom is through that door," Slow pointed towards a door at the far end of the bedroom. He was feeling a little embarrassed now he'd lost his virginity. He watched her naked, well shaped, behind, jiggle, as she walked to the washroom. He felt a slight twinge in his chest. He wondered if he was falling in love.

He sat on the bed thinking about his first lovemaking experience, when behind the roar of a car's engine, he heard a car braking hard, the tires screeching. A moment passed, and then the bedroom window suddenly exploded, the results of a shotgun blast from the street. Although the blast was aimed high, a shard of glass from the exploding window caught him in the back of the head, drawing a trickle of blood.

The blast knocked plaster from the ceiling that showered down on Slow, who'd dived to the floor, and was reaching for his pants lying near the door in a crumpled pile. He could hear Cocoa screaming in the bathroom.

The noise was deafening, as some kind of automatic weapon was firing more rounds into the bedroom, knocking big holes in the wall. Several more heavy blast from the shotgun joined the rat, tat, tat, of the automatic weapon.

Bits of plaster, and wood from the door jam, and glass from the ceiling light bulb, rained down on the terrified Slow. The barrage continued for about thirty seconds, completely destroying the window, the upper half of the bedroom door, and obliterating the ceiling and walls. None of the shots were low enough to hit Slow, who by now, was cowering half under the bed, and was covering his face, protecting himself from the debris hitting the floor, and bouncing in all directions.

Cocoa, who'd stopped screaming, had climbed into the bathtub, and got down as low as she could. Now that she realized the shots were not aimed at her, she was less traumatized, but still scared.

After the shooting stopped, Slow heard car doors closing, and the screeching tires of two cars accelerating away. He remained on the floor for several more minutes as he watched the dust in the rays of the sun coming through the broken window, and listened to the eerie silence behind the shooting. After he was reasonably sure the shooting had ceased, he called out for Smoky, and got no response.

Still a little shaken, and on his hands and knees, he crawled to the door through the debris on the floor. Putting on his now dust covered pants, he opened the door that fell half off it hinges, and crawled to the kitchen where Smoky should have been while firing back at his attackers. As he crawled, he kept calling for Smoky, and received no answer.

At the kitchen door, Slow paused, and peeped around the door-jam in the direction of the kitchen window where Smoky should have been. He couldn't believe his eyes. His long time friend was sitting with his back to the wall under the kitchen window, eyes open, but seeing nothing — Smoky was dead.

Apparently he tried to look out of the kitchen window to see who was firing at the house. One of the gunmen with the shotgun, seeing him, fired a shot in his direction, and Smoky caught a pellet from one of the 00-buck shotgun blast in the throat. He choked to death, swallowing his own blood. He never had a chance to return a single shot.

Slow crawled to his dead friend, and sat close in front of him, staring into Smoke's unseeing eyes. He reached out to close those haunting eyes, but stopped short. He couldn't bring himself to touch the dead man. He sat back, and looked at the trail of blood running down the front of Smoke's throwback jersey from the wound in his throat to his crotch. Slow noticed the shotgun resting across the legs of his friend, his finger still on the trigger, he wondering if he'd managed to get a single shot off.

Slow's eyes filled with tears, and he began to sob softly. The tragedy of the situation was beginning to sink in. He knew he'd never find another friend like Smoky. Slow began to rock back and forth, his chin on his chest, sobbing openly, the grief overpowering. He reached out with one hand as if he was trying to will the man back to life. He couldn't stop the tears. He'd lost one of his best friends. A friend he knew he'd never forget. A friend he knew could never be replaced. For the fist time in his life he felt true pain.

The excited voices of several people outside the window brought him back out of his remorse. It was at that moment he remembered Cocoa in the bathroom. Getting up and running through the bedroom, cutting a foot on the glass shards, he didn't feel the injury. He had to see if she was also hurt. He kicked in the locked door. She gave a little yelp, and tried to get even lower in the tub. She was scared and still naked.

Slow calmed her down, explaining the gunmen had left. He got her dressed in her debris-covered clothes that were on the littered bed, grabbed his stash of money and drugs, and after peeping outside to make sure it was safe, got the hell out of the house. The people, who were outside, on the side of the house, didn't see Slow and Cocoa leave through the front door, and walk in the opposite direction.

Cocoa, who was scared beyond fright, stopped Slow after they were a couple blocks from the house. She wanted her dope. The dope she was supposed to receive for the sex. She wanted to get away from him just in case the shooters came back.

Slow, who liked her, gave her a hundred dollars, and what amounted to about a half a ball of dope. He apologized for the shooting and let her go her way. He didn't expect her to invite him to her place after what just happened. He hoped, but doubted he'd see her again, as he watched her quickly walk away, her head on a swivel. *I'll be all right as soon as I find Andrew,* he thought. *Together, we can figure what to do next.*

Long after Slow and Cocoa had departed the house, the police arrived and found Smoky. They did their investigation, saying it was a typical drive-by, the results of a dope dealer's drug war, and after the body was removed, left the house as they found it. Later that evening, someone drove by the house and threw a Molotov cocktail through one of the shot out windows, burning the house to the ground.

Now, it had been rumored it was the police who burned the place. It was said burning a dope house was a sure way to guarantee it wouldn't open again. This was speculation that could never be proved, but it seemed every time someone was killed in a dope den, it always ended up in flames. Let's be clear, the house could have been flamed by the rival dealers in the area, but it was strange the burning of houses was happening over the entire city, and always after some form of violence had taken place in the structure.

In any event, that was enough for Slow. He sold what dope he had left to another of Big's dope house, the same place he once worked as shotgun, and with the money he'd saved, caught the first thing heading back south to Mississippi from where he came.

Slow's dope house was doing too well. He was taking all the customers from a neighborhood, rival's, dope house. His competitors, a gang of young thugs, decided to eliminate the competition the easy way, kill him, or burn him out, rather than step up their service, and compete fairly.

After moving back home to Mississippi, Slow tried to set up shop selling dope there. He was later arrested for street dealing. Without the contacts, he could not set up the same situation he had in Detroit. He, with the previous felony warrants, and the drug pushing charges he now had, is enjoying an extended stay in the Mississippi State Prison System. He never forgot his good buddy, Smoky, and never will.

Slow learned a valuable lesson: A life of crime could temporarily be profitable, but usually ends in tragedy. And not many people have been able to change that formula.

Chapter 11

Big-D is being watched.

After leaving Slow's, Big told the girls to quit messing around. Shirley playing with Candy's pleasure pit began as a joke on Slow, but now Candy was actually being turned on. She began moaning softly, and occasionally sucking in air as the feeling grew more intense. She had her hand on top of Shirley's, making sure the probing fingers stayed in the right spot.

Big wanted to watch, now that Candy was beginning to openly enjoy Shirley's probing fingers. He wanted the girls to save the genuine feeling until they got home where he could watch and get turned on. But he had business to transact, dope to deliver, and money to pick up.

"I told you two to not get down unless I could watch. We'll be heading home soon after I make one more stop, then and we can all have some fun," admonished Big, and continued after a little thought, "well I guess it's okay Shirley if you keep her warmed up, but Candy, you better not get yours, not until later. Don't forget, y'all is gonna want something to smoke later, so y'all better be cool," he warned.

The girls giggled. Big had no idea while Slow was still in the truck, Candy had got her cookie. They loved to perform in front of someone. Having someone watching them seemed to add a little excitement to their acts. Seemed to make what they were doing to each other, which to them was natural, a little nasty. Even if someone wasn't watching their every move, just dallying each other in the presents of someone such a Slow, turned them on, but they'd repeat their act for Big when the time came, and it would be an act with a lot of fake moaning and groaning. Hell, they knew he wouldn't be able to tell the difference, anyway.

It wasn't a long drive before Big-D pulled into the alley behind Edward's. He parked next to the vacant lot across the alley. He took a quick glance in the back seat to make sure the girls weren't going at it too heavy, but still didn't trust them to behave, and decided to separate them while he was in the house.
"Shirley, you come on and get in the front while I'm gone. I don't trust you two to behave. I shouldn't be gone no more than five minutes," Big instructed.
As he exited the truck, ever vigilant, he stared across the vacant lot in the direction of a U-hall truck parked one street over. He thought nothing of it, many people kept the trucks overnight, while moving. Satisfied the coast was clear, he went to the rear of his truck, opened one of the hidden compartments, and removed the dope he'd hidden there. He moved quickly, and deliberately, he didn't like hanging around these dope houses. He could never tell when a patrol car might luck up, and catch him in the act of delivery, or the house raided. *I should have listened to my first mind, and parked a couple blocks away, and walked to the dope house, or had Edward meet me some place,* he thought, as he replaced the seamless cover to the hidden compartment. He particularly liked having the operator get into his truck, and they drive away from the dope den the way he and Slow had done earlier. But to be honest, there was less of a chance of being caught with the drugs in his possession when walking with the drugs in hand.
He could walk, and watch for approaching police cars,

and dump the drugs behind some shrubs or somewhere at first sight. If the police didn't stop him, he could return, and retrieve the dope. If they did stop him, he'd be clean, and could return to retrieve the dope after they moved on.

He was in a hurry this time, and didn't follow his normal protocol. The girls freaking in the back seat had turned him on, and he wanted to get to his house as quickly as possible. Besides, with Edward probably freaking inside the house, he most likely would take a long time to get to any rendezvous location he might set up, and he didn't want to wait.

Edward's package in his coat pocket, he hurried up the stairs to the back door of the dope house, and knocked. Joe's, Edward's shotgun man, eye appeared in the peephole.

"Come on man, it's me, Big. Come on, I'm in a hurry," Big said, impatiently, as he glanced around quickly, still nervous about going into the place, and glancing back towards the U-Haul truck parked on the other side of the vacant lot.

Joe opened the door, and stepped out of the way, as Big entered, "Hey Big," said Joe, as he looked outside the door before closing it, and replacing the two two-by-fours running across the door. He picked up his shotgun and cradled it in his arms. There was no need for him to hold onto the weapon other than he felt powerful with it in his hands.

Big continued on into the makeshift bedroom, Edward's freak room, without saying anything. The first thing Big saw was Darlene servicing Edward. "Aw, damn, man. You had plenty of time to finish that crap before I got here," Big said, disgustedly, and Edward not paying him any attention.

As Big moved further into the room, he saw Joyce, naked, and on her knees, her head between V's legs, making loud slurping noises. They were on a twin-sized mattress on the floor, which wasn't covered by a sheet, and was filthy with an assortment of stains. A huge cockroach scampered along one side, looking for a place to hide, while another, with its antenna waving, was nibbling at an empty crack bag on the littered floor, probably sensing the baking soda, one of the ingredients used to cut the cocaine as it's being rocked.

The girl's stems were lying on the head of the mattress waiting for when Edward would give them their rocks for the show they were putting on. He couldn't help but notice a slight odor of unwashed bodies, and burning rocks, lingering in the haze filled air of the unventilated house. An electric heater sat in one corner, its elements glowing red, but seemed to be un-needed in the cramped room with so many bodies in it.

Watching the two women freaking reminded Big of a scene he'd see between his two girls when he got them home. But his show would be on a clean, king-sized, bed, and some mellow jazz playing in the background with a glass or two of Yack within easy reach.

He stopped behind the girls, and watched the action for a moment, not paying any attention to Edward. Watching two women was cool, but watching a man and woman, not his thing, unless the man was giving the woman a tongue-lashing, that he might get into.

The sight of Joyce's well-rounded bottom swaying from side to side as she serviced V, got the best of him. He reached down and ran his middle finger over Joyce's wet pinkness, and then brought his finger to his nose and sniffed — *clean*, he thought.

Joyce gave a little shiver, and raised her head to see who was caressing her. She saw it was Big. She bowed her head back towards the ceiling, and let out a loud moan. She pushed her hips back into the invading hand, and gyrated her hips as if she enjoyed his touch. It was all an act — she hoping

Big might take a liking to her and bring her into his stable with Candy and Shirley. She had no way of knowing there was no chance in hell of that happening. He was happy with his two girls the way things were, and he definitely wouldn't take a chance on having sex with no crack-whore like her no matter how hard she tried. Not only that, he noticed the long dirty toenails jutting from the rusty feet of V, which discussed him a little. *That girl really does need to attend to her personal hygiene,* he thought.

"You better stop, unless you wants to be my next victim, and get raped up in here," Joyce said, between clinched lips.

She, quickly, put her head back down on V, and resumed her licking and slurping, only louder, and accompanied by an ecstatic moan.

The activity was having the desired affect on V, who was starting to moan, and manipulate her nipples as she wreathed on the mattress. "Damn, girl, you gonna make me gush," V said in an exhaling voice, as she grabbed the back of Joyce's head, and forced it deeper.

"Move Big, you blocking my view" Edward informed, while still enjoying the attention of Darlene.

"Sorry, my man. I got a little carried away for a second there," Big apologized. "These women sure can freak" Big continued, "I'm going to get into a little something-something, myself, when we finish our business here."

"You cool, Big, I kinda lost the feeling anyway. I guess I got my mind on our business," Edward, placated, as he pushed Darlene back, and got up from his chair, his stiffness now going flaccid. "Come on, let's get this over with, so I can take another hit and get back into the mood," Edward said, as he led the way to his real bedroom.

"Can we get a little something until you comes out?" Darlene asked, Edward, before he got into the bedroom.

Edward didn't pay her any attention, and continued to the bedroom. He wanted to continue where he left off when Big arrived, and didn't want Darlene or the other two women high when he did so. He knew they would be mad about not getting their dope right now, but, also, knew they weren't going anywhere until they got what they were working for.

Big followed Edward to the bedroom, while taking one more peep at the girls on the mattress, who'd quit freaking, not having to perform for Edward. Darlene joined the other women on the mattress. Sitting with her back against the wall and her arms crossed under her naked breast. As Edward figured, she was mad he didn't give her the dope she felt she'd earned, and might have to start over again if she was going to get anything.

Once in the bedroom, Big removed the package from his jacket pocket, now in a hurry to get out of the place. "Okay," he said, "you wanted a couple marbles, right?"

"Yeah Big, that should hold me through the night," confirmed Edward, as he handed Big two-hundred-dollars in payment for the package. Edward would be able to cut up the two 8-balls into many tiny smaller pieces, and make anything from four to five hundred dollars, selling the pieces separately, depending on how large he made the pieces, and how much he gave the crack-whores to party.

"You Sure you don't want more?" inquired Big. "I don't want you calling me until after twelve o'clock, tomorrow, afternoon. I'm going to tie one on tonight, along with my two girls, and I don't want to be bothered."

"Don't worry player," Edward insisted, "This is the middle of the week, and things are slow, so I won't need anything else until tomorrow night. Go on home, and get your freak on. I know I am as soon as you get your big ass out of hear."

The two men laughed and soul hugged, Big saying, "Okay, Ed, I'll see you tomorrow night some time, cool?

"Right on, Big, my man. Now get your oversized out of here so I can get back to my business, will you?" Edward prompted.

"I feel you. I'm gone. Take care. Catch you later," Big said, as he opened the bedroom door, on his way out.

Edward remained behind to stash the package of drugs Big had given him.

As Big was on his way out, he noticed the three women sitting side-by-side, backs against the wall, still naked and re-lighting their stems, as if nothing had happened. They were trying to flame the residue of the rocks they'd smoked earlier. He shook his head while thinking this is all these girls have to look forward too — probably for the rest of their lives. *A sorry situation,* he thought.

Joe began removing the timber from the door before Big got to it. He opened the door with the shotgun still in hand, stuck his head out, and took a slow look around. Many people knew who Big was, and knew Big might have some money on him, and one couldn't be too careful. Big, knew what Joe was doing, and didn't rush him. He was also aware of the danger of leaving the rear of a dope house, going into a dark yard, while not having a burner on him.

Big exited the house after taking a quick look around for himself and with Joe watching. He sees the U-hall still parked in the same location. He makes a beeline to his truck, gets behind the wheel and starts it while leaving the alley in a hurry. Shirley would have to stay in the font next to him for the time being. His next destination, home, and some sure-nuff freaking with his girls. *Life is good,* he thought.

———

If Big knew what was in the future for him, he'd have made Edward's the last delivery he'd ever make...

Chapter 12

Big brother flexes his muscles

After writing up their reports, Officers, Robert Drake, and Ray Johnson, turned them in to their precinct's narcotics raid team. They'd taken several very descriptive pictures of the drug house, and Joe the doorman. They were sure they'd gathered enough evidence to close down the place causing so many complaints from the residents of the neighborhood. They'd also taken a few pictures of the mid-level drug supplier, and his vehicle, a good night's work, or so they thought.

When they were called into the captain's office, they figured they would receive praise for their diligence, a pat on the back, a job well done, and they did. What took them by surprise was the fact they would be asked to do more work on the case.

Usually the evidence they'd gathered was enough to get a search warrant and justify a raid on any dope house in the area. As it turned out, the picture of the mid-level supplier is what made this particular situation different.

If all the police wanted was to shut down the Edward's, the raid team would be on their way, already. The hold up was, as the captain explained, the prosecutor wanted to make a case on the higher up supplier, who they'd taken pictures of, meaning, Big, which was not a common event. To raid the crack house with the just pictures might not put enough pressure on the house operator to make him willing to give evidence on the big boy, the captain explained. He wanted more evidence to put added pressure on Edward. Make a solid case, which might lead to a long stint in prison for Edward while making him more willing to flip on Big.

The captain asked them to stop one of the crack-heads coming out of the house, threaten to arrest him, or her, if the person refused to make an undercover buy of crack from Edward with marked money. With the proof of possession with the intent to deliver, case, documented, the dope house operator, Edward, would be facing a long prison term. He'd be offered a shorter jail sentence if he gave information useful in the capture of the mid-level supplier, Big. They'd used that tactic many times before, and it usually worked unless the supplier was connected with the Mob, and then no one was fool enough to rat on their supplier. But in this case, the police knew Big was the supplier, and felt Edward wouldn't hesitate to flip.

If Big could be caught, maybe they could make a similar deal with him that would lead to the arrest of the top-level supplier, maybe lead to the person responsible for the importing of the drugs, a big score indeed, but would only work if Big's supplier wasn't Mob connected — in that case, all bets are off. Nobody would be fool enough to rat on the Mob, no matter how many years they faced in jail. Everyone knew the Mob could get to them, regardless of where they were in prison.

Officers Johnson, and Drake, knew picking up a crack-head would be easy — busting the dope house would be easy, but getting Edward to turn over on Big wouldn't be so easy, and they told their Captain as much, but they agreed to give it a try. The Captain, an old veteran, already knew he was asking his men to do the near impossible. He knew how dangerous some of the mid-level suppliers could be. He knew if one of the mid-level suppliers found out his operator had flipped on him, he'd put out a contract on that individuals head, resulting in one dead pusher. Actually, the Captain didn't expect Drake and Johnson to be able to get anybody to flip to begin with, but he had to try anyway, but who knows, they might get lucky, he hoped. The whole plot hinged on how much dope Edward was caught with, and how bad he wanted to stay out of jail. Besides, even if they couldn't, somehow, get Edward to rollover, at least his place would be shut down while satisfying the complaints of the people in the neighborhood, and sometimes, that's all he could do.

Back on the streets, the two plain-clothes officers set up to arrest a crack user who'd just exited the targeted dope house. They'd need the help of a couple marked cars to pull off catching the individual with the drugs in their possession, and not alarm the operator of the dope house. If the crack-head saw the police coming, he, or she, could dump the illegal substance, before being stopped, so to catch them dirty would take a team effort.

To catch someone red handed, it was common practice to stop a car in which someone that'd just exited the drug house and gotten into. It was much harder to dispose of the drugs when inside a car. The stop team would set up with marked cars a few blocks on either side of the dope house. The surveillance team would park near enough to the dope house in an old, beat up, car, to take down the make, model, and plate number of the offending vehicle. Dressed in work, or old clothes, the surveillance team could park within a house or two of the dope house, and radio to the marked police cars the direction in which the offending car was going.

No offending car was ever stopped near the dope house. Word spread quickly when the police were in the area. If word got back to the dope house cops were around before the undercover buy could be made, the whole operation would be a waste. Most operators, when they got word the cops were stopping people, were smart enough to not sell to anyone who'd just left their place and returned within an hour. Some dope men went as far as to post lookouts within a block of the dope house to warn the operator of approaching police or a raid team.

    Before leaving the prescient house, Drake and Johnson had obtained the $50.00 bill with which to make the undercover buy. The money had been marked, the serial numbers photo copied for later use in court. The raid team was instructed to post up at a Coney Island in the neighborhood with a large parking lot, and were put on alert, and told to wait for conformation of a successful undercover buy.

    The operation in full swing, Officers Drake and Johnson parked their old Dodge pickup one house east, and across the street from the dope house. They'd made a big deal of pushing the truck to the curb at that location, after it had stalled in the middle of the street. The truck had stalled because it had a concealed kill switch. The way they played it, it appeared as if the two men were driving an old vehicle pasted its functional life span. No one would give them a second look. Drake and Johnson took turns looking under the hood, and attempting to start the truck. It was cold outside, and they would allow the truck to run long enough to provide a little heat, but would, with the kill switch, shut it down after a little while, to give reason to stay parked in the location without drawing to much attention to them.

    The last time they watched the front of the dope house, they met with little success. It was colder outside this time, so they figured maybe someone would get lazy and ask to be dropped off closer to the dope house, hopefully in the front rather than the alley.

Their intuition proved to be correct. After about an hour and fifteen minutes of swapping places under the hood, a car pulled up and parked directly across the street from the two officers, and in front of the dope house. The driver of the car, a middle-aged male, rolled down his window and asked the officers if they needed a boost. The passenger of the car, a young, dark skinned, woman, of about 30, short, small breasted, with big hips, and her hair all over her head, got out and went around to the side of Edward's.

"No, thanks, it starts okay, but cuts off again," replied Officer Drake, who was looking under the hood, playing his part expertly. "I knew I should have replaced the coil way back before it got cold."

"You're right about that," responded the driver. "If there's anything wrong with it, cold weather will bring it out. If you need anything, I'll be here for another minute," the driver finished, as he rolled up his window.

The officers could tell the driver was nervous. He kept looking up and down the street, and then back towards Edward's. It just goes to show you, judging by the age of the driver, crack has no age limit.

The young woman came back from around the side of the house, and got into the car. The two people talked for a second and the car started. The car pulled into the driveway of the house behind the officers, and made a U-turn, and proceeded back the way it had come.

As the not too old Chevy passed the two officers, Officer Drake, who was under the hood, got a good look at the license plate. The plate was so dirty, neither officer could make out the entire plate number, but got the first three letters, which was all needed by the stopping officers. They radioed the information to the marked car covering the area into which the Chevy was going. The raid team was also listening in on the radio conversations.

The marked police car made the stop, using the dirty plate as the excuse for stopping them, but actually didn't need any other reason than it carried a passenger that had just been seen leaving a known drug house. As it turned out, an empty beer can was visible on the floorboard. The driver, not only had a suspended drivers license, but also had no proof of insurance, not to mention, neither he, nor the young woman were wearing their seat belts, more than enough to warrant a search of the car.

A search of the young woman turned up a rock hidden in her bra. In her haste to dump the drugs she must have missed one. Several more rocks were found on the floorboard of the car, on her side. After arresting the driver and his companion, and having the car impounded, the two officers in the marked car were instructed to take the young lady, whose name was, Brenda Smith, to the all night Coney island where the raid team was waiting for the go-ahead to raid Edward's. The driver was taken to the precinct. He wasn't needed for the undercover buy, and most likely, would be released with a bench warrant.

Drake and Johnson arrived at the Coney Island, and saw the police cruiser parked near the raid team's vehicles with Brenda in the back seat. The two officers in the front of the cruiser were eating, having taken advantage of the opportunity to grab a bite.

The raid team was standing around, joking with each other, trying to stay loose. Raiding a dope house, for the most part, went relatively smooth, but was still a dangerous undertaking. Joking and kidding around was a way to relieve tension while waiting on the go signal.

Drake and his partner, after having a word with the raid team, got into the back of the cruiser with Brenda.

"Hey, Brenda, how you doing?" asked, Officer

Johnson. Both men could smell the odor of alcohol on her breath, and weed in her clothes.

"I'm okay, I guess," responded Brenda, with a puzzled look on her face, her hands handcuffed behind her back, and obviously uncomfortable. She'd been arrested before and this was the first time any cop had gotten into the back of a car with her.

"You know you have a warrant out on you for failure to appear on a solicitation charge, don't you?" asked, Drake.

"Yeah, I know, I promise to go to court tomorrow if you let me go, really, I promise. I was out of town the day of my hearing," pleaded Brenda, as she looked wide eyed, back and forth, between the two officers.

"Hold on, hold on," Drake continued, "There's not much I can do about the warrant. You're going to have to go to jail on that, but there is this little matter of the rocks we found on you that's the real probl…"

Brenda cut Officer Drake off. "Those weren't mine, I don't know where they came from, and I ain't taking the rap for them," she said, still glancing between the two officers.

"Deny possession all you want, we found one rock in your bra, and several on the floor of the car, on your side. The driver claims they belong to you, and we believe him," informed Drake. He knew he could not pin the drugs on her that were found on the floor of the car, but decided to try a bluff, maybe, she'd flinch.

Drake, continued, "Put the two charges together, and you might be looking at some time. But, and this is a long shot, I might be able to help you, if, and only if you help me."

Brenda knew what officer Drake wanted before he finished saying it, but decided to hear him out.

"What we need you to do is make a buy at the dope house you just left using marked money, and bring the dope back to us. We'll drop you off a couple blocks from the place so no one will suspect anything." Drake, informed, and finished, "how does that sound?"

Brenda was ready to take any offer she could get. What the cops couldn't tell was she also had a long termed heroin addiction, and didn't want to spend one day longer in jail than she had too. "Hell yeah, I'll do it, give me the money, how much you want me to buy, hell yeah, come on, let's go. You want me to do it now? Let's go, I'm ready. Edward don't mean nothing to me," Brenda said, in rapid fire, happy to find, what she thought, a way out of her predicament.

Drake and Johnson looked at each other thinking the same thing — these crack-heads are so predictable.

Johnson got out of the cruiser and walked over to where the raid team was waiting. He informed them of what was happening. And told them to be ready to move within a minute's notice.

After releasing Brenda from the handcuffs, the three of them loaded into the old Dodge pickup, Brenda in the middle. They drove to a spot a couple blocks from the targeted dope house.

"Here's the marked money. Try to get five dimes and return here," Drake said, giving Brenda the marked fifty-dollar bill."

"You and the house are being watched by another team, so don't try to run off with the money," Officer Johnson, explained to Brenda. "Try anything funny, especially taking our money and we will throw the book at you, understand?"

"Yeah, Yeah, I got you," Brenda replied, while looking at the money, trying to see where it was marked, and could find nothing unusual. She folded it up and stuffed it into her bra, while wishing it was hers. *A nice hit would go down real good right now,* she thought, *and this is enough to buy me a blow too.*

She wasn't conscious of the plan already forming in the back of her mind to break off a piece of one of the rocks and hit it before returning with the rest, but the thought was there just the same.

"All right, go get yourself out of trouble. We'll give you thirty minutes to get back here with the drugs. When you return, we'll write up a favorable report that will help with the failed to show warrant, and we will drop the possession charge, fair enough?" Officer Drake, asked.

"Hell yeah. It won't take me no half-hour to cop. I'll try to be back in about twenty minutes. You ain't got to watch me, either. I won't try anything," Brenda stated as she stuck her finger inside her bar, checking on the location of the money. She had no conscious thoughts of double crossing the officers, *but fifty-dollars could get her high for at least an hour, if only it was hers to spend,* she mused. She was, also, thinking of her heroin addiction, and how it felt to go through withdrawal. She was really rattled when she was arrested, but was soon to find out her addiction was stronger than her fear of going to jail.

Brenda got out of the truck, and walking quickly, took off towards Edward's. She was at the back door of the dope house in seven minutes. After being let in by Joe, she bought five dimes from Edward using the marked fifty-dollar bill. Having the dimes in her hot hand was too much temptation. A craving was centered in the middle of her chest like a belch, which wouldn't come up, and growing. It was mental as well as physical in nature, and was making her nervous. The overpowering erg was beginning to make her sick. That half-baked plan to double-cross the cops began to gel — became irresistible. Was there any doubt she'd do this once the money was in her hands, of course not? All needed to be done was to figure how she'd get away with it.

She figured she could smoke one of the rocks at Edward's, and take the rest back to the two waiting officers. She'd tell them she must have dropped one in her haste to get back to them on time. She figured she'd be in lock-up, and this might be the last time she'd be getting high for a while. *And then again, the cops might not believe me,* she thought, her mind trying to override the craving, and failing. There was no way she was going to rationalize doing the right thing. Her addiction and craving had been nourished over years of drug abuse, and would not be denied.

She went to the front room, and made an offer to one of the crack-heads, who was pushing his stem. She asked if she could use his stem in exchange for a small piece of rock. She told him he could have the residue because she had someone waiting for her. The junkie was glad to acquiesce to the exchange. She put what was left of the dime into the junkie's stem, lit it, and inhaled long and deep — the high seeming to be better than usual, maybe, because it would be the last for a while.

Immediately after hitting the rock, she got paranoid and wished she'd never tried to trick the police. The whole transaction only took a couple minutes, but seemed longer to her. She was starting to panic. She couldn't decide what to do next. The drug was doing what crack does. She hurried to the back door, and told Joe she had someone waiting on her, to let her out. Joe had seen this kind of behavior many times. He took no notice, and looked at her with a bemused expression on his face while letting her out.

Back outside, she frantically started back to the waiting cops. Her hart was racing, and she was walking fast. She was afraid she'd have a heart attack, but she kept going, the panic was in full bloom. She thought about all kinds of bad things happening when she confronted the cops and wasn't able to produce all the dope they paid for. For a brief moment, she thought about not going back, but not sure she wasn't being watched, decided to go back and face the music.

Back at the truck, she got in quickly. Officer Drake started the engine, and they left the area. They returned to the Coney Island, and parked on the far end of the parking lot, next to the raid team. Officer Drake got out to brief the raid team before returning to the pickup where Johnson remained in the car with Brenda.

Officer Johnson eyed the woman for a moment, noticing the way she was wide eyed, and fidgety "Damn, you breathing hard woman, let's see what you got," he requested.

"I thought I was running late, and damn near ran back to you guys, I ain't got no watch," Brenda offered, as she poured the four rocks into Ray's hand.

"What kind of crap you trying to pull, junkie? We gave you fifty dollars. Where's the other rock? You better not be holding out on us!" Officer Johnson exploded, as he held an open hand in Brenda's face.

"Aw hell no. Damn, I musta dropped one when I was hurrying back to you guys. Take me back, I'll find it, take me back. I ain't trying to pull nothing, really, I ain't," Brenda pleaded.

"No, we can't return to the area, too dangerous. You better hope the Captain accepts your explanation, and hope the missing rock doesn't affect our case on Edward," warned, Officer Johnson, as he placed the four rocks in an evidence bag, sealing it. "We're going to have a female officer search you when we get back to station — you better not have anything on you when we get there. It's a felony to take drugs inside the police station. Is there anything you want to tell us before we get there?" asked, Johnson, as he pulled out his handcuffs to cuff her hands in the front of her, this time.

"Naw, I'm clean," is all Brenda responded, as she took a not so noticeable deep breath, and thought, *you dumb cop.*

"I bet there ain't," Johnson said. "We aren't stupid. You look as if you might have smoked that rock in the dope house before you came back, but we'd have a hard time proving it, so you'll get away with this one this time. But I have half-a-mind to cancel our deal, junkie."

Brenda could only sit with her head down and listen to the cop, as the craving was already returning. A crack high doesn't last very long. She was starting to become bold (suffer from withdrawal symptoms from the need to hit another rock, and, or, heroin. Although some say the withdrawal symptoms from Crack Cocaine are more mental than physical, it's not argued there is, to some degree, withdrawal symptoms associated with crack) but there was little she could do about that now. It would be a long time before she'd have a chance to drug again.

The undercover buy successful, everything was in place. The raid team was briefed. It was time to raid Edward's.

The caravan of vehicles rolled out of the Coney Island parking lot together. A black unmarked car containing four officers took the lead. The raid van containing six officers, with Drake and Johnson riding along, followed the lead car, while Brenda in another black unmarked cruiser, escorted by three officers brought up the rear.

Step one, the arrest of a dirty junkie, and step two, the undercover buy, complete, it was time for step three — the players position themselves for the sting. Big brother was about to flex his muscles...

Brenda had supplied the raid team with information regarding the layout of the house, how many men were armed, and their locations in the house, and approximately how many people they could expect to encounter during the raid. The two narks, Johnson and Drake, had promised her she wouldn't have to face Edward after the raid.

The raid team knew how dangerous and unpredictable a raid can be. They wanted to get in and out without anyone getting hurt, and for the most part, they usually managed to accomplish that objective. Everybody on the team road in silence. The only sounds heard inside the van were the officers checking, and rechecking their weapons and safety equipment.

Arriving on location, the van and unmarked cars held back a few blocks from the dope house. They had to give the marked cars a chance to locate, and disable any lookouts posted to warn Edward of a pending raid.

An Officer in one of the marked cars spotted a young man standing near an intersection, while pretending to talk on his cell phone. The officers pulled up next to the suspected lookout, and asked the thug looking young man to approach the cruiser.

If the young man was not in the life, he sure looked the part, having a doo-rag on his head, baggy jeans worn low around his butt, and sagging on top of his designer gym shoes, and a oversized white T-shirt, under his leather jacket, covering the jeans. Although, he may not be in the drug life, or wasn't a lookout, he still cold be rolling himself, and his appearance dictated he had to be checked out. If everything went well, the young man would be detained only long enough for the raid to get under way, and then released.

"Hey buddy, come here for a second," one of the officers in the marked car beckoned the young man.

"What? What? You talking to me? I ain't done nothing. What you want me for? I ain't breaking no laws," the young man protested.

"I didn't say you've done anything illegal, we just want to check your ID. You match the description of an armed robbery suspect we're looking for. When you're asked to submit yourself, by a police officer, you do it," one of the officers said to the thug, as booth officers got out of the car, one officer's hand on his Glock pistol.

Their plan was to hold the man long enough for the raid team to get into place, and proceed with the raid, and maybe bust him too, if he had no ID, or had an outstanding warrant for his arrest. Actually, they didn't have probable cause to detain him, but he didn't know his rights, and did as was told. As it turned out, the young thug looking man had no identification. The officers arrested him, placing him in the back of their car. An examination of the phone he was pretending to talk into would later reveal Edward's cell phone number programmed into it. He was a lookout as the officers suspected. The other marked cruiser spotted no one who could be a lookout. The okay for the raid to proceed was given.

Brenda, who was in the last, black, unmarked interceptor, watched the raid team quickly pull up, and stop in front of Edward's. As soon as the cars and van came to a stop, she watched the doors open on all the vehicles, seemingly, altogether. Four men from each car, six from the van, and two from the car she was in, leaving one behind to watch her, all poured out, and quickly proceeded to surround the house. Several of the heavily armored and armed officers went onto the porch, and front door. One of the officers at the front door carried a hefty battering ram. They had shotguns and pistols at the ready. Officers' Drake and Johnson remained behind in the van. They were just along for the ride.

Inside the house, it was business as usual. Several people in the front room were doing their thing, smoking their dope, and pushing their stems. The sex-capades in the dining room, on the other side of the sheet, had ceased for the moment. Edward, who'd gone without sleep for several days, was exhausted. He'd counted out thirty-dime-rocks, and gave them to Darlene to sell, while he took a little nap.

"Now listen to me woman," Edward warned Darlene, "I'm going to get some sleep. This is thirty-dime-stones equal to three hundred dollars if you sell them all. My money better be right when I count it. I don't have to tell you what will happen if it ain't. Understand?"

"Don't worry daddy, I'll take care of business the same as always. Can I have one for helping you out?" Darlene asked Edward.

"Yeah go ahead, and smoke one, and only one, and don't chip off the others. If I have any complaints from my customers about the size, its me and you," Edward threatened. "Come to think about it, you can give one to V, and Joyce. They put on a damn good show," Edward, instructed Darlene, as he turned to Joe, "Joe don't let her out of your sight. I mean don't even let her go to the crapper unless you're there watching. I don't trust her, she'll take an ass kicking to smoke a couple rocks," Edward said, as he started toward the bedroom.

In the bedroom, after locking the door, Edward took the large bundle of money from his pocked, and hid it in the closet. He didn't bother to hide the paper bag of rocks on the dresser. He fell on the bed, and was out almost before he hit the mattress. He was also hungry. *I'll send out for something to eat later, after I get some rest,* he thought, before closing his eyes.

Because Edward was dead tired and in a deep sleep,

and because the bedroom door was closed, he wasn't roused out his sound sleep by the sound of the front door being bashed in by the raid team. He didn't hear the raid team ordering everyone to put their hands up and to get on the floor, face down. He didn't hear the team come into the freak room, and prostrate the naked women, and Joe, before they tried to enter the bedroom he was in.

One of the officers tried the locked bedroom door. Several members of the team positioned themselves around the door as an officer with the battering ram prepared to smash it opened. The men coordinated their moves with same precision they'd used at the front door. On a count, and all together, they smashed the door open, and entered the bedroom, where Edward was sleeping with their weapons at the ready.

The sound of the bedroom door busting open shocked Edward awake. He jumped as the officers came into the room, shotguns aimed at his head. His eyes burning from the lack of sleep. It took a moment for him to comprehend what was happening.

"Don't move, punk! On the floor! Face down! Hands behind your head!" Came the order from one of the heavily armored officers.

Edward, who'd been through the routine many times before, followed their orders almost instinctively. He was glad they hadn't come while he was being sexed earlier.

He was cuffed, and led out into the dining room. The escorting officers weren't gentle while taking him to the next room. His hands being cuffed behind his back, they snatched him up off the floor by his arms, which caused a terrible pain in his shoulders. Edward protested the way he was being handled, and got no response. Taking him to the next room, they forced him onto the floor even though he was trying to lay down on his own.

He'd been manhandled like this before, which always mystified him. But had he stopped to think about the situation, he'd have understood the raiding officers were human, and under the influence of higher adrenaline levels, the result of entering a dangerous situation. They were excited, and sometimes didn't know their own strengths, and combined with their training ingraining the need to quickly take control of a situation, their behavior might be understood. It could happen to anyone when subjected to a volatile situation.

The three girls, who'd been part of the sex activity, now had clothes on, and were laying face down on the floor. Joe, the shotgun man, had thrown his shotgun into a corner, and immediately laid down on the floor as soon as he heard the police coming through the front door. He knew the back of the house was covered and there was nowhere to run. He knew the most he'd receive with he no longer on probation, and as long as he wasn't caught with the weapon, was a fine for loitering in a dope house

Everybody being under control, and in safe positions on the floor, the officers began joking amongst themselves — their way of relieving the tension, but irritated Edward.

He felt they, the officers, were treating he and his companions as less than human. He imagined himself, with superhuman strength, breaking the cuffs, jumping up, and kicking all the cops asses. He was so mad about the way the cops were stepping over him as if he were a pile of crap on the floor, he hadn't stop to think he might have been set up.

Two officers remained behind in the bedroom to search for drugs and the most important marked, fifty-dollar, bill, used to make the undercover buy.

They took the bedroom apart, tossing the filthy mattress on the floor, pulling out the drawers in the dresser and dumping the contents on the floor, causing one of the officers to jump back, as a horde of roaches scampered for cover as they hit the floor.

"Christ, how can someone live like this?" the officer said, while trying to stomp on the fleeing pest.

"Beats me," his partners responded, as he continued his search, emptying the closet, and looking into anything in which something could be hidden, all the while watching for more bugs.

It didn't take long to find the drugs on the dresser, and not much longer to find the bundle of money, including the marked fifty concealed in the closet. The officers high-fived each other. They had him now. Another officer found what was left of the rocks that Edward had given to Darlene earlier. All the evidence was placed in several evidence bags and tagged.

Edward knew he was heading to jail for an extended stay. Hell, it wasn't his first time, so he wasn't worried. But he sure was going to miss the sex thing. As he was led outside through the front door, he saw the officers questioning the prone crack-heads in the front room. After being questioned, the addicts would be ticketed, and released if they had identification. Those who were without ID would be held until they could be identified, and checked for wants and warrants.

Damn, Edward thought, as he was led out, those fools will spill their guts to save their asses. *Crap, they got me anyway — I know they found the bag on the dresser, and the rocks I gave Darlene,* he thought, *what more could they say that would make things any worse? At least I didn't party with any minors or my ass would really be in a jam,* he justified.

Outside, Edward was seated in the rear of one of the marked cars. There, he was told why he was being arrested as if he didn't know. But he didn't know they'd found marked money in with the rest of his cash. That's when he discovered someone had set him up. He later discovered he'd be taken to the nearest precinct house, and put into a holding cell, where officers Drake and Johnson would approach him with their offer to set up Big-D, in exchange for a lighter sentence and maybe some dropped charges.

Brenda watched Edward being led to the car. She tried to duck down low in the back seat in fear Edward might see her, and know she was the one who set him up.

"Relax junkie. These are dark tinted windows. He can't see you, and you'll be taken to a different station house than him. You'll be safe. We keep our word," the officer, who was in the front seat, said, consoling her.

Still a little dubious, Brenda raised up high enough to peep over the back of the seat to see Edward, cuffed, an officer's hand on his head, being placed into the back of a cruiser. She watched as several people came out of the house, each holding tickets for loitering, and going their separate ways, including Edward's three freak friends, and Joe the doorman, while others, while cuffed, were placed in the back of marked cars.

It took another hour and a half before the officers began loading up. By then, the cuffs on Brenda's wrist were beginning to hurt. The two officers, who got out of the car she was in, finally came back, got in with her and started the engine. They laughingly discussed the raid as they drove.

"Did you see them naked women when we first busted in?"

"Hell yeah. And they were all as high as anybody I've ever seen."

"What naked women?" The officer in the back with Brenda, asked.

The officer who was riding shotgun, turned to tell his

partner in the back about the women who were sitting on the mattress, smoking dope, and were all naked.

"Damn, the one time I don't go in, you guys get an eyeful, and I had to sit out here and baby-sit this junkie. Damn," the officer in the back said, as he rode by the crowd, who'd gathered to watch the raid.

The two officers in the front laughed, and teased their partner.

"Yeah, you missed it. Man you should have seen their eyes when we busted in. You aren't going to believe this, but one of those women was trying to light her stem as we were trying to get everybody down on the floor. We kept telling her to put the stem down, but she kept lighting it while watching us the whole time. Un-frigging-believable."

"You got that right, partner," the driver said, "She was going to get that last hit no matter what."

"Sure was," the other officer riding up front said, "Crack-heads ain't got the sense God gave a brick."

The three officers laughed together. Brenda sat quietly listening to them talk about people she knew, and essentially, her, as if she weren't there.

Listen to them, Brenda thought. *They thinks they is so high and mighty, like they is better than anybody else, just because they is cops. Mutha-frigging-pigs. I hate them all,* she thought, as she rode to her destiny. She'd never have guessed she'd be glad to be on her way to jail, but she was, and none too soon. Those cuffs were really hurting, and she couldn't get comfortable in the not so spacious back seat, plus she wanted to get away from the self-righteous cops. Besides, there was an odor lingering back there starting to bother her, mostly because she was in the early stages of becoming bold from the lack of drugs.

At the 9th precinct, Edward was thrown into the same

holding cell as his, so-called, lookout man.

"What the hell happened, how come you didn't warn me of the raid, like I pay you for?" Edward asked, Billy.

"Man, it wasn't my fault. The police were checking me for ID, and to see if I had a warrant. I think it was a trick to keep me from calling you because as soon as they started hassling me, the raid truck pulled up in front of the crib," Billy said. "Not only that, they found an arrest warrant on a traffic ticket from way back two years ago. That's why I'm in here now, ain't that a blip?"

"Forget that, I got to find a lawyer, and quick, those sneaky muthas made an undercover buy with marked money. Now they're going to throw the damn book at me. I'm in some deep ass crap, here, damn, damn, damn," Edward complained, angrily.

"Did they find the dope too?" Billy asked.

"Hell yeah. They found everything. Now I'm as broke as those crack-heads they busted in my place," Edward said, his head resting in his hands, elbows resting on his knees. "I sure would like to find out who made the buy from me. Whoever it was, I'll have them capped if I find out who it was," proclaimed Edward, looking at the floor.

"Damn E, what you gonna do?"

"I don't know. I guess I..." Edward was interrupted by Officers Drake, and Johnson, who appeared out of nowhere. He didn't see them coming, and wondered if they heard him talking about capping somebody.

"Edward Matthews?" one of the officers asked, as they approached and stood in front of the cell.

"Yeah that's me. What the hell do you want now?" asked Edward.

"If I were you, I'd watch my mouth. You ain't in no position to mouth off. Now get up and turn around," Drake ordered, as he unlocked the door to the holding cell, and cuffed Edward, again. "Come on, you're coming with me."

"Hey, what about me?" Billy questioned, as he got up and stepped closer to the cell doorway.

"Sit tight. They'll get to you soon enough," answered Officer Johnson, as he slammed the barred door shut with a loud clang, coming close to hitting Billy in the face.

Edward was led down several long halls, and through a couple of heavy, gray metal, locked doors, to a room with a single table in the middle. A camera hung in one corner, its unblinking eye watching every move Edward made, and seemed to be looking inside his head, Edward imagined. He was seated at the small table, and one wrist was handcuffed to a metal loop protruding from the tabletop. The table and two chairs was the only furniture in the room. A long mirror, obviously, one way see through, ran the length of one wall.

The officers took up their positions, one behind him, and the other seated directly across from him. The seated Officer Drake, laid a large folder on the table, opened, and read it briefly, while rapidly flipping pages of Edward's criminal record.

"Well Mister Matthews, you have quite a record here. It seems you're a five or six time looser. Add the several possessions of a controlled substance with the intent to deliver — the operating a criminal enterprise — the contributing to the delinquency of a minor, who was caught smoking dope in your house, as well as the two years for the possession of the shotgun we found in your place, and you're looking at maybe twenty-years," Drake informed Edward, as he thumbed through the pages, not looking up. Edward sat and listened, uninterested. He'd heard it all before, until the words twenty-years woke him up and scared the crap out of him.

"What! Aw-hell-no, you got something wrong. First, I didn't have that much dope, and second..." Edward tried to defend himself, but was interrupted by Officer Johnson, who was standing behind him.

"No my man, we got it right, you're looking at some serious time. Although, If you cooperate with us there is one, and I mean only one way out of your predicament," Johnson explained. "Do you want a lawyer, and depend on him to save your sorry butt, or do you want to help us and..?" Officer Johnson didn't have to finish.

"You don't have to say it," Edward cut Officer Johnson short. "I know exactly where you're going with this. You want me to flip on my bag man, just like that low-down, back-stabbing, rat fink, who made the undercover buy from me, right?" Edward asked, while throwing his head back, and looking at the ceiling and the florescent light that hummed and flickered, faintly. The light causing the small craters in his pocked marked face to appear deeper.

"For a smalltime, half-ass, low-rate dealer, you pretty smart, Eddie," Drake complimented, sarcastically.

Edward declined, "Are you insane, man, you can forget that. If I set up my supplier, I'd be dead in a week. It ain't happening," he said, while turning his back to Officer Drake. He looked down at his unwashed feet, and at the long, thick, dirty, toenails that were beginning to look like claws. For the first time he realized he didn't have on any shoes. He wondered how he could come this far, without noticing he was barefooted. *They got me for sure this time,* he thought.

Officer Johnson took the lead, "Dig this my man, you ain't going to have anything to worry about. For one thing, no matter how much you help us, you aren't going back on the streets. You'll be safe in jail while serving your time on reduced charges. And second, when we bust your supplier, he'll be facing a nice little stint himself," Johnson offered, and continued, "not only that, we'll make him the same offer we're giving you. We want the top man, and we're willing to do whatever is necessary to get to him. Your bag man will be so busy taking care of his ass, he won't have time to think about your insignificant butt," Johnson finished.

"And keep in mind, finks don't turn on finks," Drake, interjected.

"Um, um, um," Edward relented. "Man, you guys are really putting me on the spot. But I guess it's better than doing twenty on the wrong side. Okay, I'll do it. What do I have to do?"

He was hoping he wasn't making a mistake leading to his death. *But what choice do I have,* he thought, as he turned around in the chair, and using one finger, scratched his uncombed hair before he put his head down onto his balled up fist on the table. He was starting to get a headache. He needed something to eat, and some, way overdue, rest.

"My man, we knew you would come around. Good move," Officer Johnson said, slapping Edward on the back.

"Okay, this is how we're suggesting you do it..." Officer Drake offered...

The world of crack has no allies — only those who use, and those being used.

After making the decision to go ahead with the set up, Edward seemed to relax. He tried to lie down on the concrete bench that circled the cell, but found it cold, and hard, and impossible to get comfortable on — probably designed for that purpose.

He was doing some hard thinking, as he waited for the two officers to come and get him out of the holding cell.

Drake and Johnson had promised his relative safety. They told him Big would be too busy trying to save his own ass to worry about him. He wished he could believe that, it would make things a lot easier for him. *Maybe they're right,* he thought. He knew when Big was arrested, he'd know who it was who double crossed him, and might attempt to put out a contract on his head. No matter, he was going to do the dirty deed, anyway.

He wondered if he should ask for a lawyer, — try to get his deal in writing. *Maybe a mouthpiece can get me out of here with time served,* he thought. *Naw, I'll leave things alone for now — see what happens.* It wasn't that he had a fear of going to jail — he'd done his share of time behind bars. "Hell, they alta name the place after me, and put my name on a gold plaque and hang it over my own, personal, cell," he once said, while bragging to a crack-whore about how many times he'd been locked up. It was the idea of going to jail for a long time he didn't like.

During his wait, he witnessed several other people being brought into the holding area. Two female officers escorted what looked like a streetwalker down the hall, who loudly proclaimed her innocence, and who was obviously sick — probably from withdrawal. The woman had on too much makeup, and her blond wig was askew on her head. She never stopped claiming her innocence, even after she was locked in a cell with others of her kind.

Several young men, heads held down, and looking very scared, were put into a cell not far from him. *Damn, them boys will be eaten alive if they does some hard time,* Edward thought.

A drunk, who'd pissed on himself, was almost dragged into another holding pen, he being too drunk to walk. Edward was glad they didn't put him in his cell. *That's the last thing I need,* he thought, *a smelly, vomiting drunk being dumped in with me.*

He was very thirsty, and wanted a drink of water, and a bite to eat wouldn't hurt either. *Let's see, when was the last time I ate anything? Hell, I can't remember,* he thought. Just the thought of food started his stomach growling. He started to go back and sit down on the hard ledge, but changed his mind, staying near the bars in the front of his cell. He was hoping to ask an officer for something to eat, or at least find out how soon they would be serving something. Now that he wanted to catch the attention of an officer, the hall grew quiet, except for the drone of conversations from the other prisoners in the lockup. *Great,* he thought, *just when you need a cop there ain't never none around.*

Eventually, two officers came down the hall, joking between themselves. As they passed the individual cells they were asked several questions. Edward heard someone ask when they were going to be fed. The officers said they wouldn't be eating for another four hours. Edward returned to his seat on the ledge, his question answered. *Jesus, four hours? I'll be half-dead by then. These muthas sure don't give a damn about how they treat a man,* he thought, as he leaned back against the cold tiled wall, trying to get comfortable.

Three long hours later and just as he'd made up his mind to ask the next officer to give him a drink of water, two officers came to take him to an interview room. He quickly forgot about his thirst and hunger, as he was again led down the hall, and through several heavy doors.

Inside the interview room were several officers — maybe about fifteen or twenty? Some plain clothed, some in police uniforms, and others in what looked like SWAT gear. *This ain't no game. These guys are serious and it's going down now,* he thought.

Edward was surprised at the magnitude of the operation. He was a little unsettled being watch by so many eyes. Officer's Drake and Johnson were the only two seated at the table. Unlike the other metal table he was handcuffed too, this table was made of wood, and had no handcuff loop on the top, and had three chairs sitting at it.

Edward was seated at the table, and his handcuffs removed. That was when Edward noticed for the first time he still had the black ink from his fingerprinting on his hands. Being embarrassed, he balled his hands into fist. He'd been given a pair of those green, cloth, hospital slippers, to ware. At least he wasn't bare-footed anymore, showing his long, uncut, dirty, toenails. The escorting officers then left the room, closing the door behind them.

Officer Drake began the meeting. "This is Mister Edward Matthews," he began, "One of our local smalltime crack-house operators. He has graciously agreed to help us get a handle on his mid level suppliers, a Mister Gerald Calvin Reynolds, a.k.a. Big-D or Big. As many of you know, we've been trying to get something on this felon for some time. He's always been able to elude arrest on drug possession, or distributing charges," Drake continued, "We now have a chance to send Mister Big away to be a guest in our housing complex." Drake said, jokingly. The other officers laughed lightly, and slapped hands.

"Mister Edward's, here, has agreed to buy a quantity of crack cocaine while using our marked money. Isn't that right, Mister Edward's?" Drake asked, while getting up from his seat at the table, walking over behind and placing his hand on Edward's shoulder, and squeezing a little more firmly than necessary.

Edward, looking around at the crowd surrounding him, shook his head affirmative, and whispered, "Yes."

"What was that? Speak up, we can't hear you," came

the command from one of the plain-clothes officers.

Edward had never felt so intimidated in his life. He looked at the table, and said in a clear voice, "yes! I'll help you," while feeling his underarms grow moist and the odor of unwashed armpit wafting to his nose. He hoped no one else could smell him, but knew better.

He wished they would get on with the preparations. He was ready to get out of the room. His butt was hurting and going numb from sitting on the concrete bench in the holding cell. The wooden chair he was now sitting on was not much more comfortable, but at least he could stand in the cell, and give his ass a rest. He also knew breakfast would be served in a short while and he didn't want to miss getting something to eat.

The briefing took a couple more hours. It seemed everybody had something to add to the plans, or just wanted to be seen, or heard. By then, Edward was just about out of it. He'd been without sleep or food for a couple days before the raid on his place, and now this. The affects of the drugs he'd smoked had warn off. He was hungry, thirsty, sleepy, and leg shaking, exhausted. However, much to Edward's dismay, he wouldn't have a chance to eat or sleep for al least another four to five hours. He'd be made to get back on the street, to aid in the capture of Big.

As he was led out of the jailhouse and put into an unmarked cruiser, where he'd be taken to central to set up the buy, he noticed the Sun coming up on a new day. *Before this day ends, I'll be back behind bars,* he thought. The other prisoners had been served the morning breakfast of one slice of bologna, two slices of bread, and a cup of luke-warm, black, coffee, he missed. *Maybe I can catch lunch. They could have at least waited until after the morning meal, the dirty dogs,* he thought, his mouth watering. Not only that, his handcuffs were on too tight. *This is not going to be a good day,* he reflected, as he was driven away.

Chapter 13

The sting.

The siren on the fire truck woke Big and his companions, as it passed his medium sized suburban tri-leveled home. He and his two companions, Shirley, and Candy, were asleep in the double king-sized bed, in the second floor master bedroom. The oversized, flat screen, plasma TV suspended from the ceiling, was still on, playing quietly, and had on the morning news.

Shirley stirred, raised her head, and looked towards the bedroom window, a look of irritation on her face. Lowering her head, she put her arm over Candy's side, and cupped her naked breast. Candy cupped her hand over Shirley's, as they snuggled closer, and while spooning, tried to go back to sleep.

While on the other side of the giant bed, Big watched the two naked girls breathing softly, as they attempted to get back into dreamland. He found the remote and turned off the TV. He rolled over and ran his hand over Shirley's shapely hip, and thought about trying to get something going. Wisdom set in, and he decided it better to let the sleeping girls rest. He knew the past nights activities were enough to hold him for a while, besides he had a slight hangover. His best course of action would be to surprise the girls with a late morning breakfast. He wasn't in the mood to cook anything. He'd go out to get something from the Coney Island.

He got up, used the toilet, took a shower, got dressed,

grabbed his keys, and set out to get something to eat.

As he stood on his front porch, he looked up at the clear blue sky, and then up and down his street. The fire truck that had disturbed them earlier was parked blocking his street at one end. Apparently what had happened was somebody had run into a fire hydrant, knocked it completely off its base, and water was spaying twenty feet straight into the air. If the hydrant couldn't be shut down soon, the street would be one big ice rink. There was no snow falling, but it was still plenty cold outside.

A few of his neighbors were standing around, talking quietly amongst themselves, as they watched the firemen attempt to shut down the hydrant. Other than them, the well-maintained houses on the street were serene. *I bet they would be talking about me if they knew what I did for a living*, he thought, as he climbed into his truck, a feeling of self-content bolstering him.

He backed his Navigator into the street and proceeded to the restaurant. As he drove, he noticed, without alarm, another car back into a driveway, and fall in behind him. *That's funny, something isn't right*, he thought. He didn't notice them earlier when he looked up and down the street.

He made it to the Coney, got his order, and started for home. A quick look around revealed no sign of the car that seemed to be following him earlier. On the way back to the house, his cell phone rang, "hello?" he answered, not recognizing the number on the caller ID.

"Hey, Big, this is Edward," the caller responded.

"This ain't your number, where you calling from?" Big asked, always cautious.

"Yeah I know it ain't my phone. That's what I'm calling you about. You ain't going to believe this, but I was hit last night..." Edward tried to explain, but was interrupted by Big.

"What you mean you was hit — somebody rob you — you have a drive by — what the hell you talking about?" Big inquired.

"Damn, Big, if you hold on for a minute, and let me talk, I'll tell you what happened. The cops raided me. Can you believe that?" Edward continued. "They found a marked fifty dollar bill in with my other money. They got me man. They took everything, all my dope, and money. Somebody set me up. They made an undercover buy with marked money. When I find out who it was, I'm going to have them hit. But that's another story. What I need right now, is some help from you to get back on my feet," he explained.

This doesn't sound right, Big thought, and asked, "what are you talking about? What kind of help you need? How did you get out of jail, anyway, if they got all your money?"

"Man, I had to have Darlene pawn my bling to raise bail. It was more than enough to pay my bail, and have a little left over. That's where you come in, I got enough cheddar for one eight. What I was wondering is if you'll front me another? I know you don't give out credit, and normally I wouldn't ask, but I'm in a jam. I promise I'll have your money by the end of the day," Edward pleaded, playing his part like a pro, the police listening in, and using hand signals, coaching him.

Big listened to Edward, shaking his head as he drove. *Edward was right — I don't give credit, and have no intention of doing so now,* he thought, as he listened. Big knew when dealing with crack, or anybody, who had anything to do with it, it seems every time you allowed credit, nothing good ever came of it.

"Sorry Ed, I can't help you right now. I can get the one eighth to you when you're ready, but I don't have anything to spare. You know there's a light panic (shortage) out here right now. Do you want the eighth?" Big asked.

Big, having a slight hangover and not completely awake, was not thinking. He being in a hurry to get home with the food, and wanting to end the conversation, caused him to drop his guard ever so slightly.

He knew enough to never talk this much business over the phone. Especially to a cell phone number he was not familiar with. His normal precautions would have served him well in this situation. His entire conversation with Edward was being recorded to be used against him in court later. Not only that — the police were listening in and coaching Edward during the discourse.

"Are you sure that's all you can let me have? I wouldn't ask if I didn't need it, but if that's all you can do for me, I'll take it," Edward asked, while being prompted by the listening police to try and get Big to deliver more.

"That's it Ed. Do you want it or not?" Big was growing impatient. His empty stomach was growling. His mouth was watering from the smell of the food in the car, and he wanted to end this conversation.

"Yeah, I'll take it. I'll have to cut the dimes down a little to make a little extra money. Will I be able to get another as soon as I raise the money?" Edward inquired, playing the part a little better than even he thought he could.

"Word, baby boy. You know I'll take care of you," Big assured.

"Where you want to meet?"

"I don't know. I want some place I can see the cops coming. I know, let's meet on the Island, at the point, near the rest rooms. You know, near the fountain," Big instructed.

"Damn, Big, wake up, you know I ain't driving. Can't we meet somewhere on the eastside?" Edward reminded, being coached by the police.

The police didn't want to set up the sting on Belle Isle Park, too many intangibles like children and civilians. They also didn't want to go there for the same reason Big did. It was too open, too easy to spot surveillance or the police coming.

"Don't worry about that Edward, catch a cab, and I'll take care of it when you arrive. I'll meet you there at four this afternoon. Be on time, I don't want to have to wait. And make sure the money is right," Big instructed, and hung up the phone without giving Edward a chance to reply.

He still had that nagging felling something isn't right. Edward's explanation or pawing his jewelry didn't sound right. He, during the time he'd dealt with Edward, had never known him to have a lot of bling. Hell, Edward smoked up and tricked with all the extra money he made,. When did he buy jewelry, Big wondered? He ignored his instincts as best he could, and tried to forget about it.

His empty stomach, hangover, and desire to take a short nap after eating, helped to set up his own trap.

The arrest team wasn't happy about the location of the sting, however, they'd lost control of that, and had to go with whatever they had. As soon as the exchange location was decided, they went into action, hoping Big didn't decide to attempt to call back and change things. They scrambled to get a surveillance team in place on the Island. A male and female officer in plain-clothes, would make up the team, and would pretend to feed the seagulls prevalent on Belle Isle — a not too uncommon scenario. The island was a popular place for people in love, or who were courting, to frequent.

Staying in radio contact, the two cop's job would be to confirm his arrival, and the dope exchange that probably would take place inside of Big's dark windowed SUV. After the exchange, Both, Edward, and Big, would be allowed to leave the Island.

The police not knowing to what extent Big would be willing to go to get away, wanted to make the stop in the city in case Big decide to fight it out with gun play. In the city, because of the buildings, the chance of a stray bullet traveling a distance, and hitting an innocent victim was lessened. Edward would be picked up once he was back in the city, and out of sight of Big.

Big would be followed by the surveillance team until he crossed the bridge, and his general direction could be determined. He'd be stopped, searched for the marked money, and arrested in the city proper. They had pictures of him going to the hidden compartments in the back of his truck. But busting him with only the photos wasn't good enough to really nail him. If he was just caught with the drug in his possession, the most he could be charged with is possession with intent to deliver, but once Edward made a buy, they would have him for actually trafficking, a more severe offense.

The plan wasn't too complicated, so everyone relaxed until it got near the meeting time. Some of the officers went out to get a bite to eat, while others went to inspect their equipment. Edward was taken back to his cell, to wait for his time to perform, and still hadn't had anything to eat.

―――――

Big was not stupid, but he, like anyone who decides to

deal drugs, can and will be caught, sooner or later...

———

Back at the house, Big found the girls showered, dressed, and in the kitchen looking for something to eat. He got home with the food not a minute too soon. They had the volume on the plasma TV in the livingroom turned up so they could hear it in the kitchen. One of the news channels was on.

Big searched for the remote, found it, and turned down the volume. "Damn-it, I told you hard headed women don't play the TV so loud," he said, as he entered the kitchen, carrying the meals.

"Oh, daddy, you so sweet, you brought us something to eat," Candy, who saw him first, said, as she gave him a peck on the cheek, "Sorry about the TV, we won't do it again."

"Yeah, yeah, I've heard that before. Eat up girls — I'm still a little sleepy. After I finish eating, I'm going to take a little nap. That fire truck woke me up early, and I have a hangover. Wake me up around 3 o'clock, I have some business to take care of, and you girls be ready to go with me. And please keep the TV at a reasonable level. Okay?"

"Sorry, daddy. We'll try to keep it down." Shirley promised.

After eating, he never did get back to sound sleep . As soon as he went upstairs to take his nap, the girls turned up the volume on the TV. He thought about going downstairs and unplugging the television, but just buried his head under his pillow, and tried to sleep as best he could, and cursing under he breath, he vowed to get into their cases later. As he began drifting off, the feeling something wasn't right about the conversation with Edward still plagued him, and was also partly responsible for his inability to get back into deep sleep.

In what seemed like one minute to him, a faint knock

at the bedroom door roused him from his semi-sleep. "Time to get up sleepyhead. Its three o'clock," Candy said, as she cracked the door.

"Damn, already? I just closed my eyes," Big said, with a yawn.

Wrestling his, still hung-over, and tired butt to a sitting position on the side of the bed, he sat looking at the late afternoon sun stream in past the side of the window blinds. *I'm getting too old for this mess*, he thought. He threw on some clothes, and headed downstairs to gather the women. He had to get to his stash of drugs on the Westside to fill Edward's order of one eight-ball.

During the drive to the Westside, he called a couple of his other dealers whom he supplied with drugs. His first call was answered on the second ring. "Hey Roscoe, this is Big, I'm out and about, need anything?" Big asked, one of his lesser pushers, who happen to smoke also. Roscoe, also, ran a dope house much like Edward, but could never generate the same traffic as Edward.

"Naw, Big man, still got something left, check with me tomorrow," Roscoe responded, sounding half-asleep.

Probably smoked up his profits. He's never going to make any money, Big thought, as he searched through his phone numbers to find his next call. A call to AJ, a dude who rolled out of his apartment, went unanswered. *Typical*, he thought. *Sometimes, these guys stayed up all night, and slept during the day. I'll call later.* A third call to Ben, an older dealer who pushed out of the back of his barbershop, met with success.

"Hey Big, glad you called, I was about to call you," Ben said. "I'm running low. Them rocks rolling out of here like a landslide, mellow. Bring me a couple, or three, marbles. Yeah, you better make it three. How long will you be?" Ben asked.

"Got to make one stop. Let me check to make sure I got enough product to fill your order. If I don't, I'll bring whatever I've got. I should be there by four-thirty. That okay?" Big replied.

"Sounds good to me. See you then, Big," Been said, and hung up.

Now that's what I'm talking about, Big thought. *I need to get more older guys like him to handle business. He's always on point.*

Two more calls went unanswered. *The hell with it,* he thought, *I'll let them call me, and let them wait on me to deliver. Now watch, as soon as I get to Boss-man's place, and get into a heavy card game, them fools will start calling, wanting some more weight,* he imagined, *it never fails.*

The drive to the Westside apartment took about twenty minutes. Good time for this time of the day. Usually the freeway was jammed with people on their way home, and would be locked solid in the early rush-hour traffic.

Once in the apartment, Big asked Jesse, the live in, how much product did he have cooked up?

"Bout five balls, bagged, and on top of the safe. Don't know what you got inside the safe," Jesse replied.

"Cool, I've got a large order to fill. I'm going to have to re-up, myself, some time tonight. I guess about two K's (kilograms) should be enough, " Big said, as he went to his safe in the closet.

Big, after removing the available rocked dope, which was in individual dime sized bags inside larger plastic bags, each holding an eight-ounce, he asked Jesse if there was anything he needed.

"Naw, Big, I'm cool. Got enough to eat, and drink. Might have me some company by later. Might need a few dimes to kind of get things going. That okay with you?"

"Hell yeah, Jesse. You're doing a great job here. Go ahead and have some fun. But I got to warn you to not let any of them rock-stars know about the stash. You know you can't trust most of them. Follow me?"

"Way ahead of you Big. You have a nice day, and good looking out. Catch you later, player."

"Word, buddy. See you later. Probably tomorrow, so you don't have to worry about me walking in on something," Big said, as he left and locked the door behind him.

His business complete in the apartment, he took the dope down to his SUV, and stashed it in one of the hidden compartments. Back behind the wheel, he turned on the CD player and set it to front. He didn't want to disturb the girls, who were watching something on the headrest DVD player in the back seat. He drove to his meeting with Edward, listening to some mellow jazz. He didn't notice the, innocuous, conversion van, pull in behind him at the next corner, follow him onto the expressway, and then exit, where another, newer, but plain looking car took up the tail.

On the island park, Big arrived at the rendezvous location early. Having a few minutes to kill, he decided to walk over to the water and watch the waves from the Detroit River splash on the rocks put there to prevent erosion. He breathed some refreshing early winter air that seemed to clear his head a little. Another couple were feeding the Seagulls, and paid him no attention, or so he thought.

He watched as a large freighter, carrying gravel, its rusty sides showing neglect, passed slowly up the river, sending large waves onto the rocks. He took a step back to keep from getting wet as the waves broke over the rocks and splashed a little. *This is nice. I have to come out here more often,* he thought.

After a while of sitting on a picnic table and watching

the boats and the seagull feeding couple, and planing his entertainment for later that evening, he decided to wait for Edward in the warm truck. He had to remove Edward's bolder from his hidden compartment, anyway. The girls in the back were asleep again, the movie still running. *Damn, I wish I could go to sleep any time I wanted,* he thought, as he laid his head back on the headrest, and closed his eyes for a moment.

It wasn't long before Edward, in a cab, pulled in behind his truck. Big watched him get out of the car, and come to his driver's side. "Made it Big, I need twelve-thirty for the cab," Edward told Big, while glancing back at the couple who were feeding the gulls.

"Here, give him fifteen-even," big said, while handing Edward the money.

After paying the cab driver, and telling him to wait, and returning to and getting into the passenger side of Big's truck, Edward started to get a little nervous. Talking to the man face to face is a lot different than talking over the phone. It's not everyday you set up your dope supplier for a police sting. "Hey, Big," Edward said, talking a little faster than he normally would, "did you change your mind about giving me the two I needed?"

Big lied, "I was going to take a chance on you, but I got a call from one of my heavy hitters, who wanted all I had. But since I promised you the one, and you know I always keep my word, I brought you the one, and gave him the rest," he said, as he handed Edward the wad of dope wrapped in clear plastic wrap.

"Well, thanks anyway. I'll chop this up real good, and try to make a little extra," Edward said, taking the bag of rocks, and handing big the marked money, and then made a move to get out of the truck, without looking at what Big had handed him — not normal.

Any time someone is handed some dope, it doesn't matter who It's, dealer, or user, they always eyeball it carefully, turning it over in their fingers, checking to see if they got what they paid for. The fact Edward didn't do what Big had observed many times before, didn't alarm him. Again because he wasn't thinking clearly.

"Whoa, baby boy, what's your hurry? The cab can wait a little longer," Big said, grabbing Edward's arm. "Besides I ain't give you the money for the ride back."

Edward was jittery because of what he was doing to Big, not to mention he was afraid Big might discover he was wearing a wire.

"I... I, just want to get back and chop up this marble, and find some place to roll it. I got a lot of work in front of me. You know I can't go back to my old place. Somebody else is probably in there, anyway," Edward said, still talking fast.

"I hear you, Ed. But what I wanted to know is if you had any idea who might have set you up? You know I can take care of them for you," Big said, looking Edward straight in the eyes.

Now conscious of the fact he was wired, Edward didn't want any part of a conspiracy to commit a murder that was being recorded.

"Naw man, I wish I knew. Whoever it was, it had to happen while I was asleep," he lied, "Darlene did the transaction. I ain't had a chance to talk to her yet, and she is probably still in jail, but no, I don't know."

One of the officers who was listening to the conversation via the wire Edward wore, cursed at the mistake Edward just made. He was hoping Big didn't question Edward as to how Darlene was able to bail him out if she was still in jail?

"Okay Ed., blow your horn, (phone) if you need my help. Take care, and try not to take anymore marked money, all right?" Big said, while handing him twenty more dollars for the return ride, and letting Edward out of his truck.

Edward noticed the money Big gave him for the cab, was out of the marked money he'd used to pay for the drugs. *I hope the police marked all of the bills, and don't try to blame me for the missing money,* he thought, as he got in the cab, and headed for the bridge. As he rode away, he watched the two cops, who were still feeding the gulls, for any sign he'd done a good job. Of course, none was forthcoming.

The gull feeding surveillance officers watched the whole transaction, but couldn't see what transpired inside of the truck, because of the tinted windows, but they noted the location of the hidden compartment. That information would be radioed to the rest of the arrest team as soon as Big was on the move.

The worried officer, who was concerned about Edwards mistake, relaxed. Big didn't catch the error — the sting was still on.

Big watched the cab motor down Strand Drive on it's way to the bridge. The feeling something isn't right was like an itch in between his shoulder blades where he couldn't scratch.

He couldn't explain the feeling. Everything seemed to be okay, but this feeling just wouldn't leave him alone, and seemed to get stronger since he met Edward. He waited for the cab to get out of sight before starting his engine. He looked around, and took note of the vehicles in his area, before pulling away from the curb on his way to deliver Ben's order.

He kept looking into his rear view mirror, checking for following cars. He thought he spotted the same car the couple, who were feeding the gulls, were driving. He decided to go around the Island one more time, this time, cutting through the woods to make sure he wasn't being followed.

He took the shortcut to the bridge, rather than drive the six or seven miles it would take to drive all the way around the Island. The short cut would take him through the woods and pass a nine hole golf course, bringing him out near the beach, and a short drive to the bridge from there. As he drove, he constantly checked the rear view mirror, and saw nothing suspicious.

Now on Riverside Drive, while checking his rear view mirrors one last time, and not seeing a tail, he decided it was okay to cross the bridge. On the Gen. Douglas MacArthur Bridge, more commonly called the Belle Isle Bridge, which was the only way on, and off of the Island by car, he got into the right curb lane that would take him eastward on Jefferson, a street more or less following the river to lake St. Clair.

On Jefferson, he'd driven a few blocks when he saw a black, unmarked, police car, pull in behind him. The cops in the unmarked car seemed to be looking him straight in the eyes through his rear view mirror. He started to panic. His heart began beating faster. He still had the three eight-balls in his car for Ben's order, which was enough to send him away for a long time. The feeling something wasn't right grew even stronger. Normally, he'd rely on his hidden compartments to protect him against detection. His license, registration, and proof of insurance were in order, yet he was uneasy, and didn't know why.

He decided to pull over to the curb, get the girls out of the car, and let the unmarked car pass. If the police cruiser followed him to the curb, he'd know what was up.

Pulling over to the curb, while still watching the rear view mirror, Big woke the two women in the back seat, "Shirley, Candy, wake up! Here, take this hundred, and catch a cab back to my house. I'll meet you there later," Big instructed, handing the girls the cash over the back seat, his hand trembling.

The unmarked car behind Big continued down the street. The officers in the car looked straight ahead as they passed. Big, let out a silent sigh of relief, but was still a little uneasy. The voice in the back of his head was trying to tell him something, but was more like a little, nagging, fruit fly, buzzing in his ear, and could not be understood. The mistake Edward made was picked up by his unconscious mind, but the lack of sleep, combined with the hangover, wouldn't let his conscious mind register it.

"What's wrong daddy, is everything okay?" Shirley asked, as she untangled from Candy, and stretched while yawning, before opening the rear door to exit. "Its cold out here, do we really have to get out of the truck?"

"Yes you do. Now get out. I'll call you at the house and explain later," Big said, as he watched the cruiser behind him continue down the street.

Just as the car behind him passed, two more cruisers, one marked K-9, and another unmarked, approached and passed from the opposite direction. The officer in the K-9 car shot him a quick glance, as he passed.

Big's, the crap's about to hit the fan instinct was now on full alarm. He could almost hear what the tiny voice in the back of his head was trying to tell him. He was sure his mind wasn't playing tricks on him — or he wasn't being paranoid because of the dope in the car. He'd driven around many times with weight on him, and had never felt like this before. He had the feeling if he did get stopped, it wouldn't be a normal stop.

They must have something on me, he thought.

He was really becoming concerned. A bead of sweat formed on the side of his head and ran down to his chin where he wiped it away with the back of his hand. He rolled down the driver's side window. The cool breeze cooled him for a moment, but his nerves overrode any calming affect he received.

Had he not panicked, he'd have thought to remove the drugs from his truck, and drop them down the nearest sewer before anyone could get close enough to him to stop him, but his mind was not hitting on all cylinders at that moment, again do to the lack of sleep, and the fog clouding his mind, the leftover affects of drinking to much the night before.

How the hell is he going to get the drugs out of his truck, he wondered? What would he do with them, if he did? He knew he was being watched. The hidden compartments would do nothing to stop the dogs from finding the hidden 8-balls of crack. He had to do something, and he had to do it now.

He pulled away from the curb, making his tires chirp a little — got into the left turn lane, and made a left on the next cross street. The maneuver was fruitless. Two cruisers, their cherries and blues glowing, idling at a 90-degree angle to his path, were waiting for him at the next corner. He drove by them, not looking in their direction. They fell in behind him — the leading car giving him a little chirp of its PA speaker. There was no denying it — they wanted him to stop. He had to stop. An unmarked car was approaching from the front. It was lit up like a Christmas Tree with lights flashing all over the interceptor. They had him boxed in, no where to run, no where to hide. He stopped, put the truck in park, turned off the engine, and put his hands on the steering wheel. In all, about six cars converged on his location. Police officers were everywhere, including the K-9 unit.

"Turn off your engine, put your right hand outside the window, open the door with your left, and exit the vehicle," squeaked the command from one of the cruiser's PA speakers.

Big did as he was told, and was immediately set upon

by several officers with guns drawn.

"Why am I being stopped?!" Big asked, no one, in particular.

"We will explain in a moment," replied one of the officers, who had a smirk on his face.

He was handcuffed, and searched. Anything in his pockets was removed, including the marked money. He was then stuffed into the back seat of one of the marked cruisers.

Wile leaning to the side because of the tight handcuffs, he couldn't see much from his seat in the back of the cruiser, but he could see several officers looking at his money with a funny looking, blue, light. That's when it hit him — he'd been set up, and it had to have been Edward.

I knew it, I knew something wasn't right, he thought, leaning his head back on the seat, and gazing at the dirty headliner of the car, his teeth clenched.

It wasn't long before an officer came to the side of the car he was in, and opened the door. "Mister Reynolds, we have a warrant to stop you, and searched your vehicle. You are now under arrest for trafficking cocaine, and possession of cocaine with the intent to deliver," the officer informed Big in a monotone voice, sounding like Sergeant Friday from the famous, old, cop show, Dragnet. "It seems you accepted marked money in payment for a quantity of cocaine you delivered," the officer continued. "The money was found in your possession, and was checked with a UV lamp for verification. We've also found a quantity of rock cocaine in a compartment in your vehicle," the officer finished. "you need not say anything at this time. You'll be read your rights, taken to the ninth prescient, and booked. There you'll be given a chance to call an attorney, if you choose. Just hang tight a little while longer and we will be on our way."

Big watched, as his truck was hauled onto a flat bed tow vehicle, and taken away. He knew he'd never see that truck again. But he wasn't worried. He still had the money and the dope in the safe, which was in the apartment, to get back in business as soon as he was released.

A crowd of onlookers gathered, and chatted, and pointed at him, some laughing. They were glad to see someone with such a nice truck being taken down a peg or two. Two officers finally came and got into the car he was in, their radios squawking, and giving him a glance, headed for the 9th.

He had to admit they had him. There was little he could do, or say, to get out of the mess he was in. They'd played their hand well, but he had a hard time believing he could be caught so easily. In the back of his mind, Big always knew something like this could happen, but he didn't expect it to happen this soon. *Reality is a mutha,* he thought, as he wondered how much time he'd receive?

The drug life claims another victim, — maybe not as innocent as others, but a victim just the same.

The dope Edward had in his pocket was making him a little edgy — working on his addiction. He was sure once he was over the bridge, and back in the city, the cops would be waiting for him. *This cab is moving too fast, I need time to think,* he thought. *How can I dodge the cops,* he wondered, *and where could I go to hit a little piece, and what would I use to smoke it?*

He knew it would be his last blast for who knows how long. And yet, after turning on Big, he was kind of looking forward to a stay in the pen. No telling how Big would react to being set up, and jail might be a kind of sanctuary against

Big's wrath.

Even better yet, he reconsidered, *maybe I could lay low for a while. Hide somewhere neither popo or Big's hit men could find me. I could then leave town, keeping the dope or the money from selling the dope, and have my freedom. Yeah, that's what I can do, make a break for it, and hide out somewhere.*

He told the cab driver to go east on Jefferson and make a left on Conner, forgetting about the hidden microphone he was wearing. His head was on a swivel like an owl's, looking for the cops, but saw nothing in sight. He relaxed and sat back in the seat, thinking he was home free. Nothing could be further from the truth.

Yeah, I'm free. Free as the birds in the trees. Those dumb cops don't know who they is messing with. Fast Eddie, that's who, he thought. No sooner than the cab made the turn onto Jefferson Street, the cab driver, while looking in his rear view mirror, cursed loudly.

"What wrong?" asked Edward.

"The damn cops are pulling me over. Hell, I ain't done nothing wrong. Why they messing with me?" the driver replied.

Edward snapped his head around so quickly, looking out the rear window, he almost gave himself whiplash. A sinking feeling came to his stomach. There, on the cab's bumper, in an unmarked car, cherries and blues flashing through the grill, where his two friends, Officers Drake and Johnson, looking him straight in the eyes, and seeming to be grinning as they shared a private joke.

"Don't sweat it bro, it's me they want, pull over," Edward told the driver.

The driver pulled over and stopped. The unmarked car pulled along side them and stopped. The officers didn't bother to look around. Edward knew what to do. He got out of the cab without paying the driver.

"Hey, brother, where you going? You ain't paid me yet," the dreadlocked driver protested.

Edward was trying to pull a fast one — hoping the police' presents would allow him to get away without paying the fare. He got back into the cab and paid the driver. *Now is not the time to start some crap,* he thought, as he paid the exact fare and not a penny more.

He got out of the cab and into the back seat of the patrol car, and settled back for his ride to jail.

Once seated in the cruiser, Officer Drake turned to speak to the sick Edward. "Eddie, my boy, you weren't thinking of trying to make a break for it, were you? We heard you, over the wire, tell the cab to turn on Conner."

"Who, me? Hell, naw, man. I knew you guys were behind us and listening. I was telling you which way I was going. I was just waiting for you to make the stop. Honest, man, I didn't know what to do next," Edward lied, as he handed the balled up package of dope to Officer Drake.

Officer Drake, a seventeen-year veteran in the department, the last five in the narcotics division, took the dope and examined it, hefting it in his hand. And giving Edward a quick look over his shoulder, he asked, "I know you weren't fool enough to pinch off this were you?"

Why the hell is he asking me that, Edward thought? *I know he don't think I'm going to tell him, yeah, cop, I was going to bust me a big o' piece off that marble, and do me a big, mind-blowing, hit. Get my head in the right place. Damn, these cops are stupid.*

Edward, tipping his head to one side, and faking an injured expression, responded, "Come on man. I know I ain't too bright, rolling the way I was, but I ain't no idiot. If I did break off a small piece, where was I planning to smoke it? And I know it's a felony that would stretch my stay in jail, if I brought the crumb into the station house. Give me a break, man. And, when you going to clean this mutha? It stinks back here, smells like vomit." he concluded, as he turned his head and watched the free world pass by for the last time. *Should have got out of that damn cab when I started too,* he thought, *I could have borrowed a lighter and a cigarette from someone, and had me a good hit by now.*

His empty stomach was turning flips, partly from the odor in the back of the car, and partly from the craving for the crack just a few feet away. *So close and yet so far away, and so much of it too. Damn, I want a hit,* he thought.

"Good answer," is all Officer Drake said, ignoring the remark about the odor. He dropped the contraband into an evidence bag and labeled it. He too, turned to watch the free world go by, but not for the last time.

"Sit tight, Ed," Officer Johnson, added. "We'll remove the wire when we get to the precinct. You did well. You can relax now. Big will be in our hands in a few minutes, and while in the joint, you can start your recovery from your addiction. I hope you learned your lesson, Eddie. There's no way you're going to roll in this city. Think about that while you're in your cell cooling your heels. We've busted you before, and know you. When you get out in a year or two, don't try rolling again. We'll bust you again. And next time, we ain't going to offer a deal, you'll do your full time."

Officer Johnson turned back around and said no more. He knew Edward wasn't going to take his advice, but at least he had his conscience covered by offering it. *I wonder how long it will be before I bust him again,* he thought?

Cherries off, the cruiser sped eastward on Jefferson, headed towards the 9th precinct, and Edward's destiny.

The formula holds true, again — to do the drug, or sell

the drug, equals tragedy.

Chapter 14

Candy and Shirley only want the rock.

Candy and Shirley, after getting out of Big's SUV, watched him make the left turn onto the side street. They ran down to the next corner, and looked down the street he'd turned on to see if they could see which direction he was going. Big sped away from the curb so fast, after letting them out, they were a little worried. He'd never done anything like that before, and they knew something serious was up.

As they reached the corner, they could see what looked like a hundred, cherry and blue, police lights going. They couldn't see Big's truck but they knew he had to be the reason for the spectacle. They decided to not go down the street. Big would be angry if he saw them there. Instead, they decided to do as Big told them — catch a cab back to his house and wait on his call. Of course, there was nothing wrong with them picking up a little something to smoke on the way home, they agreed, as they flagged down a taxi.

Back at the house and while they were smoking and drinking a little Paul, the police came crashing through the front door without knocking. The officers had a search warrant. They ignored the girls, and began destroying the house, looking for Big's stash of drugs. It was a wise decision Big made to keep his product in the apartment on the other side of town.

When the police couldn't find anything, they turned their attention on the girls, asking them if they knew where

Big kept his supply of dope. Of course the girls couldn't tell the police much. The police didn't believe them, so they wrote the girls bench warrants for the possession of drugs and drug paraphernalia. It didn't matter, the women didn't intend to keep their court date, anyway — they'd have to be caught. That's the way it is in the drug life.

They decided they'd, after not hearing from Big in a couple days, catch a plane to Chicago while hoping they could hook up with a big-time dope dealer there. After all, they were, now, essentially, homeless. The police told them they had to move out of the house after it'd been searched. They were told the house would be seized and forfeited as prescribed by the Michigan Drug Laws. The house and its contents would be auctioned, and the money used to fight drug proliferation.

Shirley had to beg the officer in charge of the investigation to allow them to collect their clothes before they were locked out. She really wasn't worried about her clothes. She knew where Big hid his jewelry. *I'll be damned if I let them take that,* she thought. *Besides, we'll need the money in Chi-town until we can find someone else to take care of us.*

The Sergeant in charge agreed to let them collect their clothes and no more.

While upstairs in the master bedroom, and while under the watchful gaze of an officer, they went about the task of gathering their clothes. Shirley whispered to Candy to create a diversion so she could get to the hidden bling, and hide it in her suitcase.

"Mr. Officer, Sir, I need to go down into the basement to get another bag to put my shoes in. Is it all right with you?" Candy asked the officer, while putting her hand on the officer's shoulder and giving him her best come-hither smile.

"Yeah, I guess it's okay, but I'll have to go with you," the officer replied, and told Shirley, "You stay here, I'll send another officer up to keep an eye on you."

By the time Candy and the officer had taken their second step down the stairs, Shirley was in the closet removing the false back on the top shelf, and feeling for Big's shoebox, in which Big kept his jewelry. She was able to find the box, and tuck it away in her suitcase just as the second officer reached the top of the stairs.

She turned around, and gave the entering officer a look of disgust, as she threw some sexy underwear at her suitcase, a thong, landing on the floor. A little embarrassed, the officer diverted his eyes — the desired effect she was hoping for.

She pushed down hard on the suitcase lid, but couldn't get it latched. The shoebox full of jewelry took up a lot of room. Asking for assistance from the officer, they were able to get it closed and latched.

By then, Candy and the other officer were returning from the basement. "Shirley, do you know what Big did with that blue travel bag?" Candy asked.

"No, and I don't give a damn." Shirley replied, while faking anger. "Get your crap together and let's get the hell out of here. Leave them shoes, they ain't no good anyway."

"What do you..." Candy started, but was interrupted by Shirley.

"I said let's go, bitch, now!" Shirley demanded, nodding her head towards her bags.

Candy, now understanding, and saying no more, hurriedly completed her packing. The two officers help them carry their 10 bags of clothes down the stairs, where they waited for the cab they'd called, Shirley taking the bag with the hidden jewelry. At the bottom of the stairs, Shirley hoped the cops didn't search her bag, and they didn't, as they stood around talking about how nice Big's house was, and how he'd hate loosing it.

The cab arrived, they, with the assistance of the cab driver, whoes eyes were glued on the two women's butts, helped loading the vehicle, and they all got in. They headed straight to the pawnshop to get what they could for the jewelry. They had to hurry, the pawnshop would be closing shortly.

The two-thousand-dollars they were able to get for the bling was enough to catch a cab to the Metropolitan Airport where they caught the first thing flying to the Windy City. The hell with waiting two days for Big to contact them, they discussed in the first class section of the jetliner. Both women agreed if Big was caught dirty, it would be much longer before he was able to take care of them. If Big's house hadn't been seized, they might have hung around and smoked rocks for a few days, while sexing each other up, but not having a place to stay, except, maybe, Boss's whorehouse, they agreed going to the windy city and trying to hook up with another high roller was a better option. Besides, Boss-man might want them to go to work turning tricks in exchange for a room, and they both agreed they didn't want to get back into that. Big had spoiled them, and tricking with a bunch of old ass men didn't appeal to either of them. Hell, if they could have gotten out of giving Big a little booty every now and then, they would have.

In the drug world, close alliances are only as good as what someone could do for the persons involved.

Jesse the live in, who Big had protecting his Westside apartment, was beginning to become worried. Normally Big would contact him at least once a day. It had been two, going on three, days, since he'd heard from Big — not normal. He was getting jumpy. He was afraid the cops would come busting through the door in any minute. He decided to get out of dodge. He packaged the last of the dope Big had supplied, and not knowing the combination, left it sitting on top of the safe in the closet. If Big returned, he'd find it. If he didn't, the hell with it, not his problem, he reasoned.

He threw what clothes he had, along with his small five inch TV into a plastic bag, and locking the door as he left, walked to his brother's house three miles away. If Big wanted him, he could call him on the cell phone. *Big shouldn't be angry,* he thought, as he sat the heavy bag down to take a break, while walking, *as long as I didn't mess with his dope, he'll understand why I had to leave.*

Resuming his trek, he threw the heavy bag on his shoulder and leaned against its weight. As he walked, he wondered what he was going to do if Big had got busted, or killed? His situation, living in the rent free apartment, cooking the dope, and occasionally giving a small quantity to a female visitor in exchange for sex, would be hard, if not impossible, to replace.

About a month later, the rent due, and not hearing from Big, and getting no response from repeated knocks on the door, the landlord decided to get a lock smith to open the door to the apartment in which Big had changed the locks.

There wasn't much furniture in the place other than an old couch with an ancient coffee table in front of it, a refrigerator and stove, and a twin-sized bed in the bedroom. Other than that, everything seemed to be in place. He decided to go to one of the closets to see if there were any clothes in it

— a good way to tell if someone had abandoned the unit. He found no clothes in the closet, but did find the locked safe with a large quantity of rock cocaine on top. Being an upstanding citizen, the landlord immediately called the police. He was surprised Mr. Reynolds was into drugs. *Big seemed to be such a nice man,* he thought, as he dialed 911.

The police, judging from the drugs on top of the safe, and feeling the safe was used in some kind of criminal activity, pulled the safe from the floor, and carted it to the station house to be opened. The justice department's locksmith, upon opening the safe, found the large sum of money and more drugs, all of which was seized. They didn't know whose money it was, but were sure no one would come in to claim it. It didn't matter — whomever it belonged too would never see it again. As is customary in situations like this, any money seized during an investigation of illicit activity, and if forfeited because of that investigation, is put into a kitty and used to further fund future criminal investigations.

The crooks pay to catch other crooks... Cosmic.

Chapter 15

Big gets a dose of reality.

After being held in the lockup for several days to stew, as the police called it, Big was made the same offer Edward was given. If he agreed to aid the police in capturing his top-level supplier, the prosecuting attorney would go easy on him. To sweeten the offer, Big was told if he turned states evidence, he wouldn't do any time, only put on probation for a few years.

Big was no fool. If he flipped on his supplier, his life wouldn't be worth the breath it took to snitch, and that was not conjecture, it was a fact. No jail would be safe, and probation would only make it easier for them to get to him. Those guys commanded a lot of money, and money walks, talks, and gets people dead. Big knew the most he'd get was eight to ten-years, and he'd probably be released in seven with good behavior, and he'd made up his mind he'd be the superstar of model prisoners, and he told his lawyer as much, even though the lawyer wanted him to plead not guilty and take his chances with a jury, which could result in him receiving a longer sentence if convicted. Big decided to throw himself on the mercy of the court, and told his attorney to enter a plea of no contest.

Big kept his mouth shut, and decided to take his punishment. *Who knows, with the overcrowded jails, I might get out even earlier,* he thought? *It's much better to be alive in seven years, than to surely be dead in less than one.*

Hell, with my contacts still intact, I'd be back in business within a month of being released, he assured himself. *Besides, I still have the money and dope in the safe. That would give me a leg up on getting back into business. I'll get hold of Jesse when I get situated in prison. Tell him the combination to the safe, and have him take what money and dope I've got in there to Boss-man's. Yeah, Boss will hold on to it until I get out. It'll be safe there,* he thought, *and who knows, when I get out, I might be able to get in contact with my buddy, Edward, and properly thank him for my vacation, the mutha frigging, back stabbing, dog.*

At least I'll get a chance to contribute to society, he imagined. *I'll eat everything they throw at me in prison. There won't be any wasted food as far as I'm concerned. I sure hope the food is better than this crap they is serving me here in the county lockup. Oh, I can't forget to call Candy and Shirley, and tell them to move in with Boss-man. I'll tell Boss he can deduct their room and board out of the money he'll be holding for me. I don't want my women tricking with nobody but me,* he planed. *Yeah, they'll like that.*

―――――

Of course Big was right about ratting on his supplier. They would not hesitate to kill him if for no other reason than to make an example of him, his death serving as a warning to the others they supplied, to keep their damn mouth' shut.

―――――

Even with his optimism, the day D began serving his sentence of fifteen years in the St. Louis, State, Correctional Facility, in St. Louis, Michigan, and the heavily barred door slammed shut with the unmistakable resonance of reality, his resolution to do his time was already weakening. He looked around the tiny space in which he'd spend the next decade and a half of his life, and a cold chill ran through his body. Already, the damp gray walls seemed to be closing in on him. The angry, menacing, stares, some of the prisoners gave him as he was being led to isolation, terrified him. The large black water bug crawling on his bunk, and looking at him with an antenna waving defiance, discomforted him. He decided to leave the bug alone. He didn't like roaches, and this was the King-Kong of roaches.

He walked to the front of his cell, and gripping the bars with both hands, listened to the other inmates screaming at each other out of boredom. It was apparent at that moment several questions had to be answered. Could he do what he was so determined to do before being locked up — does he really know how terrible being in prison is — would he change his mind and set up his supplier to get out, and what would be the outcome if he did? These are all questions that wouldn't take long to answer. For understandable reasons, the offer to aid the police was beginning to sound very appealing.

He turned to find the oversized bug on his bunk, and found it gone. Now he was wondering how he was going to be able to sleep with that big-assed insect roaming around his cell. It would be a long first night for him. In any event, he'd have been wise to take heed of the maxim, and you've all heard it, and know how true it is: "If you can't do the time, don't do the crime."

The End?

CPSIA information can be obtained
at www.ICGtesting.com
Printed in the USA
LVHW021118031222
734518LV00027B/1154